SAM'S SALVATION

WAGNER BRIGADE

BOOK FOUR

ASHLEY A QUINN

TCA PUBLISHING LLC

One

People milled on the busy Las Vegas Strip just outside the shop window. Sam Brackley crossed his muscled arms and watched the people passing by while waiting for Edie's fiancé, Jordan, to pick out a wedding ring. Vegas was a study of humanity. In one glance, he saw several nationalities and ethnicities, as well as multiple fashion styles—some of them bordering on obscene. He doubted there was another place on the planet where a person could see so much diversity in one location.

"What's wrong with them?"

Jordan's question drew Sam's attention. He turned to see him talking to one of their other friends, Dean, and tip his chin toward Sam, and Max, who stood nearby.

Dean looked over, then grinned. "I imagine Max is having flashbacks. And Sam gets hives at the word commitment."

"What?" Sam glared at him. "I do not. This is all just too —" He swirled a hand, frowning as the word he wanted refused to come out. He clenched his teeth, hating that his mind didn't want to work right. Damn brain injury... "You know what I mean." He folded his arms again and glared. "It's too frilly. I don't do frilly." That still wasn't the word he wanted, but it would have to do. Shopping for women's jewelry was not his thing. Even when he had a woman. He preferred to show his appreciation of her in different, more personal ways. Though, this shopping excursion was necessary. Most women expected a wedding ring when they got married.

Max laughed. "I don't think any of us do."

Sam rolled his eyes. "Oh, whatever. I caught you wearing a tiara and nail polish last week when you watched Margot's twins."

"That's different. They're kids. I'll do frilly for kids."

"For *those* kids, you will." Those two little girls had Max wrapped around their little fingers. Their mother did, too, for that matter.

"What's that supposed to mean?"

Sam turned to face him. "It means—" He stopped as something outside caught his attention. He squinted, frowning. "What the—" He stepped closer to the window. Was that —? No. It couldn't be.

"What is it?" Ford asked. Sam felt him move closer.

"I thought I saw—" Sam shook his head. "But that's not possible." He stared a moment longer at a woman on the other side of the road who had stepped out of a restaurant. She just looked like someone he thought he used to know.

"Saw what?" Ford asked.

"Nothing." Sam continued to stare down the street. The woman looked up from her phone as she stepped into the throng of people. Sam's heart stopped. It *was* her. Ten years older and with darker hair, but he'd never forget that face. He turned toward the door. "I'll meet you guys back at the hotel later."

"What?" Ford took two steps after him. "Sam?"

Sam waved and hurried out the door. He couldn't lose her. Dashing across the street, he wove between people, bumping into a few as he ran after her. Even in four-inch heels, she was moving at a good clip. She'd always been a fast walker.

Ten feet behind her, he called her name. "Audra!"

She didn't react. Muttering a soft curse, he skirted around a group of young women already dressed to party hard, even at four in the afternoon. With another long stride, he reached out and touched Audra's arm. "Audra."

She stiffened beneath his touch, pausing to turn. Coffee-rich brown eyes met his. They widened slightly before her expression blanked.

"I'm sorry. I think you have the wrong person."

Sam frowned. That was her voice—minus her accent. "No. I don't. What happened to your accent?"

Her nostrils flared. "This is how I always sound." She backed up a step, and her gaze darted to the side. "I'm sorry." Turning her back on the direction she'd looked, she kept backing away. "Don't follow me, Sam." Her lilting British accent returned. She stared at him for another long moment, then spun on her heel and hurried away.

Sam's eyes followed her as she briskly walked away from him. When she reached the other side, a man in a dark suit stepped away from an elegant black car. Sam backed up, fading into the crowd, but kept them in sight. The man said something to her. She pinned him with a glare, said something, then slid into the backseat of the vehicle. Closing her door, the man glanced up, scanning the crowd. Sam melded into the shadows behind a potted palm. With a fierce frown, the man rounded the hood of the car and got into the driver's seat. A moment later, the car pulled away from the curb. Sam stepped away from the palm as they drove past, taking note of the license plate.

Audra turned her head, meeting his gaze. Sam frowned, watching her leave.

Audra, what did you get yourself into now?

Two

Standing at his balcony window, Sam gazed down at the bustling street below. Even at eleven p.m. the city was wide awake. He flipped the lock holding the door closed and pulled on the handle, opening it the inch the bar in the track allowed. Wind rushed in. The cool air smacked him in the face, but it did little to calm his racing thoughts. All evening, Audra's wide brown eyes had lurked in his mind. What was she doing here? And sounding like an average midwestern American? It was an act; the switch to her normal voice had proven that. But why? British intelligence didn't operate in the U.S. Not like that. It was possible she was working with a U.S. agency, but which one? And why?

He blew out a breath and crossed his arms, still staring down at the street. The Sphere lit up the sky, the image shifting from an ad for the new Disney movie to a sleeping emoji face. That thing was an eyesore, even if the technology was impressive. But it played into the Vegas experience, so it fit right in.

Sam rolled his neck and stepped away from the window. He needed to move. Crossing to the small duffel he brought for the one-night trip, he dug out some running gear and quickly changed. Maybe pounding the pavement would pound Audra out of his head.

Downstairs, he exited the smoky lobby straight into a cloud of marijuana-scented air. Wrinkling his nose, he took off, hoping he could escape the smell. He knew he'd never find the clean, fresh air of home, but something that resembled a normal city would be nice.

Audra's face kept pace with his footfalls as he ran, refusing to leave his brain. He ran faster. Why couldn't he get her off his mind? It had been ten years since he'd seen her. Ten years since their little interlude in Rota. Sure, their time together had been amazing, but they'd both known it was temporary. When he left to rejoin his unit, he'd had no regrets. Over the years, he'd thought about her. What man wouldn't revisit some of the greatest sex of his life? He'd even inquired about her a time or two, making sure she was doing okay. A month before Sam's convoy was ambushed and his life changed, she'd gone off the grid. After he left the service and joined Ford in Costa Rica, he'd asked Asher to check into her whereabouts. He couldn't find her.

Which brought him back to why the hell was she in Vegas pretending to be an American? She was either deep under-cover, or she'd crossed over to the dark side. He was betting on the former, but she had a reckless streak, so he couldn't rule out the latter.

Turning a corner, he found himself on the same street where he'd been earlier that day when he saw her. He slowed his pace as he came up to the restaurant. Tipping his head, he read the sign. Byrne's. Sounded British. Or Irish. He didn't stop. No need to attract attention in case someone was around who might have seen him earlier.

Instead, he crossed to the kebab shop across the way. He'd get a late-night snack and watch the place for a bit. After placing an order, he sat down at one of the tables tucked behind a pillar and turned his chair to face Byrne's. He knew the odds were slim she'd show up again, but he could probably learn a bit about what she was up to by who came and went. It was none of his business, and he didn't know what he'd do with the information. But he had to know. He had to be sure she was safe.

Twenty minutes later, he had a decent idea of what was going on. Several men with mafia tattoos had pulled up and entered the restaurant. He'd bet his pension it was a front for the Irish mob.

Sam scowled. How the hell did she get mixed up with them? And why? The New IRA had been quiet as of late. Even if they weren't, it would make more sense for her to be embedded with them in Ireland or the United Kingdom. Not in the U.S.—with an American accent.

The restaurant's front door opened. Audra emerged, dressed in a short black cocktail dress and a black fur coat. A man out front asked her something, to which she shook her head and walked several yards away. She dug into her small black clutch and pulled out a piece of chewing gum, stuffing it into her mouth. Sam smiled, remembering her habit of chomping on spearmint Extra every time she was annoyed.

He got up from his seat, tossing his trash in a can as he jogged down the sidewalk. There was an alley twenty feet behind where Audra stood. It was a long shot, but maybe he could get her out of sight and get some answers.

Keeping an eye on her, he went several storefronts down before he crossed the road again. When he reached the alley, he leaned on the corner of the building closest to her, then started whistling the song they'd danced to the first night they'd spent together.

She straightened away from the building where she'd been leaning. She stared straight ahead, but Sam knew her eyes were looking everywhere but at the jewelers. He kept whistling. After a few moments and a glance at the restaurant, she stuffed her hands in her coat pockets and wandered his way, looking like a woman just out for a stroll.

Audra passed him without a word, but turned into the alley. She wandered into the shadows. He only knew she stopped because he could no longer hear her heels clacking on the asphalt. With a quick survey to make sure no one was paying them any attention, he followed.

Three

Darkness descended on Audra Ridley, wrapping her in its arms, much like her heavy coat. Normally, she liked being able to see, but tonight she was thankful for the shadows. She didn't want anyone to see her—see them. And she didn't want to have to look into Sam Brackley's eyes. She'd drown in the midnight blue pools. Of all the people she had to run into... Why the devil was he here?

Soft footfalls approached. Backlit by the bright lights on the street, Sam's tall, imposing figure walked toward her. She tensed.

"Are we alone?"

His low baritone rumbled over her nerve-endings, sending a low voltage of electricity humming through her veins. How could he still do that after ten years?

She quashed the feeling and answered him. "Yes."

"Good. Care to tell me what's going on?"

"No. Why are you here?"

"Uh-uh. I asked first."

"Yes, well, I'm not at liberty to say."

He crossed his massive arms. Even in the shadows, she

could see him raise that eyebrow at her. It was infuriating—though adorable—ten years ago, and it still was today. She crossed her arms and stared back.

He huffed. "A friend of mine got married today. I'm here for the wedding. Your turn."

Audra swallowed and looked away. "It's complicated."

"It always is with you. Just—" He stopped and let his arms fall to his sides, propping his hands on his waist. "You're safe, yes?"

"Yes. I'm safe. It's an assignment. I really can't tell you more than that."

"I figured. And I've drawn my own—" He stopped again, circling a finger in the air, and growled. "Dammit," he muttered softly.

Audra frowned. "Are you all right?"

"Just dandy."

She tried to read his expression, but it was too dark. "Are you sure?"

"Yes. Words... don't always like me anymore." He shuffled closer. "I'm glad you're doing well. I tried to keep track of you, but you disappeared." He brought a hand up and skimmed her face with the back of his knuckles. "It's good to see you, Audra."

"It's Alexandra." Telling him her undercover name was an inane and dumb thing to say, but his touch short-circuited her brain cells. "In case you feel the urge to call my name in public again."

He shuffled even closer. "If I say your name again in this city, I don't plan for anyone but you to hear it."

That low hum in her blood grew louder, and a shiver went down her spine. "Sam..." Her voice held a note of warning. They couldn't spend any more time together than the few stolen minutes in this dank alleyway. Liam was expecting her back. She'd only stepped outside to cool down.

It was hot in the restaurant, but she refused to take off her coat. Having Liam's hand on her bare skin made her skin crawl.

Sam's hand snaked into her hair. Tingles raced through her skin, feeling much different from what she was used to recently. Her eyelids fluttered for a moment before she forced them to stay open. She couldn't let herself succumb to his charm.

With a gentle tug, he pulled her closer. "I know we only have a few minutes. Might as well make the best of them." His head dipped.

Audra knew he intended to kiss her. She wanted him to, even though it was a terrible idea. She didn't need thoughts of him clouding her mind. Not now. But just like their time in Spain, she was powerless against his magnetic pull.

His lips touched hers. Audra raised her hands and clutched at the soft material covering his powerful chest. She was tremendously happy she'd worn colorfast lipstick. Having to explain color smeared over her face would not go over well with her betrothed.

Sam slid a hand under her coat and around her waist, tucking her against his muscular body. Audra leaned into him, savoring the feel of his hard length pressed against her. She'd missed this. Missed him. Even after ten years, she still thought about him quite often. No one else had ever come close to making her feel the way he did.

Which is why she had to stop this nonsense. The timing wasn't right now any more than it had been in Rota. She broke the kiss and extended her arms, putting some space between them. She didn't let go of his shirt, though. Her fingers refused to uncurl just yet. Audra inhaled a deep breath, letting the faint, damp ammonia smell of the alleyway clear her head. She forced her fingers to open. "Go back to your hotel, Sam. Forget you saw me."

He let out a snort. "Fat chance of that. You sure you can't sneak away and come with me?"

Oh, how she wanted to. "Tempting, but no. I need to get back before someone comes looking for me."

"Who?"

"I can't tell you that."

"Why are you involved with the Irish mafia? And in America? What's going on?"

Her eyes widened, and she was grateful for the darkness, so he couldn't see her reaction. It shouldn't surprise her that he'd figured some of it out. The man was far from dumb. "I don't know what you're talking about." She backed up, unwilling to confirm his—correct—assumption.

"Audra—"

"I can't, Sam." Her voice was soft. She backed up another step.

He huffed a harsh breath. "Fine. Just—be careful."

"I am." She drank him in for another long moment, knowing it might be the last time she ever saw him. Rolling her lips inward and pressing them together, she blinked and spun on her heel.

"Audra."

She paused, glancing back into the darkness, barely making out his silhouette.

"If you ever need anything. Look me up. No matter what it is, I'll do what I can to help."

She nodded once. "Thank you." Squaring her shoulders, she willed her emotions back into their cage and walked away.

FOUR

Three months later...

Audra slipped out of the overheated ballroom into the quiet hallway at Liam's house. She was done schmoozing with his buddies and investors. If one more man tried to look down her dress, she was liable to smash his face in. She didn't know why they tried. She never wore anything too revealing. It was part of the persona she'd crafted over the last two years. Demure, intelligent, but deferential. It was the perfect combination of what Liam Brogan wanted in a wife and what she was comfortable giving. Thankfully, she'd managed to put off sex with the man until their wedding night. A wedding night that would never happen. It didn't stop his hands from roving, though. He made sure to stake his claim whenever they were in public. Yet another reason she'd crafted Alexandra Burton to be a demure lady. It meant she could wear sleeves and necklines higher than those that barely covered her nipples.

But her escape had another motive. Her fiancé had

conducted a business meeting earlier with those same investors. She needed to find out what they'd discussed. Even though she worked for his company as his "assistant," she hadn't been privy to this meeting. That told her it wasn't on the up-and-up.

The door to the ballroom opened. She glanced up. Dismay filled her, but she kept it off her face.

"You can't disappear yet, my dear. The party isn't over." Liam strode toward her. In his monochromatic dark suit and shirt, he cut a handsome figure. It was too bad his soul was as dark as his clothing.

"Sorry. I got a little warm."

"Ah. How about a stroll in the garden, then?" He walked forward and held out an arm.

Audra clenched her teeth. There went her chance to search his office. Plus, she did not want to be alone with him outside and away from the guests, but a refusal would arouse his suspicions. So, she pasted a bright smile on her face. "Sure." Taking his arm, she let him lead her down the corridor, into the living room, and out the French doors to the back patio.

"So, how is the wedding planning coming? My mother said you looked lovely in your dress."

"It's fine. Things are on schedule." They were supposed to get married in three months. She'd had her final fitting yesterday. His mother had declared herself Audra's stand-in, since her own fake mother was dead. Siobhan Brogan was a true matriarch. The woman could be kind when she wanted to be, but, even though technically Liam was in charge, she ruled the family—her son included—with an iron fist.

"Good. I'm looking forward to it."

She glanced over at the heated tone of his voice. His brown eyes glittered with a dark heat that sent a chill down Audra's spine. She was glad she'd never have to sleep with him. All indicators suggested it wouldn't be a pleasant experience.

Looking away, she let a lock of her hair fall over her face, shielding it from view. She took every opportunity she could to play up the demure lady persona. Her operation hinged on being the rich man's sheltered daughter. Thank God she wasn't a party animal.

"I still think we should test the waters." He stopped under a tree, drawing her into the shadows. "Make sure we're compatible. It'll be a lonely marriage if we can't keep things spicy in the bedroom."

Audra fought another eye roll. Like that mattered? He'd been stepping out on her since she agreed to this arranged marriage. "My father wouldn't like that. He insisted we wait, remember?" It had been one of her stipulations for taking on this role. They might have had Sean Burton dead-to-rights on a number of charges, but she had threatened to put a halt to the entire thing if he didn't insist Liam wait to deflower his "daughter." She would do a lot for her country, but pimping herself out to a mob boss wasn't in her job description.

Liam hooked a hand around her waist and tugged her forward. "He'll never know. He's all the way back in Chicago. None of my people will tell him." He leaned in and nuzzled her neck with his nose.

Bile rose in her throat. "What about your mother?"

"She'll be going home soon. It's getting late, and she's not the partier she used to be. Especially without father around to insist she stay." He licked the skin behind her ear.

As delicately as she could, Audra put her hands on his shoulders and pushed him back. "I made a promise, Liam. If I break it, I'll feel guilty every time I'm around my dad. I can't do that."

The passionate glitter in his eyes hardened. Audra was happy she knew how to defend herself and that she wasn't really the innocent Alexandra Burton. That woman was happily living her quiet life in witness protection while Audra assumed her identity.

"The longer we wait, the more the—urge—to taste this delectable body of yours gets hold of me." He raked his dark eyes over her body. She'd deliberately chosen a dark dress to hide some of her curves. It hadn't done much good. The men had actually seemed to look at her harder, trying to see through the black fabric.

"Well, that will just make our wedding night that much more exciting. I'm sure you'll be ready to do all kinds of wicked and delicious things." She gave him a coy smile.

Some of the steel disappeared from his gaze. His lips softened into a rakish smile. "How about we save the big act for then and have a preview now?" He slid a hand between her thighs.

Audra deftly side-stepped. "No." She sent him what she hoped was a sexy look; her disgust was reaching new heights. "I want the anticipation. It will make it so much better."

He growled and snatched her close again. His lips landed on hers with punishing force.

Don't bite the arsehole's tongue.

Don't do it.

But, oh, how she wanted to. Instead, she swallowed her disgust and parried her tongue with his, hoping she showed the appropriate level of interest. When he grabbed her breast and gave it a firm squeeze, she faked a moan and pulled back. "That's far enough. Anymore will have to wait."

"You're a tease, Alexandra. And I will delight in teaching you what happens to that kind of woman on our wedding night." He rubbed his palm over her nipple and thrust his hips into her belly.

Audra felt the hard ridge behind his fly. She faked a sultry laugh. "I'm sure we'll both enjoy it," she said, playing the naïve heiress. From the look in his eyes, she doubted he would be kind to her body. No, he planned to take what he wanted as hard and as fast as possible. Oh, she couldn't wait to take this man down. She almost had what she needed. If she could get details of his business meeting, she could potentially close the book on this chapter of her life that had lasted far too long. She was ready to be herself again.

Liam slid a hand down over the curve of her butt and squeezed, then let her go. "Come on. Let's go back to the party."

"Could you give me a few minutes? I'm still a little warm."

A smirk lifted one side of his mouth. "I guess since I heated you up, I can give you a few minutes to gather yourself."

She smiled at him. "Thank you."

"Don't take too long, my dear. The night is still young."

Audra kept her smile in place until he walked away. Once he was out of sight, she let it fall with a grimace. "Bleck." She shivered and shook out her limbs. Keeping one eye on his path to the house, she took another through the garden to the patio that came off his bedroom. Earlier, she'd slipped in and made sure the doors were unlocked.

She sent a glance over her shoulder as she reached the doors. A breeze whispered through the trees, and she could hear the party going strong in the ballroom. With a quick twist, she opened the French doors and let herself into Liam's bedroom.

Stillness surrounded her as she shut the door. Her heels sank into the plush cream carpet as she crossed the room to open the door a crack. Peering into the hallway, she saw no one. Audra slipped off her heels and stepped out onto the tiled hallway floor. Her feet made soft scuffs as she strode toward Liam's office. This part of the house was off-limits to guests, so she was unlikely to meet anyone. It also lacked surveillance, which she didn't understand. A man in Liam Brogan's position should have cameras everywhere. He had a few, but most of them were on the perimeter of the property. He wanted to see people coming, not who was already there. She wasn't complaining, though. It made her job easier. A bug would have made it even easier; she'd already know what the meeting was about. But she'd learned early on that while Liam wasn't the most security conscious mob boss, he did order periodic sweeps for listening devices. Thankfully, she'd learned that little tidbit of information before she'd planted anything.

When she reached the office, she set her shoes on the floor and reached under her skirt to the tool belt strapped to her upper thigh. It was a special one she'd had custom made. Low profile, it hugged the crease of her thigh and hip. Liam had roving hands, so she'd wanted it tucked up as high as she could get it. So far, he hadn't ever gotten a hand high enough to reach it.

From the belt, she removed a set of lock picks and made quick work of unlocking the door. Grabbing her shoes, she went inside, closing the door behind her. She gave the lock a quick twist.

Safely ensconced in the room, she turned and surveyed it in the dark. Through the light coming in from the windows, she could see Liam's solid oak desk looming on the far side. A long conference table took up most of the space to her right. Bookcases and a small seating area occupied the area to her left. She shook her head. It wasn't her first time in here, but she still marveled at the size of the room. It was bigger than her living room and kitchen combined at her flat in London.

Audra moved to the desk. Any information would be locked away in the drawers. She'd seen him stow some files in the bottom once and lock them up. Using her lock picks again, she turned the flimsy latch and slid the drawer open. Audra took the small penlight from her thigh belt and shone the beam on the drawer's contents. On top was a small journal.

She lifted it out and opened it. Lines of code stared back at her. She repeated the top entry to herself. "350G TS DTC." Frowning, she shook her head. "Gobbledygook. That's what it is." Audra took her phone from her dress pocket and photographed the pages. She'd send them to her handler and let the analysts figure out what it all meant.

Once she had pictures of every page, she went through the rest of the drawer's contents, photographing everything. When she was done there, she opened the drawer above it, but it was just office supplies. Feeling along the bottom of the desk and the tops and backs of the drawers, she found nothing else of note.

She peered out the window, then closed the blinds before sitting down at the desk to open the laptop. Reaching into her little thigh pouch again, she took out one of the USB sticks her handler gave her and plugged it in.

"Come on, come on, come on," she muttered as it did its thing to crack the password. She drummed her fingers on the desk and glanced at the door. She needed to get back to the party before Liam went looking for her.

The screen changed and the desktop icons appeared. She clicked on the file explorer and then the documents tab. Her gaze raked down the contents, stopping on one with her alias. "What?"

Audra clicked on it. Images of herself popped up. Most of them were of her running errands. A few were through the blinds at her house. One showed her walking through her living room in her underwear and a t-shirt. She remembered that night. That was the night she ran into Sam. When she got home, she'd been too keyed up to sleep, even after a shower. She'd wandered out to the kitchen to get some wine and ice cream, hoping the comfort food items would help settle her mind so she could sleep. It hadn't helped. The ice cream had just made her think of decadence and the wine had stoked her hormones. She'd had some vivid dreams that night once she finally fell asleep. Had one of Liam's bodyguards seen her with him? Was he afraid she was cheating?

But the pictures went back further than that night. He'd had her under surveillance for months, it appeared. How had she not seen someone watching her? Better yet, why hadn't her handler, Theo? He lurked around sometimes, just to check things out. Did he know about this and just hadn't said anything?

That felt like a more real possibility. So long as it was harmless, she could see him keeping it to himself. If she'd known, it might have made her more guarded, especially when she was out by herself. Her mysterious stalker would have picked up on the change and reported it to Liam.

Audra plugged a second USB device into the computer and copied the contents of the folder. She went back to the documents tab and looked at the other folders. Only one looked promising. It had some of the same code as the ledger: DTC. She opened it.

Muffled voices came through the door. Her head shot up. "Shit." She was out of time. With a few clicks, she copied all the files to the USB drive. Clicking back to the hard drive tab, she scanned it quickly, making sure she hadn't missed anything, then ejected her device, exited all her windows, and closed the laptop. Stuffing everything back into the slim pouch around her thigh, she grabbed her shoes and padded silently to the door. She could still hear voices. They were down the hall, but she couldn't risk leaving.

With a soft curse, she glanced at the window. *The blinds.* She'd forgotten to open them when she shut the laptop. *Good move, Aud.* She crossed to the window and turned the stick.

The voices grew louder. One of them was Liam's.

Audra bit back a frustrated groan. She should have been out of here already, but that damn folder had distracted her. She bit her lip and weighed her options. Going through the door was not one. She could hide under the desk or behind the sofa and pray they didn't find her if they came inside.

She glanced at the window again. Or she could go out that way.

Shadows moved through the light coming in from under the door. There was no time to waffle. Get out or hide.

She chose out. Ducking under the blinds, she flipped open the window lock and tugged. The sash slid up with a soft swish. Audra lifted a leg through the opening. Metal clicked on metal at the door. Her heartbeat rose several notches. She only had seconds left. Wiggling her other foot through the window, she hopped to the ground and spun around, whisking the window closed before diving into the bushes lining the house below it. She crouched in the shadows and kept her head down, thankful for her dark hair. She wished she had a shawl, though, to hide her gleaming white shoulders.

A light came on, illuminating the yard beyond. Audra stayed put. In this position, someone would have to practically press their face against the glass and look down to see her.

Minutes passed, and the light stayed on. Her legs started to tingle, the blood flow restricted by her position. She chanced a glance at the window. No one was visible. She snaked her left leg to the side, following it with the rest of her body. She needed to get back to the party and would have to chance moving. If she stayed against the house, she could likely make it out of view.

With slow, deliberate movements, she kept up her sideways walk, staying low to avoid the windows. By the time she reached the edge of the house, her thighs burned. She peeked around the bushes and glanced out. The shadows in the garden shifted as the wind ruffled the trees. No people-sized shadows moved, though. Audra gave the area one last cautious look, then stood and walked out from behind the hedge. She paused long enough to put her shoes back on, then wandered back to the party.

She made it through the rest of the evening without incident. Liam returned to the ballroom about ten minutes after she did and proceeded to hang all over her. He'd had a few drinks in his office. She could smell the whiskey on his breath that wasn't there when he kissed her in the garden. When it came time to leave, she made sure to say goodbye with others present so she didn't end up pressed into a dark corner. She really didn't want to maim him and blow her cover. Not when she was so close to bringing him down.

Cool, dry air hit her skin as she left his house. It felt wonderful after the cloying atmosphere inside. Too many bodies wearing too many different perfumes. She'd wanted to escape to the garden again, but didn't dare. Not only because she didn't want to invite Liam's advances, but she also didn't want to arouse suspicion. So, she stayed. Now, though, she had a splitting headache.

The valet opened the driver's door on her black BMW Roadster and Audra slid behind the wheel with a quick smile and a murmured word of thanks. The engine purred softly. She would be sad to give up this car when her op was over. She loved this little thing.

Buckling up, she put the car in gear and headed for the high-end condo her alter ego lived in. The trendy neighborhood was nice, but Audra missed her flat back home. Her building was ancient and had the old-world charm she loved. Soon, she hoped to be back in it.

The miles whizzed by in relative quiet. At this hour, traffic was light. Fifteen minutes after she left Liam's, she pulled into her garage. Exhausted, she climbed out of her car and went inside. She desperately wanted to go to bed, but she needed to get a message to Theo that she had a copy of Liam's laptop first. She'd copied it twice before. Once when she first arrived, then again a few months later. She honestly hadn't expected much on it after the last two times of getting nothing. The pictures of her were a surprise.

Audra entered the small mudroom off the garage and kicked off her heels. "Oh, that's better," she sighed. She didn't care that they cost more than her rent; they were killing her feet.

The marble tile was cool underfoot as she crossed the threshold to the kitchen. She stopped for a bottle of water from the fridge, then headed upstairs. The third step creaked as it always did. It was the only spot in her flooring that did. It was a great reminder that even things wrapped in the shiniest packages weren't perfect.

She stripped out of her clothes and unfastened the strap around her thigh, letting it all fall to the floor. She'd take a quick shower, then contact Theo. She could still smell Liam on her; it was making her queasy. The longer this op went on, the lower her tolerance for him became. It took a superhuman effort anymore not to stab him in the eye.

The rain head shower shot to life as she twisted the knob. When the water warmed, she dipped her head in the spray with a sigh. She spent fifteen minutes standing under the steaming torrent, scrubbing herself down with her honey and jasmine-scented body wash until her skin was red. The hot water relaxed her muscles and helped ease her headache. Reluctantly, she shut off the water. She couldn't stay in the shower all night.

After wrapping her hair in a towel and donning some underwear and a heather gray t-shirt, she scooped the pouch containing the USB drive off the floor, picked up her phone, and went downstairs.

Audra caught sight of her reflection in the living room

window. She marched over and pulled the cord for the blinds, then twisted them shut. No one would be peeking in on her through the curtains tonight. With the room secure, she picked up her laptop from the table and sat down on the sofa. She logged in, then inserted the USB drive into the port and hit download. She wasn't supposed to make copies of the information she gathered, but there was absolutely no way she was turning over the drive without making a backup. Not with what she found on it. She'd always been a bit of a rule breaker, anyway. She looked at the backups she'd made throughout this mission as insurance. A lot could go wrong on an op of this magnitude.

A gray box popped up; the blue bar at the bottom slowly crept toward the opposite side. When it was done, she saved it to a private server that only she had the password to, then deleted the file from her computer. Connecting her phone, she copied all the pictures she'd taken of the ledger and loaded those to her private server as well before she copied them to the USB stick and deleted them off her hard drive and her phone. With that finished, she logged into her agency's server and sent a message to her handler, asking to meet in the morning.

Blowing out a breath, Audra ejected the drive and shut off the computer. She set it on the table and stood. Her bed beckoned her.

A soft trill came from upstairs. Audra groaned as she recognized the ringtone. It was Theo on her burner phone. "Dammit." Why couldn't he wait until morning? She just wanted to go to sleep.

Audra dashed upstairs and dug the phone out of the shoebox in her closet. "Are you aware of what time it is? When I said in the morning, I didn't mean right now."

"You're still awake, so what does it matter? Put some pants on and meet me at the park."

A frown creased her brow. "How do you know I'm not wearing pants?" Her mind flashed to the images on the drive.

"I've been sitting in your neighbor's bloody hedge for the last two hours. You gave me a full show when you snapped the blinds closed. Blue's your color."

"Oh, sod off, arsehole." She hung up on him with a huff. Putting the phone back, she grabbed a pair of black leggings off a shelf and slid them on. After thrusting her arms into a matching black zip-up hoodie, she stuffed her feet into a pair of plimsolls and headed outside with the USB drive in her pocket.

She stuck to the shadows as she walked. This time of night, someone would notice her just strutting down the street. With her head on a swivel, she quickened her pace.

It only took her about five minutes to reach the park. She cursed Theo the entire way. Even in the more comfortable canvas shoes, her feet still hurt. And she could hear her bed calling for her, still. The only good thing about meeting tonight was that she could now sleep in tomorrow. She didn't need to be anywhere until lunchtime. Liam's sister wanted to go over the seating for the wedding. Audra needed plenty of sleep to pretend she cared.

A soft coo drew her attention. She walked toward it, recognizing Theo's signal. The shadows shifted, and he stepped out of the darkness he'd been melded to. Palmetto fronds fluttered as he moved through the plants that filled a landscaping bed. His black long-sleeve shirt, black pants, and black running shoes had made him nearly invisible.

"Don't scowl, Aud. It's not a good look."

"Again, sod off. You look like a burglar, so you've little room to talk. Here." She took the thumb drive from her pocket and thrust it at him. "Take this so I can go home and sleep."

He took the drive and slipped it into his pocket. "It's not that late. You've partied harder in the last year."

"Yes, well, he was particularly handsy tonight. And several people wore clashing perfumes. I have a raging headache and a low tolerance for people now."

"Well, hopefully the drive will have what we need on it, and you can get out of there."

"I hope so too. Speaking of its contents, he's been keeping tabs on me. I found a file folder full of pictures."

Theo's gaze sharpened. "Of you doing what? He didn't catch us meeting, did he?"

"No. It's mostly of me running errands or lounging around at home. I was careful coming here too. If someone followed me, they're far better at this spy thing than me."

Theo's mouth flattened. "Okay. We shouldn't linger, then. Go home. I'll be in touch."

"Find something, Theo, and get me the hell out of here." With a hard look at him, she turned and jogged away.

Five

Humming to herself, Audra whipped her roadster into a parking space outside of Byrne's. She'd had more fun at lunch with Hannah than she thought she would. Liam's sister was an energetic, chatty woman who, most days, was only concerned with herself. She could be funny, though. And she lived for parties, which was why Liam's mother, Siobhan, put her in charge of her eldest son's wedding. While Audra had still stifled yawns as they went over details, she'd enjoyed Hannah's company.

Which was the only reason she could think of why she'd agreed to run to Byrne's and fetch a box of table linens for a different party Hannah was in charge of this evening. Hannah had seemed frazzled—the caterer had called her shortly before she left to meet Audra for lunch and informed her there would be a change to the menu; one she didn't like—so Audra volunteered to help so she could go and straighten that out.

She sighed as she stepped out of her car, shaking her head. At least she didn't have anything to do after this until she had to meet Liam for dinner at seven. She could go home, slip back into her comfy clothes and read a book.

Entering the restaurant, she waved at the hostess and walked toward the back. The din of the lunch crowd receded and was replaced by the sound of the kitchen staff. Her heels clacked on the tile floor as she headed for the stockroom.

"Hey, Alexandra. What are you doing here?"

She paused and smiled at the day manager, Miles. "Hannah asked me to pick up some tablecloths for her."

"Oh, yes. They're all boxed up and waiting. Let me show you."

"Thanks, Miles." She followed him into the stockroom.

He hefted a box from a stack in the far corner. "I'll carry it out for you."

"Are you sure? I can take it."

"I'm sure. It's heavy."

She didn't argue with him, even though she was more than capable of carrying the box. Alexandra wouldn't argue.

They wove back through the kitchen and out the front doors. Her roadster beeped as she pressed the button to unlock it. She opened the trunk and stepped back so he could put the box inside.

"There you go."

"Thank you, Miles." She slipped him some cash, then got into the driver's seat and pulled into traffic.

Her drive took her across town to Liam's neighborhood. The party was at a neighbor's house. Some fancy businessman Audra was sure was under FBI surveillance. Most people in this particular neighborhood led some shady lives. She didn't really want to go into the house—or even pull into his driveway—and end up on their radar, but she didn't have a valid reason for turning Hannah down. Especially not now that she knew Liam had her followed. She didn't want it to get back to his sister that she lied. She'd just call Theo later and tell him to be on the lookout for an inquiry about her alias.

Turning into the circular driveway, she parked and

hopped out, grabbing the box. Picking her way over the cobblestone walkway to the front door, she poked the bell with her pinkie.

A maid answered the door. "Yes?"

"Hi, I'm dropping these off for Hannah. It's tablecloths for tonight's party."

"Oh. I'll take them."

"You're sure? It's heavy."

"Yes. Mr. Kimball doesn't like strangers in the house."

Audra's brow puckered, but she stayed silent. She was hardly a stranger in Kimball's social circle. She'd never been in his house, though. And she didn't really want to spend more time than necessary on this task. But there could be relevant intel inside. She thought quickly.

The maid reached for the box. Audra deliberately fumbled the handover and the woman's hands slipped off. "I think you should just guide me where you want this." Audra readjusted the box. "So we don't spill them all over the ground."

Biting the corner of her lip, the maid nodded. "Yeah. We can't get them dirty. I suppose it would be okay. You'll only be here a moment." She stepped back, pushing the door wide. "Come in."

Audra stepped over the threshold. She kept her gaze straight ahead until the maid turned around and started deeper into the house. Then, Audra put her head on a swivel and took in everything she could. The dark walnut floor underfoot stretched down a long hallway to her left. To her right, she glimpsed a small parlor with a champagne damask settee and a mahogany leather wingback chair grouped around a gleaming cherry wood coffee table and a plush cream rug. Ahead, the foyer opened into a large, airy living room filled with shades of gray and white. It was like walking into a magazine spread. On the far end, to the right, was the kitchen, which was also done in shades of gray and white. High-end appliances gleamed, nary a fingerprint in sight.

How do people live like this? Audra shook her head at the thought. It didn't matter how much she cleaned or picked up after herself, her condo, and her flat in London, always looked lived in. Perhaps it helped to have a maid who could trail around after her employers and put everything back to rights the moment it was knocked askew.

They passed down a short hallway and into a solarium. Plants lined the perimeter, soaking up the sun streaming in through the glass walls and ceiling.

"You can set the box over there." The maid pointed to a spot where someone had piled other party supplies.

Audra crossed the room and set her load atop a short stack of boxes, then flexed her fingers. They'd started to cramp.

Movement outside caught her attention. Two men exited the house and strolled toward the small bar set up poolside. One was Jackson Kimball. She didn't recognize the other. The way he was dressed, though, struck her as odd. Even in casual clothes, she could tell that Kimball's outfit was expensive. But the stranger's didn't have the same look to it. He looked ordinary.

"Thank you for bringing the tablecloths."

Audra glanced away to look at the maid. She stood in the doorway, a polite smile on her face. Her eyes darted to the window.

"You're welcome." Taking her cue to leave, Audra walked toward her. The maid stepped into the hall and started back the way they came. Again, Audra paid close attention to her surroundings. Nothing stood out to her, but she took mental snapshots of the house's interior. Smiling at the maid, she exited the house and went back to her car.

As she pulled away, she mentally went over what she'd seen inside as well as the man with Kimball. When she got home, she definitely needed to call Theo. Something about that guy bugged her.

She shook her head. *Not your problem, Aud.* She needed to leave that one to the FBI. Maybe she'd tell the agent working with her on Brogan's case about it. Moran could pass along the intel to whoever had Kimball under surveillance.

With the daytime traffic, it took her a little over twenty minutes to reach her condo. Parking in her garage, she went inside and headed upstairs to fetch her secure phone. She sat down on her bed and dialed Theo's number.

"What's up?" he asked when he answered.

"I just made a delivery to Jackson Kimball's house. You'll probably get a hit on my alias from the FBI or whatever alphabet soup agency is watching him."

Theo sighed. "What did you deliver?"

"Tablecloths."

"You're sure?"

"I didn't look in the box other than to peek through the flaps to see the top layer was just that. Miles carried it to my car and watched me drive away. If it had anything important, I'm sure he called ahead, so a delay wouldn't have been wise."

"Did you talk to Kimball?"

"No. He was there, though. With another man. I didn't recognize him, but something about him set off my radar."

"How so?"

"I'm not sure. He just didn't look like he was in the same class as Kimball. He was dressed nice, but his clothes were more—working class, I guess. Not expensive, like we'd expect of his associates."

"Maybe it was someone who works for him. An accountant or something."

"Maybe. But I don't think so. Even the accountants and other office type people that surround men like Kimball and

Liam dress in more expensive clothing. This guy's looked like he bought them off the rack at Target or something."

"All right. Well, keep an eye out for him. We can't do much, because Kimball's not the focus of our investigation. But if you see this guy with Brogan, I'll do my best to get an ID."

Audra sighed. That really was the best she could hope for. Sometimes, it irked her to not have the U.S. agencies looped in on their investigation. Someone, somewhere was aware, she knew that. But the local guys in the field weren't likely to know, and she couldn't risk her cover and tell them what she saw. "Fine. Can you let Moran know? He can pass it along within the FBI."

"Sure."

"Did you get anything on those files I brought you?"

"We're still working on it. I'll let you know if we find anything you need to know."

Audra rolled her eyes. That was code for she wouldn't be getting anything unless the circumstances were dire. She was happier more than ever now that she'd made a copy of the pictures. She wasn't completely useless when it came to information and image analysis. "All right. Thanks, Theo."

"You're welcome. What's your plan for the rest of the day?"

"Nothing until dinner this evening. Liam's taking me to some new place that opened up at the Bellagio. Thankfully, it's not just us. We're meeting some of his associates."

"Good. I hope you get some good intel."

"That's the plan." That was always the plan. It's why she was here.

"Report in when you get home."

"I will."

They said goodbye and hung up. Audra stowed the phone, then changed. For the next several hours, she refused to think about work. She desperately needed a break. This assignment was really beginning to wear on her. She was ready to end it and get back to her normal life.

The afternoon flew past as she whiled away the hours, reading a romance novel. It was her little secret passion. There was nothing wrong with reading romance, but she preferred not to let Liam or Theo know she liked the books. Liam would belittle her, making her angry, and then she'd just have to suppress the urge to tell him where to shove it. Theo would roll his eyes and tell her it was a waste of her brain power. It wasn't. The books were an escape from reality. They reduced her stress, which to her, made them more valuable than all the couture clothing in her closet.

All too soon, the alarm on her phone went off, letting her know it was time to slip back into Alexandra Burton's shoes. Quite literally. In her real life, Audra rarely wore heels. She was tall enough without them. Plus, she disliked blisters. Since taking on this role, though, she'd developed callouses on her heels and the sides of her toes. But the first month had been painful. She wanted to tell herself that she'd wear high heels more often when she went back to London, now that she had her feet conditioned to the shoes, but she knew herself too well. She much preferred sneakers and boots to dressy heels. No matter how good they made her legs look.

With a huff, she got up, leaving her book on the end table beside the sofa. Upstairs, she painstakingly applied her makeup and donned a royal purple, sleeveless dress that she topped with a three-quarter sleeve gold bolero jacket. There would be no exposed skin on her upper body that Liam could touch. She learned early on it made her skin crawl, so now she usually covered everything above the elbow.

At six-fifty, she heard the horn from the limo outside. Liam never came to the door. Sometimes, he wasn't even in the car. Since they were meeting people, she doubted he was tonight. He was likely at the restaurant, making sure everything was to his liking. When it came to social events where others could judge him, Liam left very little to chance.

The chauffeur offered her a smile as she neared.

"Good evening, Ms. Burton." He opened her door.

"Good evening, Rowan." She slid inside. As she'd expected, the car was empty. Her shoulders relaxed.

But the reprieve was slight. Within fifteen minutes, they were pulling up to the restaurant. Rowan opened her door, and she slid out. Giving her name to the maitre'd, she was shown to a circular booth tucked into a corner. She took stock of the people at the table before they saw her. Two men, both dressed in nearly identical gray suits, sat on one end, a blonde woman with a blank stare on her face sandwiched between them. She held a long-stemmed wineglass in her fingers and toyed with the rim as she stared into space while the men talked. On the other side of the second man sat another woman. This one had dark hair, and unlike the blonde, her gaze traveled the room. Liam sat at the other end of the booth, talking to the men.

Liam glanced up as she approached and smiled. "Ah. There you are, my dear." He stood, motioning her to sit.

Audra sat down, hiding a grimace. She didn't like being closed in, but there was no way Liam would let anyone box him in. He always sat on the end.

Audra smiled at the strangers. "Hello. I hope I didn't keep anyone waiting. My driver ran into traffic." She wasn't about to tell Liam that Rowan was a few minutes late. She liked her chauffeur. He was a kind, older man.

"You're fine, my dear." Liam laid a hand on her thigh. "We chatted a little while we waited. No harm done."

"Good." She lifted her water glass and took a drink so she didn't pluck Liam's fingers off her leg.

The dark-haired woman nodded in agreement, smiling at

her; the blonde perked up slightly at the conversation. From the glazed look in her eyes, Audra guessed she was high. She could also see the faint outline of a bruise on the woman's jaw. There were likely more hiding beneath the sleeves of her jacket. The woman flinched when the man to her right reached up to rest his arm across the back of the booth.

Anger burned in Audra's chest. She catalogued his face and noted his name as Liam introduced her to the table. When she got home tonight, she'd do a deep dive on him and see what she could find. It would be her pleasure to stick this man in federal prison. She'd hand him to the FBI on a silver platter. She didn't care if taking him down wasn't part of her assignment. The men who beat women got her blood pumping harder than just about any other kind of criminal. Only child molesters angered her more.

Audra was the last to arrive. Shortly after she sat down, a server appeared to take their orders. She hastily glanced at the menu and picked something that sounded decent—an exotic stew. Then she sat back and did what Alexandra Burton was supposed to do. Look pretty. It was the perfect cover. While Alexandra appeared uninterested, Audra's mind took in everything. From names mentioned, to business transactions. Tonight, however, there wasn't too much of that. It seemed to be more of a get to know you type of dinner. The two men, Simon and Geoffrey Powell, were brothers who owned a distribution company in Las Vegas. Why Liam would be looking for a new distribution company intrigued her, but the three of them spoke little about business. It was mostly about themselves and their interests.

She was actually thankful they didn't talk business. The dark-haired woman with Geoffrey, Celine, was chatty. Audra hadn't been able to pay as close attention to the men's discussion as she would have liked because Celine kept engaging her in conversation. By the time the meal ended, Audra had learned little else about the men besides some background info.

"Did you enjoy your dinner?" Liam asked as they left the restaurant.

"It was fine."

"Only fine?"

Audra shrugged. "Yes. It wasn't anything special. It was like a lot of the higher end restaurants we go to. All the food is the same."

His mouth flattened. "Good to know."

Something in his expression made her frown. "Why?"

"I invested in this place." He tipped his head toward the building behind them. "I hope it doesn't fail."

"Oh. Well, I'm sure it will be fine. The food was good, it just didn't wow me. Not many places do anymore. Like I said, it's all the same." Rowan opened the limo door. "There's no originality," she said as she got in.

"I suppose I see your point." He got in beside her.

Audra pressed her knees together and tucked her ankles to the side, resting her hands and her small clutch purse in her lap. She did not want him to get any ideas while they were alone back here. She'd rebuked him before in the back of a limousine.

He rested an elbow on the window and stared out. "If I were to invest in another restaurant, what would you want to see?"

"You're asking for my opinion?"

"Of course." He looked at her. "You'll be my wife soon. People will look up to you. You'll have your own social responsibilities in that role, and others will respect your opinion. If you don't like a restaurant or call it dull or unoriginal, others in our circle won't go there. So, what would you like to see?"

"More flare. Exotic ingredients used in exciting ways. That place had the ingredients, but they put them in a stew and used the same herbs and spices you'd get in any traditional stew, so it didn't taste any different."

He nodded. "Perhaps I'll suggest a change to their menu."

Audra stayed silent, not wanting to get in the middle of it. That chef likely worked hard to not only create the dish, but to secure Liam's backing and that of other investors. She would not be the one to derail his or her business.

Liam peppered her with other questions as Rowan drove toward her condo. She answered as diplomatically as she could. When he broached the subject of a menu for a new restaurant rather than a current one, she answered more freely, feeling more comfortable when it wasn't someone's livelihood on the line. It made the drive pass quickly, for which she was grateful. When they pulled up outside her home, he looked surprised.

He tipped his head, eyeing her thoughtfully. "I had a nice time this evening."

Her brow wrinkled. "You don't normally enjoy my company? This bodes well for our marriage, Liam," she said with a chuckle.

A quick smile flashed over his face. "I guess I haven't really taken the time to get to know you as well as I should. Ma arranged this marriage, and I went along with it because she's right. I need an heir. You're beautiful and come from a good family, so I never looked much further than that at you. But you've got a brain hiding behind that pretty face." His expression turned quizzical. "Why did you agree to this marriage?"

Crap. Why now, of all times, when they were so close to bringing this operation to a close, did he want to get personal? She dredged up the backstory they'd come up with for her, then lied through her teeth. "My father's business put our entire family in danger. Your mother offered us a way out. I have younger siblings. They don't deserve to suffer. Plus, I've grown accustomed to a certain lifestyle. And let's be honest.

You're not exactly hard to look at." She lifted a shoulder, playing the part of a spoiled heiress. "No one was going to want some bankrupt mogul's daughter. No one of any standing, anyway. It was a win-win for both of us. My father saves his business and our family's status, I get to keep my lifestyle, and you get access to my father's business contacts and a spot on the board of his company. It was a no-brainer."

A slow smile spread over his face. "Why, Alexandra. I never knew you were so calculating. I like it."

Audra's stomach turned. That should not be an attractive quality to anyone. She swallowed the bile and pasted a naughty smile on her face. "Yes, well, when you grow up in our world, it's a good quality to have."

"Indeed." He slid a hand over her knee. "Can I persuade you to let me come in tonight?"

Her stomach churned so hard she feared she'd be unable to choke down the vomit this time. She clenched her teeth, swallowing as inconspicuously as possible, and covered his hand with hers. "No. I might be calculating, but I also love to torture myself by denying myself things I know I would enjoy until the time is right. And I'm sure I'll enjoy our first night together, which is why I want to wait."

A hardness entered his eyes, turning them cold. "What if I decide I no longer wish to wait?"

You'll find yourself without your bollocks. Audra barely bit back the words. She forced a sickly-sweet smile onto her face. "Now, why would you want to do that? A willing woman will always make the experience more fun." She leaned in and ran a finger under his jacket lapel before injecting a low, sultry note into her voice. "There are things I can do that you'll only get from me if I'm a willing participant. Wicked, naughty things."

The cold glint in his eyes heated, and Audra knew she'd averted disaster.

"Such as?"

She sat back and ticked a finger back and forth. "A woman never gives away her secrets. You'll just have to wonder."

He growled. "You're not as innocent as your father would like me to believe."

"No."

"I like that."

Audra only had a moment to steel herself before he grabbed her and fused their mouths together. Her dinner threatened to make an appearance, but she tamped it down and forced herself to participate in the kiss. When he slid a hand up the outside of her thigh and under the hem of her dress, she pushed him away, her hand planted in the middle of his chest and her arm extended. "Nice try. Haven't you learned I can be stubborn when I want to be?"

He chuckled. "I'm learning many things about you. Forgive me if I'm eager to learn more." His fingers dug into her thigh.

"We have plenty of time for that." She swung her legs away and slid toward the door. "I'm going in now before things get any more heated."

Liam sat back in his seat and rubbed himself through his pants. "Give me a taste, at least. Bend over and flip up your skirt. Let me see that pert little ass of yours."

Gross. She hid her disgust with a chuckle. "You can watch it walk away." She pushed the door open and got out. As she walked up the sidewalk to her front door, she put some extra sway in her hips. Once she crossed her threshold and locked herself in, she let out a hard shiver. "Bleh! Disgusting pig." She dropped her clutch purse and keys on the entryway table and shucked her shoes. Like the night before, she went upstairs, but this time, instead of hopping in the shower, she grabbed her toothbrush and cleaned her mouth. She could still taste him.

After brushing twice and rinsing—and gargling—with

mouthwash, she stripped out of her clothes and stepped into the shower. Tonight's wash was a quick one. She didn't want to linger. She wanted to dig into the two men from dinner.

Dressed in her standard sleeping attire of a t-shirt and panties, she made herself some tea and sat down on the sofa with her laptop. Gathering some intel would tell her if the men were worth putting surveillance on. Though she was bringing Simon down, no matter what. The man deserved whatever charges she could make stick.

Absorbed in her search, it took a moment for the loud squeak of the back fence gate to register. When it did, her head popped up, and she froze, listening. Everything stayed quiet, but that gate wouldn't have made noise unless someone opened it.

Audra closed her laptop and set it on the coffee table. She stood up and rounded the sofa, reaching into the small chest on the low bookcase against the wall to her left. The thirty-eight caliber handgun nestled snuggly in her palm as she crept toward the sliding door.

The trill of Theo's ringtone echoed through the condo. Audra jumped, then muttered a soft curse. She gave the back garden another glance, then dashed upstairs to answer. The ringing stopped as she reached the landing, then immediately started again. She ran into her room, crossing to the closet, and dug it out of its hiding spot just before it rolled to voicemail again. "Hello?"

"I chased someone out of your garden, but now I think I'm being followed. Get out here. I'm headed toward the park," Theo said.

"What?" The line clicked in her ear. "Theo?" She looked at the phone to see he'd hung up. Groaning in frustration, Audra set the phone down and grabbed a pair of leggings and hastily put them on. As she shrugged into a zip-up hoodie, a sense of déjà vu hit her. She hoped tonight turned out as innocuous as last night.

Slipping on some shoes, she picked up the burner phone and her gun and ran downstairs and outside. For a moment, she debated taking her car, but she wouldn't be able to drive it through the park. She'd have to park, then jog down the trail to their meeting spot. It would be faster if she ran from the start.

Audra took off at a steady jog. It was still early enough the neighbors wouldn't think it weird to see someone out running. It was late, but not late late.

Her feet pounded the pavement in a steady rhythm. Her calves protested the exercise after being strained by her four-inch heels earlier, but it didn't take long for the muscles to stretch and warm. She neared the last intersection before she reached the park and slowed, looking for Theo or anyone suspicious. Cars lined the street, parked near a multi-story apartment complex. Nothing moved. She turned, jogging up the road. The concrete walkway ended, and she veered into the street.

A car started behind her, and she heard a quick squeal of tires.

Audra drifted to the side to get out of the way. Near the edge of the pavement, she glanced back.

Headlights flipped on only yards away, blinding her. Alarm rang in her head. She tensed, her muscles flexing to propel her out of the way, but it was too late.

The car clipped her hip as it sailed past and sent her flying to the berm; her head smacked the pavement.

Audra's lungs refused to work, the muscles frozen from the impact. Her vision went fuzzy, and all the sound around her receded behind the *swish-swish* of her heartbeat in her ears. She laid on the ground, not moving, and closed her eyes.

A soft thud penetrated the fog in her mind. She cracked

one eye open and saw a blurry pair of feet coming toward her. As they neared, they came into focus. Black running shoes. Jeans rested on the tops.

The person stopped a few feet away. Audra screamed at her muscles to move. To reach for the gun tucked into her pocket. Her fingers twitched, brushing the edge of her jacket. She didn't have the strength to do more.

Suddenly, the feet turned. A moment later, they ran away. Audra fought the darkness edging her vision, but it was too strong for her. A second squeal of tires was the last thing she heard.

Six

A buzz filled Audra's ears. Her eyelids fluttered, and bright light burned her retinas, making her moan.

"Hey, there. Can you open your eyes and look at me?"

The female voice reverberated through Audra's head. She moaned again and tried to roll away from the noise. A sharp pinch in her hand stopped her and brought a bit of clarity to her mind. What was going on?

"Open your eyes, honey. You're in the hospital."

Hospital? Why? Audra struggled to remember what happened, but her head ached something fierce. Another low moan escaped her. She raised her other hand to touch it, but someone pulled her hand down. Panic shot through her. Instinctively, she rolled her arm inward, breaking their hold, then lashed out. She connected with someone's chest, and they let out an oomph.

"Let's not do that, hon. We're here to help you," the loud voice said.

"Stop shouting. Blimey."

"That's a pretty accent. How about you look at me and tell me where you're from."

Audra groaned and blinked, then scrunched her eyes closed. "Can you turn the lights down? My head's about to split." She groaned again, but not from the lights. She'd spoken to the nurse in her native accent. Blimey was right. She'd blown her own cover.

"Claudia, hit the lights," the nurse said. A moment later, the room dimmed.

Audra blinked again, and this time, was able to focus. A woman around her age, wearing navy-blue scrubs who had her blonde hair scooped into a messy bun, smiled at her. "Hey, there. My name is Gabby. Do you remember what happened?"

"No."

"How about your name? Can you tell us that?"

"Amber Carter." Claiming she was Alexandra Burton wouldn't work now that they'd heard her accent, but she wasn't about to give them her real name. Amber was another of her identities. If anyone searched it, it would come back to a marketing executive living in Vegas.

"Good. How about what day it is?"

Her pulse pounded in her temple as she tried to remember. "I don't know. Friday?"

"Close. It's just after midnight on Sunday morning."

Audra let out a grunt as memories flitted at the edge of her mind. "What happened? How did I get here?"

"Best we can tell you got hit by a car while you were out running. The police would like to talk to you."

She bet they would. Some of the night's events came back to her. "Someone hit me."

"Yes. You were running and were struck by a car."

"No. I mean deliberately."

"What?" Gabby's voice turned sharp. "You're sure?"

"Yes. I need my phone." She touched her side, but realized she was in a hospital gown. "Where are my clothes?" A touch of panic set in as she remembered what else had been in her pocket. "Shit." She closed her eyes and rested her head against the pillow. The cops probably had *a lot* of questions for her.

"We had to cut them off of you. But don't worry, we won't send you home in a gown. Let me get the doctor to come take a look at you since you're awake. I know you have questions. Someone will be in soon, too, to take you down to CT." The woman spun away and disappeared before Audra could protest.

She took the quiet moment to take stock of herself. A chill ghosted over her skin; the thin hospital gown and blanket doing little to keep her warm. With each passing moment, her head cleared a little more. It pounded, though. And throbbed. For that matter, so did her hip and side. Tentatively, she pressed a hand to the crest of her hip. Air hissed through her teeth. "Oh, yeah. Not doing that again."

The door whisked open, and a young woman in a burgundy scrub top walked in. "Hello. I'm here to take you down for your CT scan." She walked to the foot of the bed and took off the brake.

Audra's stomach somersaulted as the bed rolled forward. She pressed the back of her hand to her mouth. "Go slow. I'm nauseous."

"Got it. No racecar driving."

The girl expertly steered her out of the bay and down the hall. Audra scrunched her eyes closed against the bright lights and bit back a moan. The gurney swung sideways, and they passed through a doorway into a chilly room that was thankfully dimmer.

"Hi, there. I'm Kate. Misty and I are going to transfer you onto our table. You just stay still. Let us do all the work."

"No problem." Audra closed her eyes. The room spun less that way.

The technicians made quick work of putting her on the table and running her through the scanner. In less than five minutes, Audra was back on the gurney and on her way back to the emergency department. Misty rolled her into her original bay, then bid her farewell. Audra lifted a hand, but didn't open her eyes.

Vaguely, she was aware of people coming in and out. Sometimes they asked her to open her eyes and answer their questions. Mostly, though, they left her alone to rest. She wasn't sure how much time passed before the doctor came in to talk to her.

The door slid open and the man's greeting startled her awake some time later.

"Hello, Ms. Carter."

Audra pressed her palm to her forehead and eyed him with a steely gaze.

He seemed unphased by her ire and smiled. "It's nice to see you awake."

Audra did her best to wipe the grimace off her face and studied the mid-forties doctor who'd walked in. A polite smile crinkled his eyes. "Hi. How long was I out?"

"Not too long. Longer than I'd like, but your head CT looks fine. Can you tell me what happened?"

"Someone hit me with their car."

"The nurse said you think it was deliberate. Is that correct?"

"Yes. Could you tell me what other injuries I have? My hip is killing me."

"I suspect it's just a bad contusion. I'll have another look, but I didn't see anything concerning. All your scans were clear. You're a lucky woman. You escaped with little damage." He came toward her and pulled a penlight from his pocket. "Let's check your pupils. They looked good when you were brought in, but your extended time unconscious has me a bit concerned."

"I'm fine. You said my scan looked all right. My brain likely just decided it wanted the sleep. I don't do that much."

He hummed. "Humor me. Follow the light with your eyes." He drew a cross in the air with the light, and Audra did as he asked.

"Good. You have a bit of a horizontal nystagmus. Is that normal for you?"

"No."

"Okay. Nystagmus isn't uncommon after a head injury. It should resolve on its own with time. I would recommend you see an ophthalmologist, though, if it's not improving after a few weeks. They can recommend some eye exercises and run other tests to pinpoint the problem."

"Oh. All right." She wasn't too worried about it. That might be because she still wasn't thinking too clearly, however. The pounding in her head and the fire in her hip were taking up most of the space in her brain. The rest was concerned with the state of her op. Who tried to kill her? And why? Did someone find out who she was? How? And more importantly, who? She never slipped up. Outside of her house, she was Alexandra. Audra ceased to exist.

"The police would like to talk to you. Do you feel up to it?"

Audra closed her eyes and drew in a breath. She didn't, really. But the sooner she got them off her back, the sooner she could get out of here and figure out what happened. "Sure."

"They're right outside. While you speak to them, I'll work on getting you situated. I'd like you to stay for observation. Hang on."

A frown drew her brows together. Observation? "Wait, I—"

The doctor stepped out before she could fully protest, and she broke off with a low growl. She did *not* want to stay here tonight.

A moment later, two police officers came in. One wore plain clothes and had a badge hung around his neck. The other was in uniform. The man in plain clothes brought the rolling stool over and sat down beside her bed.

"Hello. I'm Detective Closterman." He flipped open a small notebook and clicked a pen. "Can you tell me your name?"

"Amber Carter. Look, I know you have questions, especially with the items in my pockets. Before I say anything, I need to make a phone call."

The detective lifted an eyebrow. "To whom?"

"Just—someone who can help."

"I'm going to need more than that. An attorney?"

"No. And no, you don't need to know more."

He blinked, startled at her push back, and stared at her for several moments. "Are you an American citizen?"

"No."

"What are you doing in the United States? Do you live here?"

"I do."

"Why?" He crossed his arms.

"Why what?"

"Why do you live here?"

"Work."

He rolled a hand. "What kind of work?"

"Marketing. Where's my phone?" She was done answering his questions. She needed to talk to Dee.

He cast a quick look at the officer by the door. "We have it."

"Perfect. May I have it?"

"No."

Audra frowned. "Why not? I'm not under arrest. I've done nothing wrong."

"You mean besides carrying a concealed handgun?"

"I'm a woman alone at night."

"Without a permit?"

"How do you know I don't have one? Until a moment ago, you didn't know my name."

"You're required to carry your license on you when you conceal carry. I've seen your belongings. You had a cellphone and a handgun."

"Again, I need to make a phone call." She would not admit to the man she didn't have a permit. She didn't technically need one, but he didn't know that.

"How will that help?"

"Just..." Audra closed her eyes and sighed at his persistence. "Just trust me. It will. There's much more going on than you know. I really can't tell you more than that. I'm done talking now."

The detective glanced at the officer, who stood near the door, silently listening.

"Okay. I can't force you to talk. But you can't go anywhere until I get some answers. You're being detained, Ms. Carter."

"Great. Get me my phone, so I can make that call and get this straightened out. You'll be able to undetain me, then," she shot back.

The wheels clacked as he rolled back and stood up. He motioned to the officer. The other man produced her phone from the cargo pocket on his pants and handed it to her. "You should call a lawyer, if that's not who you're calling."

She gave him a flinty look as she snatched the phone. "Thank you." She stared at them, waiting for them to leave. When they didn't, she lifted a hand and made a shooing motion. "Goodbye."

The detective flattened his lips. "We'll be right outside, Ms. Carter."

"I'm sure."

They left, closing the door. Once she was sure she wouldn't be overheard, she unlocked the device and called Theo. The line rang several times before it rolled to voicemail. She huffed, then left a short message. "Where are you? What the hell happened?" She hung up without asking him to call her back. He knew.

Next, she dialed the number for her division head in London. It was early in England, but she was likely awake.

"Thompson."

"Dee, it's Audra."

A short pause came over the line, then, "Go."

"Someone tried to take me out with a car. I can't reach Theo, and the cops are here, asking questions."

Dee cursed. "Where's here?"

"Hospital. In Vegas."

"Tell me everything you remember."

"It's not much, I'm afraid. I got knocked unconscious, so things are fuzzy." She closed her eyes and forced herself to think about the last few hours. "I remember getting home from dinner with Liam. I did some research on the men we ate with. A noise!" She opened her eyes. "I remember hearing a noise. I went to investigate, but Theo called before I could check it out. He said he'd chased someone out of my back garden and that he needed help." Her brow wrinkled as she tried to remember more.

"And?"

"I'm not sure what happened next. I have a vague memory of running and some bright lights."

"Did you find Theo?"

"Not that I recall."

"Okay. What else?"

She closed her eyes again, searching her addled brain. "Black shoes."

"Black shoes?"

"Yeah. I remember black trainers." Unbidden, another image flickered through her mind. This one of Theo. Wearing similar shoes. Her eyes snapped open. It couldn't be.

But the thought wouldn't go away. Something—

"Anything else?" Dee's voice interrupted her thoughts.

Audra cleared her throat. "No. Look, can you get me out of here without having to explain to these cops who I am? I gave them my Amber Carter alias. I was too addled to speak without my accent when I came to. They're grilling me about the handgun I had on me and the lack of ID and a CCW permit."

Dee let out a soft groan. "Yes. I'll get on it. Don't say anything else."

The line clicked in Audra's ear. She lowered the phone and sagged against the bed, fatigue taking over again. No problem.

What felt like seconds passed, but it was actually nearly an hour later when her phone rang. She startled awake with a hard jerk. Pain lanced her side. Audra winced and pressed a hand just above her injured hip. "Ow." The phone continued to trill. She lifted it, seeing the U.K. country code, and answered. "Yes?"

"Do you need to stay in hospital?" It was Dee.

"I don't think so." Even if she did, she wasn't.

"All right. I'll send a car to pick you up. Your investigation has been compromised, so I want you on the first flight back to London."

"What? I can still investigate here without—"

"No. Come home, Officer Ridley. That's an order."

Again, the phone clicked in Audra's ear. She pulled it away to frown at it. What? That didn't make any sense. She couldn't stay in her condo, but that didn't mean she needed to leave the city. She had valuable knowledge and insights into Liam's business. It would facilitate efforts to bring him down if she were contributing to the investigation here and not in London. They'd lose over half a day just in the flight, not to mention the time difference.

Audra's mind whirled. Something wasn't right.

She tried Theo again, but he still didn't pick up. Cursing, she stabbed the icon to end the call. Audra thought furiously. She couldn't go home. To her condo or to London.

The door opened, and the detective came in, a dark glower on his face. "I've been told to let you go."

He walked closer and held out a white plastic bag with the hospital's logo. Audra could see the outline of her pistol inside.

"For the record, I don't like giving this back to you. I don't know who you are or what you're really doing here, but it's above my paygrade."

She took the bag. "Thank you, detective. I'm sorry to have caused problems. And I promise I'm one of the good guys."

He stuffed his hands in his pockets. "I certainly hope so." With a nod, he left.

Audra lifted her phone and tapped the screen. The generic background lit up. She touched the phone icon, ready to call Theo again, but the image of black trainers flitted through her thoughts. Logically, she knew many people owned black athletic shoes—she did. But she still couldn't shake the feeling that it was the same pair of shoes. Something was going on, and she didn't know who to trust.

Instead of dialing Theo's number, she typed in one she'd memorized a few months ago. The line rang four times.

"Hello?"

Audra swallowed hard at the sound of the sleep-roughened deep voice and closed her eyes. A tear leaked out. Hearing his voice was like a warm blanket. It banished the worry trying to take hold.

"Sam? It's Audra. I need your help."

A short pause came over the line. "Aud? What's wrong? Are you all right?"

"Um, sort of." She sniffed and swiped at her face. "I just—Can you come to Vegas? I don't want to explain over the phone. But I need you," her voice trailed off into a strangled whisper.

"I'll be on the next flight there. Where do you want to meet?"

A wave of relief flooded her veins at his willingness to come to her aid without question. "I'm not sure yet. I'll text you."

"Okay. Are you safe at least?"

"For now."

"Good. I—" He stopped, and a beat of silence passed.

Audra could tell by the soft grumble he made that he had more questions, but was holding back. She was thankful. Now wasn't the time for her to answer anything. That was best done in person.

"If that changes, call me. I know people who know people. I won't let anything happen to you."

Another tear slid free. "I know."

"I'll see you soon."

"Okay," she whispered, emotion clogging her throat. She swallowed around the lump and clenched her teeth. Her head injury was really messing with her mind. She wasn't normally so emotional.

He said goodbye and hung up.

Audra lowered the phone to her lap. Several more tears trickled down her cheeks, both from relief that she had an ally she could trust and from the fear and uncertainty of the last few hours.

The door swished open and the nurse from earlier reappeared. "Okay, Ms. Carter. Let's get you upstairs to a room. I bet you're ready to relax and get some rest."

"I'm not staying."

The nurse frowned. "What? The doctor said he's admitting you for observation."

"He didn't give me a chance to say no. I'm not staying. He said I have a concussion and some bruises, and that my scans are fine. I'm not staying," she reiterated. "Please bring my discharge papers. And some clothes, since you cut mine off."

"Ms. Carter, I highly advise—"

"I am aware I'm leaving against medical advice. Please bring my discharge papers," she repeated, giving the nurse a steely look. They'd have to chain her to the bed to get her to stay.

"Have the police cleared you to leave?"

"Yes."

The nurse sighed. After another moment's hesitation, she turned toward the door. "Give me a few minutes."

"Thank you."

The door swished shut behind the nurse, and Audra huffed out a breath. The woman was right about one thing: she was ready to relax. That wouldn't happen anytime soon, however.

Twenty minutes after she left, the nurse returned with the doctor in tow. Audra clenched her teeth and met his polite smile with a glare.

She held up a hand before he could speak. "Don't waste your breath. Just sign my discharge papers. Unless you've suddenly discovered an active bleed on my CT scan, I'm leaving."

He sighed, the smile leaving his face. "You're sure? It wouldn't hurt for you to stay a night and let us watch you."

"I'm fine."

He pressed his lips together, then nodded. "Okay. I can't force you to stay." He sat down at the computer and logged in. With a few keystrokes and the addition of a quick note, he got up. "Your discharge papers are printing. If you feel like you're getting worse, please come back and get checked out again."

She nodded once, even though she had no intention of doing so. They'd have to pick her up unconscious from the street before she'd come back.

Seven

Audra hobbled into the lobby from the ED, discharge papers in hand. Her leg hurt; so did her head. She was grateful it was still dark out. The sun was likely to split her skull in two. But she was free. After the doctor left, the nurse had unhooked her from all the medical equipment and found her some clothes to wear. The baggy sweatpants and oversize t-shirt didn't fit the greatest, but they were clean and she was covered.

Outside the ED doors, Audra glanced back and forth, looking for a taxi. A man holding a sign caught her attention. The name "Carter" was scrawled over it in bold, black lettering. She was quick to turn away. Getting into the car Dee sent was not the plan.

"Ms. Carter?"

"Dammit!" she growled through clenched teeth. Dee must have sent a picture too. She turned back and pasted a polite smile on her face. "Hello."

"Hi. I'm Kevin. My car's over here." He gestured to a black sedan about ten feet behind him.

Audra nodded and walked forward. He held the door for her, and she lowered herself onto the seat.

The driver got in, then turned to look at her. "The car hire notes say to take you to the airport. Is that correct?"

Oh, bless him for asking! Now she could alter her destination. And Dee was on something if she thought Audra could get on a plane right away. She had her Apple Wallet identification on her and that was it. It was possible her boss would charter a private aircraft, but Audra would still need a passport when she entered the U.K.. "No. I need to clean up and get a change of clothes before I get on a plane. Could you take me to the Venetian, please?" It was far enough from Liam's main operating territory she felt safe walking around long enough to get something to wear.

"Of course." He started the car.

Audra sank into the leather upholstery and closed her eyes. Lulled by the motion of the car, she dozed off.

"We're here."

The driver's voice jolted her awake, and she sat up. "Sorry."

"No worries, miss. Would you like me to wait?"

"No, thank you. I'll catch an Uber or a taxi to the airport." She reached for the door handle. "And I'm sorry, but I don't have any money on me to leave you a tip."

He smiled. "That's all right. It's been taken care of."

Well, at least Dee hadn't slacked on the hire car. "Great." She pushed the door open. "Have a good day." Wincing against the pain in her hip, she got out. Without a backward glance, she went inside.

Keeping her head down, she wandered into the resort's mall and entered the first reasonably priced store she saw. With a tight smile for the salesperson, she plucked a lavender t-shirt off the rack with the resort's logo. They had some soft lounge shorts, too, so she grabbed a pair of those in gray. Audra topped her haul with a dark gray ball cap.

The young woman manning the register eyed her with skepticism. "You okay?"

"Fine." Audra took her phone from her baggy sweats' pocket. "Do you take Apple Pay?" She prayed they did, because her wallet was locked in her condo.

"We do."

"Great." She gave the woman a tight smile. Her leg ached, and she needed to sit. She also needed a bottle of water. Her mouth felt like she'd gone out into the desert and ate it.

Still giving her a look that told Audra she looked as bad as she felt, the woman rang up her items. Audra paid and selected the cash back option, getting enough to book a room with cash, then thanked her and left. Moving as fast as her hip would let her, she headed for the Venetian's check-in desk.

Audra paused in front of a mirrored window and tried to tame her hair before she approached the desk. She was sure they were used to all kinds of people, but she'd prefer not to be too memorable. All she had was her digital ID—her real one—and she'd rather they not remember her name.

"Ugh, I'm a mess." She sighed and smoothed her hair once more. "I guess that'll have to do." Sighing, she turned and headed for the desk.

A man smiled at her as she approached. "Hello. How may I assist you?"

Audra stretched her lips into a smile and hoped it didn't look too garish. "I'd like a room, please. Just for tonight." What was left of it.

"Certainly. We're past our normal check-in window, though, and the next check-in time isn't until three o'clock. There's an additional fee if you'd like to check-in early."

"I guess I'll hang out in the casino or wander until then." She had no intention of ever stepping foot in the room, so it didn't matter, and she'd rather not pay the resort's early check-in fee.

"Okay. I just need an ID and a method of payment."

She opened her Apple Wallet on her phone. "All I have is my digital ID. My purse was stolen." She injected a quiver into her voice and forced some tears into her eyes as she lied. It wasn't hard. She was still upset her op had gone topsy-turvy.

"Oh, I'm so sorry. I can waive the early check-in fee if you'd like?"

"Really? That would be great." She still had no intention of using the room, but refusing his offer would appear strange.

"Of course. It's good your phone wasn't in your purse."

"Yeah. It was in my pocket. I guess the mugger didn't stop to search me after he knocked me down. I don't remember. I hit my head and passed out."

"Do you need anything else? I have some coupons for a free meal at several of the buffets in the area."

"No, that's okay. Save them for people who really need them. I still have access to my money." She waved her phone.

"All right. I'll hurry you through the check-in process, though. I imagine you're ready to just drop."

Audra didn't have to fake a tired smile. "Thank you."

A few minutes later, she scrawled her name over the check-in slip, and he handed her a room key. She thanked him again, then headed for the lifts.

Out of sight of the main desk, she changed direction. Dropping the key in the tall box they used for their key return, she exited the hotel. An agonizing ten minutes later, she was across the street and inside. Here, she intended to pay cash and use the room. She just hoped the Mirage check-in staff would be as sympathetic as the Venetian staff.

Taking a deep breath, she approached the desk, ready to put her acting skills to use again.

Luckily, it worked.

Exhausted, she trudged toward the lift. With every step, her feet grew heavier and her hip ached more. Her body was officially done.

Riding the lift to the third floor, she found her room and let herself inside. Audra sagged against the door, closing her eyes for a brief moment as the world faded away. For the moment, she was well and truly safe.

With a mighty shove, she pushed her fatigued and bruised body off the door and walked into the bathroom, where she turned on the water. Tendrils of steam swirled as she stripped out of her baggy clothes. In the wide mirror over the sink, she caught sight of her hip. Deep purples and blues streaked with red scratches marred her skin. She didn't dare touch it to see if it was tender. Just moving told her it was. When she woke, moving would not be fun, but she needed rest more than she needed to stay limber.

Audra stepped into the hot shower. Water cascaded over her tired muscles, easing some of the soreness and relaxing her mind. Using the shampoo and soap the hotel provided, she scrubbed herself clean, then turned off the water and wrapped herself in a scratchy towel. Picking up her phone, she went back out into the main room, where she set an alarm for a few hours from now, then dropped the towel. She pulled back the bedcovers and slipped between the sheets, naked.

Her eyelids fluttered as she settled in. Later, she had a lot to think about. Like, who she could really trust and how she could salvage her op. And where to meet Sam that was busy, but away from anywhere Liam's people might see her.

Right now, though, it was time to sleep. She forced her mind to blank and let sleep claim her.

Dreams plagued her slumber. Some were pleasant, like seeing Sam's smiling face as they strolled together on a beach. Others made her heart race and startled her awake. Like the one of the car coming at her. That one jolted her from a sound sleep and left her heart racing.

When her alarm went off, she smacked at the phone to silence it and contemplated staying where she was. She could feel the stiffness in her hip that had set in while she slept.

Rolling to her side, she sucked a sharp breath between her teeth when a shard of pain stabbed her. Fire raced across her pelvis and down her thigh. "Dear God," she muttered. First order of business after she got up and dressed was to find a shop that sold painkillers. And water. She still hadn't had a drink.

With a groan, she pushed herself into a sitting position, then slowly stood, bracing her hands on the wall to let her muscles adjust to the new position. Muttering under her breath about stupid cars and evil people, she made her way into the bathroom, where she put on her new clothes and went through an abbreviated morning routine.

The more she moved, the more her muscles loosened, and by the time she emerged in the lobby downstairs, she could walk without the hobble. She still wanted painkillers, though.

It didn't take her long to find a shop. She used most of the cash she had left to buy some medicine and a bottle of water. She wanted food but decided to wait; she'd get something to eat and sit down after she figured out where she was going and reached her destination. By that point, she'd be ready to be immobile for a while.

Exiting the shop, she pulled up a map of the Strip. There were several areas she needed to avoid or be vigilant in. At this hour, Liam's people would soon be out, going to dinner before they headed to the clubs and casinos. He was no doubt wondering where she was. Whether that had translated to him telling everyone to keep an eye out for her, she didn't know.

One thing she had going for herself, though, was she

looked nothing like Alexandra at the moment. That woman wouldn't be caught dead in the clothes Audra currently wore.

With a sigh, Audra decided the best place would be the Paris hotel. Down in its bowels between it and its sister hotel, the Horseshoe, she could hide in a dark corner and wait for Sam. Plus, there was food down there.

She opened her messaging app and texted Sam where she'd be, then powered the phone down and stripped the back off before removing the battery and stuffing the pieces into her shopping bag. Twisting her hair up, she set her hat over top and tugged the cap down.

As she left the Mirage, she dumped the phone pieces into a public rubbish bin. From here, Dee would have to pick her up on CCTV cameras if she wanted to track her down. Audra wished her luck. She'd need it.

EIGHT

Sam hopped out of the cab, pulling his small leather duffel with him, and paid the driver. He glanced up at the elaborate façade of the Paris Hotel. Lights on the Eiffel Tower danced in time to the fountains going off across the road at the Bellagio. He ignored it all and hurried inside, knowing Audra was waiting for him.

When he got her call, he hadn't asked questions. He'd simply called his bar manager, Martina, and left her a message, asking her to run things for the foreseeable future, then coerced a local pilot to fly him to San José. There, he'd booked himself on the earliest flight to Vegas he could get, which, luckily, began boarding only twenty minutes after he made it through security. He'd landed in Vegas just over seven hours later to voice messages from Dean, but he'd yet to call him back. He wanted more details first.

Smoke filled the air, giving the casino floor a hazy look. It stung his eyes. Trying to breathe as little as possible, Sam strode across the wild, geometric-patterned carpet, past Gordon Ramsay's steakhouse and the glam Vanderpump restaurant. He entered the corridor connecting the Paris to its sister resort, the Horseshoe. Stopping outside of a coffeeshop and creperie, where Audra said she'd be, he peered inside. At the back of the dining area, he saw a woman in a dark ball cap, sitting alone. With her head tipped down, he couldn't see her face, but he'd know the graceful line of Audra's neck and shoulders anywhere.

His heart stuttered in his chest. She was really here.

Readjusting his grip on his bag, he crossed the tile floor.

She looked up. Again, Sam's heart stuttered. She was so damn beautiful. Even worn out and looking like she could use some sun and twelve hours of sleep, she was gorgeous.

"Hey." He stopped beside her table.

A soft smile crossed her face. "Hey. Have a seat." She motioned to the chair across from her.

Sam sat.

"You hungry? They've got good food here."

"No. Tell me what's going on." He reached over and brushed his fingers over her knuckles. "Are you okay?" He didn't want to waste time on pleasantries. He wanted answers. If she was calling him for help, something went terribly wrong with her mission.

She sighed and nodded. "I'm fine. I took a knock to the head and have a bad bruise on my hip, but—"

"A knock to the head? What? Start at the beginning. All you said on the phone was basically that the shit hit the fan. How did you get hurt?"

"I got hit by a car."

"What?" Sam's voice rose in volume. His eyes roved over what he could see of her body. She was pale, but otherwise looked all right.

Audra shushed him. "I'm fine. A concussion and some bruises. Nothing that won't heal on its own with time. I got lucky."

"Was this on purpose?" He leaned in, fists clenched, lowering his voice.

"I think so, yes." She pulled the corner of her bottom lip in and chewed on it.

Sam narrowed his eyes. Something about her expression told him she knew more than she was saying. "You know who did it, don't you?"

"No. I mean, I have my suspicions, but—" She broke off and shook her head. "I don't want them to be true."

Sam propped his elbows on the table and rubbed at his eyes. He still felt like he knew nothing. "Okay. Back up. Does this have to do with what you were playing at when I saw you in February?" He assumed it did, but wanted confirmation.

"Yes." She chewed on her lip again, then sighed. "What I'm going to tell you has to stay between us. You can't tell anyone. Not even your friends in Costa Rica."

"How did—" He stopped, frowning. "Wait. How deep did you dig into my life?"

She picked at the napkin beside her plate. "After I walked away that night, I couldn't stop thinking about you. I needed to know that you were doing all right, so I did some digging. Besides, you told me to contact you if I ever needed help. I figured it couldn't hurt to look into you, so I did, and I memorized your number. I never intended to use it, but..." She shrugged. "I discovered you lived down there with several other former military members. That's as deep as I went."

"Okay." His head bobbed in understanding. "Continue."

"So, SIS sent me undercover as the fiancée of Liam Brogan, the head of the Las Vegas branch of the Irish mafia."

"Fiancée?" Sam's gut churned. What all did that entail? He hated the thought of her having to let some crime lord touch her in the most intimate of ways. "That's why you were involved with the Irish mafia?"

"Yes. I bear a striking resemblance to Alexandra Burton, oldest daughter of Sean Burton, a right arsehole of a real estate developer in Chicago. He got into some financial trouble a few years ago and turned to the Irish mob to bail him out. Except he fell behind on his payment schedule. The U.S. authorities had been keeping tabs on him for some time. They had a boatload of evidence on him, but wanted bigger fish. When they realized he was between a rock and a hard place, they played their hand and offered him a deal. He'd maintain his independence for now, plead on lesser charges when it was time, and give them an in with the mafia. The original plan was to get someone on Brogan's payroll through Burton's recommendation."

She reached for her water and took a drink. "We keep tabs on all the various Irish mafia sects. It was just happenstance that we got involved in this. My boss, Deirdre Thompson, was in the U.S. for a security conference and talked to one of the agents who's part of the Burton op. He mentioned the case and asked her if she had any insights. When Dee looked over the files, she saw a picture of Burton's daughter and realized we had an amazing opportunity. There was chatter that Brogan's family wanted him married off to secure the line of succession. He was thirty-seven at the time and didn't have any children."

"Whoa." That was unusual. Most of those guys married young.

"Yeah. Burton's daughter did not like being in the public light. She shied away from it like she'd get burnt, so there aren't many pictures of her out there. It was perfect. We proposed Burton offer his daughter—played by me—as a suitable wife for Brogan in exchange for debt forgiveness."

Sam's eyebrows slammed down. "And he agreed?"

"Only because he knew Alexandra wouldn't be the one actually offered up. The real Alexandra Burton entered your witness protection program. Quite happily, I might add."

"So, you've been Liam Brogan's fiancée for how long?"

"Almost two years. Only one of that has been here in Vegas, though. We laid groundwork the first year. I stayed in Chicago under the pretext of needing to wrap up my life there. I've been able to play the part of spoiled heiress and somehow keep our relationship fairly platonic."

"So, you haven't—" Sam rolled a hand.

"No. He's tried, but thankfully, I'm smarter. I've been able to manipulate him into being content with some kisses and some mild groping." Her face pulled in disgust.

Sam's face turned red as he thought about the slime ball putting his hands on her when she didn't want him to. He hoped he got the chance to smash his fist into the bastard's nose. "That's bad enough. How did things go south?"

"I'm not sure. Friday night, he hosted a party. I snuck into his office while he was distracted and downloaded the contents of his laptop. It's nothing I haven't done before. But this time, I found a file full of pictures of myself. They were surveillance photos. I don't know who took them or why he had them. He never hinted that he knew I wasn't who I said I was."

Sam straightened. "Do you still have the pictures?"

"A copy of them, yes. I turned the drive over to my handler later that night. I have copies of the rest of the files I downloaded too. And I took pictures of a ledger I found in the desk. I wasn't supposed to copy any of it and keep it, but this op was too big of a risk for me to follow the rules. I needed to be able to look through the intelligence myself in case there was something there I needed to know and everyone else neglected to share it with me." She paused and shook her head. "Anyway, I'm not sure if what happened last night is related to those files, but it's awful coincidental."

"What did happen?"

"I was home, doing some digging into some of Liam's new associates, when I heard noises outside. Theo—my handler—

called shortly after that and said he'd chased someone out of the garden, but now he was being chased and needed help. I ran after him. Once I got down near the park, I had to jog on the road to get to our normal meeting spot. That's where I got hit. Thankfully, I saw the car coming and tried to jump out of the way. It clipped my hip. I hit my head on the pavement when I fell." She shifted in her seat, her brows turning down as a worried look settled over her face. "What's bugging me are the shoes."

"The shoes? Whose shoes?"

"Before I lost consciousness, I saw a man come up to me and he had on black trainers. A car coming spooked him and he ran off. I passed out after that. What's bothering me is— and I still can't believe it—but Theo had on the same ones Friday."

Sam's eyebrows shot up. "You're sure?"

"Mostly?" She groaned and scrubbed her hands over her face. "I don't know. I can't tell you for certain if they were the same brand. My memories are too fuzzy. But something is linking the two in my head. I can't discount the feeling. Not with my life and my investigation on the line."

"No." He reached across the table and squeezed her hand. "You're right to question it. It wouldn't be the first time a handler has turned on their operative."

She offered him a tremulous smile and squeezed his fingers before folding her hands in her lap. "Definitely not. It's rare, though. Exceedingly. But I... I can't get the thought out of my head. And I don't want to be wrong and trust the wrong person. Hence why I called you."

"Have you said anything to your unit head? Thompson, you said, right?"

"Yeah." She snorted softly and picked up her fork, jabbing at her crepe. "She ordered me back to London. Said my cover was blown. She's right. Someone somewhere knows who I am

—or at least that I'm not entirely who I say I am. But it doesn't make sense for her to order me back to London. Just because I can't be in the field doesn't mean I'm not useful to the operation here. I have a lot of insider knowledge. It wouldn't make sense for me to be thousands of miles away on an eight-hour time difference."

Sam agreed. Things could move quickly now, and if he were in charge, he would want immediate access to one of his most valuable resources. "What does the person running the op here think?"

"I don't know. I haven't talked to him. Dee sent a car to pick me up. They were supposed to take me to the airport, but I argued that I needed clothes and a shower first and had them drop me off down the Strip at the Venetian. I bought clothes in their mall—thanking my lucky stars I linked my debit card to my Apple Pay so I could not only pay but get some cash back—booked a room in the hotel, then walked across the road to the Mirage where I booked another room with cash. I showered and slept for a few hours before I texted you to tell you where I'd be. Then I left my phone in a trash can without its battery and walked here. I'm sure if Dee tries hard enough, she can track me down from all the video footage in this city, but it'll take some time."

"You *walked* here from the Mirage? After getting hit by a car?"

"It's just a concussion and some bruises."

"Still, Aud. Damn." He shook his head, admiring her toughness. "Why come here, though, instead of a smaller hotel off the Strip? Aren't you worried one of Brogan's guys will see you?"

"Not really. I look very different right now than I typically do around them. And they stick to the restaurant they normally operate out of and some of the high-roller casinos and clubs. Down here in the bowels of the Paris? And with a hat?" She touched the brim of her weathered dark gray cap. "I'm good. Plus, it's easier to blend in when there's a crowd. I'd stand out too much at a small hotel. Someone might remember me there when I check in."

Her logic made sense, but he still didn't like her being out in public. They needed to get somewhere private. "So, what's your plan?"

"Get out of Vegas to one of the smaller cities nearby. Regroup. Figure out who tried to kill me. I called you because I need someone I can trust. Someone outside of the op. I know it's a lot to ask, but will you help me?" She wrapped her hand over the back of his and speared him with her dark brown eyes.

Sam's gaze roved over her tired face, taking in the deep purple circles under her eyes and the paleness to her cheeks, even as he spoke. "Of course I will." He didn't need to think about it. Their relationship—and he used the word lightly—might have ended ten years ago, but it wasn't on bad terms. Their lives just went in different directions. Memories of their time together had gotten him through some of the worst moments of his life. He was happy to repay her in any way he could.

"Finish that." He turned his hand over, giving hers a quick squeeze, then untangled their fingers and pointed to her plate. "We should get out of the public eye. I think I have a plan."

Nine

Audra finished her crepe and disposed of her trash on their way out of the café. Sam laid a hand on her back and guided her through the light crowd as they walked toward the Horseshoe to go downstairs to take the monorail. He wanted to get off the Strip, and now that they were together and looked like a couple, she'd be less conspicuous than a woman alone.

They boarded the train and rode it one stop to the MGM Grand. From there, they snagged a taxi for the short trip to a hotel adjacent to the airport. Normally, he'd walk, but Audra was limping. The trek to the train station had been enough.

"What's your plan?" Audra asked as they exited the cab and walked toward the hotel's front doors.

"We're going to check in as a newly married couple. Put that Claddagh ring you always wear on your other hand." He glanced down at her hands. Audra tugged the ring off and put it on her left ring finger.

"Once we get into a room, I'm calling my friends. I know you don't want the details out, but one, I need to tell them where I am. And two, I think they can help."

She frowned. He could see that she wanted to ask more questions, but her curiosity would have to wait until they were alone.

He smiled at the young man working the front desk while Audra hung back. She looked a little ragged from her ordeal, and they didn't want to rouse the clerk's suspicions. "Hello. We need a room for the night."

"Of course. One bed or two?" the young man asked.

"One. We just got married." If Audra didn't want to share a bed, he'd sleep in the chair, but they needed to keep up appearances. Newly married people didn't typically ask for a room with two beds.

The man smiled. "Congratulations." He turned to the computer screen. "Let's see what we've got here." His fingers fluttered over the keyboard. "I'm afraid all I have right now is a double queen suite with a balcony."

"That's fine. Do you have anything on the first floor?" He wanted to be able to make a quick exit if need be.

The clerk's hands moved over the keys again. "I do."

"Great. We'll take it."

"Okay. I just need your license and a credit card."

Sam handed both over. The clerk entered his information and ran his card, then passed over a paper for Sam to sign. He scrawled his name on the page, acknowledging the charges, and handed it back.

"You're in room one fifteen. Breakfast is served in our dining area from six-thirty until ten. Enjoy your stay, and congratulations, again." The young man passed a small folder with two key cards across the counter.

"Thank you." Sam took the keys, then Audra's hand, and headed down the hall.

Their room was just off the main lobby. He let them in with a soft snick of the lock, and flipped the light switch, then threw the bolts once they were inside. A yellow glow illuminated the entryway, and the lamp between the beds cast dull shadows on the beige carpet.

"Okay, explain how your friends can help. I know they're all former military, like you, but what can they do?"

"Actually, they're not all former military." He set his bag down on the red, gold, and copper bedspread of the bed closest to the door. "We have a former CIA analyst as part of the group. Asher Horn. He's a whiz at finding information. If it's online, he can find it. Anywhere. And my friend, Ford, has contacts all over the world. So do the others. And me, for that matter. We can help."

She pursed her lips and studied him. "I don't know, Sam. I could lose my job. I could get charged with disseminating classified information if I read them in on this. I still could because I told you."

Sam wrapped his hands around her upper arms and peered into her face. "I won't let that happen."

She scoffed and tipped her nose up. "How do you plan to prevent it?"

A crooked smile tipped his mouth. "Like I said, we have contacts all over the world. I think the most they'll do to you is give you an official reprimand."

"That's enough. I'll get stuck behind a desk."

"Would that be so bad after the last two years?"

Her brows knit together. She shrugged off his hands and fluttered hers. "Don't be logical on me. It's not helpful."

He barked a short laugh. "What?"

She sighed and ran her hands over her face. "Sorry. I just feel very—out of sorts. Part of it is not knowing who I can trust and part of it is I feel like my brain is scrambled."

"That's your concussion." He stepped closer and reached out to push a lock of her hair back. His fingers traced the soft skin of her cheek. A pang of longing shot through him. He'd missed her. It had been ten years, but everything they'd had, everything they'd experienced, all rushed back. "Do you want to rest? I can make my phone calls outside so you can sleep."

"No. I'll sleep better knowing we have a solid plan in place. And you might have questions for me."

"Does that mean I can call my friends and get them up to speed?"

She rolled her lips in and sucked in a deep breath, then nodded. "Yes. I hope I don't regret it, but I don't know what else to do. Something's not right."

Sam reached for her hand and squeezed it briefly, then let go and took his phone from his pocket.

Finding Dean's name in his contacts, he called him.

"Where are you?" Dean didn't even bother with a greeting.

Sam winced. He should have called sooner.

"Martina said you sent her a message in the middle of the night asking her to cover for you, then you never answered my texts or calls," his friend continued.

"I'm in Vegas."

A short pause came over the line. "Why?"

"It's a bit of a long story. Can you get the others rounded up and call me back?"

Dean groaned. "We're going to get shot at again, aren't we?"

Sam chuckled. "I hope not. Round everyone up and call me back."

"Fine." Dean hung up without saying goodbye.

Audra huffed as he lowered the phone. "That's it?"

"For now. It's easier to explain it all at once."

She grunted. "True, I guess. Does that mean we have time to find me some more clothes? As comfortable as my I Love Vegas sweats are, I'd rather not look like a tourist who partied too hard and was forced to buy the first available clothing she could find because she vomited all over herself."

Sam barked a laugh. "I see your concussion hasn't dulled your sense of humor."

"It's enhanced my sarcasm. I'm not in the mood for anyone's bullshit."

"Noted. Why don't you take a—" He broke off, the word getting stuck in his brain. An image of her showering had crossed the wires and held up the word he wanted to say. He clenched his teeth and rolled his hand. "Go bathe. I'll get you some clothes."

A tiny frown formed between her brows. Sam could see the question in her eyes, but she didn't voice it. He was glad. He didn't feel like explaining his brain injury. He preferred she remember him the way he used to be, and not as a man who occasionally struggled to vocalize his thoughts. Eventually, he knew she'd ask. But he was glad it wasn't now.

Stepping around her, he headed for the door. "I'll be back soon."

"Don't you want to know what size I wear?"

"I can... guess." The words "figure it out" stuck, so he went with the simpler term.

"You're sure?"

"Yes." He turned the door handle and left, eager to escape before his mind locked up on him again.

TEN

Audra huddled into the fuzzy hoodie Sam had bought her and stared out the hotel window at the planes moving around the airport runways. There were still hours until bedtime—and she'd had a decent nap earlier—but she was exhausted. The adrenaline had ebbed and the effects of her injuries were kicking in. A fiery throb pulsed in her hip, and a drum line pounded a deafening tattoo in her head. She needed several more hours of solid sleep and some strong painkillers. She had ibuprofen and coffee. It would have to be enough.

Sam's phone buzzed. She turned away from the window to look at him. In the light and not in some dark back alley, she could see how the years they'd been apart had aged him. There was a hardness to his eyes that wasn't there before. He'd lost some weight but gained muscle, leaving his face more angular. Mostly, there was just a matureness about him that he didn't have a decade ago.

He shifted in the desk chair he'd perched in earlier and removed his phone from his pocket to answer it. Putting it on speaker, he laid it on the desk. "Hello?"

"Sam, you have all of us on speaker," a male voice said.

"Good. You're on speaker too." Sam looked at her. "With a friend of mine. Aud, say hi."

"Hello," she called.

"Well, hi," the man said. "I'm Dean."

"Ford," another voice said.

"Edie," came a woman's voice.

"Max," said another man.

"Asher," a second man said.

"Jordan," said yet another.

"Brooke. I'm the last one here," another woman said.

Audra looked at Sam. "How many of you are there? I only remember five other names."

"Brooke and Jordan aren't part of the original group. Jordan is Edie's husband. They're the ones who got married when we ran into each other. Brooke is Ford's fiancée," Sam said.

"Wait, is that why you ran off at the jewelry store?" Ford asked. "Because you saw her?"

"Yes. Long story short, Audra and I knew each other a decade ago. When I saw her, I couldn't believe it and had to verify it was her."

"Okay, so what's going on now?" Max asked.

Sam glanced at Audra. "Do you want to explain, or do you want me to?"

She got up and came over to sit on the bed by his chair. "I will." Crossing her legs, she leaned her elbows on them. "My name is Audra Ridley. I work for the Secret Intelligence Service. I'm assuming with your backgrounds you all know what that is?"

There was a chorus of yeses until Jordan chimed in.

"Um, no. Civilian, here. I'm guessing you're a spy, though? And British?"

"Yes. It's what many people call MI6. We call it SIS. I'm in Las Vegas undercover as the fiancée of the head of the

Irish mafia's Vegas branch. Last night, someone tried to kill me."

A collective murmur went through the line.

"Are you all right?" Brooke asked.

"I'm okay. A little banged up, but I'll heal. I called Sam for help because I think my handler might be in on the plot to kill me. Two nights ago, we met so I could hand over some intelligence. Last night, he called to tell me he'd just chased someone out of my back garden and was now the one being pursued. I went to help him and was hit by a car. While I was lying on the pavement, barely conscious, I saw a man come up to me. He had on black trainers. Friday night, Theo—my handler—had on the same shoes. I don't know if he was the one who came up to me last night, or if he did, but wasn't the one to hit me and then ran because people were pursuing him too. I just have a gut feeling something isn't right."

"Why didn't you contact your superiors? Or have you?" Ford asked.

"I did. She ordered me back to Britain. That's a ridiculous notion. We're very close to bringing down Liam Brogan—the Irish mob boss. Even if my cover's blown, I'm a valuable asset to law enforcement here. No one has more knowledge of their operations than me."

"Did she give you a reason why she wanted you to go back?" Edie asked.

"No. But there was a tension in her voice that bothered me. Like she was irritated." Audra sighed. "I know my reasoning is thin, but I've spent my adult life reading people and situations. Something is off."

"What's your handler's name?" Asher asked.

"Theo Anderson."

"And where did you get hit by the car?"

She told him the area.

"Okay, thanks."

Audra frowned and looked at Sam, a question in her eyes.

He smiled. "Asher's the computer whiz, remember?"

Her expression cleared. "Ah. Yes. I don't know what you hope to find with that information, though. He used an alias with everyone except me. And I don't know what it is. That's on purpose. I also doubt there are any news articles about my hit and run. Dee, my boss, would squash those stories."

"I'm not looking for news. At least, that's not all I'm looking for. Vegas has cameras. Everywhere."

"Probably not there. It's a ritzy part of town."

"You'd be surprised. Did you get a look at the car that hit you?"

"No. They turned their headlights on just as I looked back and blinded me."

"What else can you tell me about Theo?"

"Like what?"

"Anything. Age. Background. Physical characteristics. Hobbies. All of it."

Audra massaged her temples, the headache the ibuprofen had dulled roaring back to life. "He's forty-two. Dark hair, hazel eyes. About six feet tall. Fit. He's from Chipping Norton. Never married—that I know of—and no children. I don't know about other family. He runs a lot and likes a good curry. We didn't get all buddy-buddy, so I can't tell you much more than that."

"That's plenty." Asher's voice sounded distracted.

"He's busy now," Dean said. "What can we do for you guys? What do you need?"

"Mostly for you all to use your contacts to make some discreet inquiries about who might want to go after an SIS officer," Sam said. "We're staying in... we're staying here for... a few days, at least. Audra will be safe with me until we can stop Brogan and his goons. After that, we'll see. Maybe come down there."

She frowned at him. She'd noticed he tripped over words. He didn't use to. And she could tell it bothered him; his jaw clenched and worked every time he stopped to think.

Audra pushed her questions about that to the side for now and turned back to the phone call. "If it *is* Brogan. If Theo's involved, there might be a mole in the SIS. Maybe I got too close to unmasking them. Though I don't know how. I haven't come across anyone who raises my suspicions. Not like that, anyway. I have some files we need to go over. I took them off of Liam's computer. Maybe there's something there that will give us a clue."

"Is it a hard copy or online?" Asher asked.

"Online."

"Can you send it to me? I'll start working on it."

"If Sam will let me use his phone to log in to my cloud server, yes."

Sam nodded. "Of course. We need to get you a new phone."

"Okay," Ford said. "Sam, send us your flight itinerary if you decide to bring her home with you. One of us will pick you up. If anything changes, let us know."

"I will."

Suddenly, Asher cursed.

"What?" Ford asked.

"We might have a problem. Vegas PD found a body near that park early this morning. No ID, but male. They estimate late-thirties. Dark hair, about six feet tall."

With wide eyes, Audra met Sam's gaze. "Oh, hell."

"Oh, hell is right," he said. "If that's Theo, who's the man in the black sneakers?"

Eleven

"Audra, do you know where Theo was staying or what kind of car he drove?" Asher asked.

"A silver Honda sedan. I don't know where he was staying. We always met in public places." She glanced at Sam again. A concerned frown pulled his brows down, wrinkling his forehead. Audra balled her fingers up, so she wouldn't reach out and try to smooth them away. This was the downside of asking Sam for help. Her attraction to him. She needed to maintain her composure so she could think. Sam was a distraction she didn't need, and she was rethinking involving him. Except if she left, she didn't know where else to turn. She didn't trust her boss now. There were other people in the SIS she could go to, but no one she knew well enough to be certain they wouldn't pass her concerns on to someone else.

Asher hummed.

"He's busy again," Dean said. Audra could hear a smile in his voice.

"Don't mock my process," Asher commented. "It gets results. I'm going to try to track his movements through the city. See if I can at least get a neighborhood where he was living. Audra, send me that file."

"I will as soon as we hang up."

Sam picked up the phone. "We'll go through it here too. See if anything jumps out at her."

"Sounds good," Asher said.

"If you need anything, call," Ford said.

"We will."

"Keep us posted." Ford ended the call.

Sam opened his web browser and passed the phone to Audra. "Here."

She took it and stared at it for a moment. The screen wavered in her vision. She blinked hard and rubbed one eye.

"You okay?"

"Yeah." She wasn't, but she was well enough to do what needed to be done. Her head hurt and she felt like she was swimming through a thick fog. Blinking again, she tapped the screen and typed in the address for her private server. After logging into it, she opened another window and pulled up the email account she kept that no one else knew about. "What's your friend's email address?"

Sam told her, and she typed it in, attached the files, gave him the password to access them, then hit send. "There. It's sent." She logged out of everything, then handed Sam back his phone.

He pushed it back to her. "Open the files."

"Oh. Right." She logged back into her server. Her brain was still struggling. "Sorry. My brain's a little slow today."

"Don't apologize. I know how it feels."

Something in his tone made her look at him. A sad understanding lit his gaze. Suddenly, his difficulty with words made more sense. Something had happened to him in the ten years they were apart.

She opened the first folder on the list. "You want to talk

about how you know?" She sent him a glance through her lashes.

His expression closed. "Not really. One day, I'll tell you. Right now, let's focus on you."

"I'd rather not. Talking about other things helps distract me from the fact someone tried to kill me."

"You're a spy, Aud. The possibility of death comes with the job."

She let out an inelegant snort. "That doesn't mean I'm not still rattled. You were a SEAL. You can't tell me it didn't bother you to get shot at."

"Point taken."

"So, distract me."

"No." He stood. "Scoot over."

She did, and he climbed up on the bed next to her. Audra tried not to notice the clean scent of his soap as he leaned in to see the screen.

"What all is in the files?"

"I'm not entirely sure. I didn't have a chance to go over everything. I found the pictures of myself when I was looking through his computer to make sure I copied the right things. I got interrupted before I could look further, so I just copied the entire hard drive. At home, I only looked at the pictures before I copied the drive's contents and turned the USB stick over to Theo."

"Who else knew Theo had the drive?"

"Probably our boss. Maybe an analyst, if she gave it to one. Possibly the feds here. We were working with the Violent Crimes division of the Vegas FBI branch. Chicago's field office played a role too. This operation was a big deal. Planting me was an opportunity to take down a significant chunk of the Irish mob in the U.S. and in Europe. Liam's a big fish. If this is an inside job, it could be in either agency. Theo and Dee might have nothing to do with it." A thought struck her. "It's possible she suspected a mole and was trying to protect me by recalling me."

Sam's hand landed on hers. He curled his fingers around her hand. "You did the right thing by listening to your instincts. If she's not involved and was trying to protect you, she'll understand when this is all over. It's your life on the line, not hers."

Audra studied his eyes, thinking about his words. She pressed her lips together and inhaled a breath. "Yeah. I know you're right, but part of me feels like I've let her down. And the relationship between us will never be the same. Even if she's innocent, she knows now that I don't trust her." Any way this situation shook out, Audra had a feeling she would be looking for a new job. Or at least end up transferred to a different division.

"It's better than dead."

That still didn't make her feel any better.

She pushed those thoughts away and focused on the files. There had to be an answer somewhere in all this stuff.

An hour later, she handed him the phone. "I need a break. We need a bigger screen. That one's killing my head." Leaning forward, she leaned her elbows on her crossed legs and pressed her fingers to her tired eyes.

"I didn't bring my laptop. I just threw some clothes in a bag and got on a plane."

A lump of emotion formed in her throat, making it diffi-cult to breathe. She swallowed hard and blinked back the sudden moisture in her eyes. "I appreciate that." More than he'd ever know. When she'd called him, she'd half-expected him to say he was too busy. But he hadn't. He'd dropped everything to come help her.

He sat up beside her on the bed; his hand glided down the back of her head to weave through her hair. "Anytime, Aud." Tenderness colored his voice.

She looked at him.

"I never forgot you, you know," he said, his voice quiet.

"Me either," she admitted. Their time together had been a highlight of her life. It had ended much too soon. But back then, neither of them had been ready for a commitment. Hadn't been able to commit. Their jobs were too demanding, and neither wanted to give that up. She didn't regret walking away from him, just as she was sure he didn't regret walking away from her. They'd been in a different place then. They still were.

That didn't stop the emotions from rushing back, though. Finally. She'd wondered when it would happen. Wondered when all the hunger and need she'd felt for him so long ago would come flooding in. It had, and now it was like it had only been days since they'd been together and not a decade.

His hand spread over the back of her head under her hair, holding her steady as he leaned closer.

"Aud."

She laid a hand on the side of his neck and traced her fingers over his jaw. "We shouldn't get involved, Sam."

"Probably not." His head dipped lower. "But like the last time, you're irresistible."

The low rumble of his voice washed over her. Her scalp pricked as her nerve-endings came alive. Why was it that this man had such an effect on her? From the moment they'd met, he'd made her body wake up and take notice. Ten years apart hadn't done anything to change that. If anything, she wanted him more now than she did then.

She shifted, leaning in to align her lips with his. Pain shot through her injured hip. She hissed and pulled back.

Sam kept his hand on the top of her shoulders. "Are you all right? Is it your hip?"

Audra nodded and shifted again, putting her weight on her other side. "Yeah. Sorry."

"Don't be. You probably just kept us from getting royally frustrated. I don't want to stop at a kiss, and you're not well enough for more."

She met his eyes and saw the fire blazing in their blue depths. An answering heat curled in her belly, silencing some of the throbbing in her hip. She looked away. "How about we try to sneak into my condo? Get my laptop and more of my clothes."

"What?"

She looked over to see the raw desire in his eyes turn to confusion, then understanding.

He shook his head. "That's not a good idea. If someone's watching the place, we're just creating problems for ourselves."

"That's why I said sneak. I'm trained at covert surveillance. So are you. We can do some recon before we go in and find anyone watching."

"Unless they've set up electronic surveillance. We might not find that."

"I don't think whoever this is is that smart. They ran me down in a public place, where there could be witnesses. If it really is Theo who the police found in the park, they murdered him in the same place. I'd say they're more likely to personally stake out my condo."

"Maybe so, but it's risky. We don't *need* the laptop. Or your clothes."

"No, but I do need the documents in my safe so I can leave the country, if that ever becomes the plan."

Sam groaned.

"I left my condo without any ID last night. I need those documents."

"Won't they get flagged and your boss will find out where you're headed?"

"No. I have an identity she doesn't know about."

He chuckled. "Why am I not surprised?" Blowing out a

breath, he got up and held out a hand to her. "Come on. Let's go rent a car and get your stuff."

Moving gingerly, she let him help her off the bed. "This means I have to take off this hoodie." She shrugged her shoulders, bringing the soft, light blue material up around her ears. "It's comfy." It might be close to a hundred degrees outside, but in their hotel room, it was only seventy. The hoodie was doing more than keeping her toasty warm. It was like a safety net, holding her emotions back. So long as she was warm and comfortable, she could pretend everything was all right.

"I mean, you can sweat if you want and leave it on." He grinned.

She scrunched her nose and pulled one arm out, resigned to leaving her cocoon. "No, thank you."

Twelve

Sam steered their newly acquired black sedan into Audra's neighborhood. He drove past her condo, cataloguing the vehicles parked on the street. Only one piqued his interest. A man sat in the driver's seat of a late-model luxury sedan. When Sam passed, the man turned his face away, like he was looking at something in the center console. "Okay, who are you?"

"Did you see something?" Audra asked from her position sprawled over the backseat. They'd decided it would be best for her to stay out of sight initially.

"Maybe. There's a man in a dark blue Audi sedan. Is there normally one parked across from you?"

"No."

"Okay. I'm going around the block. We'll check out the street behind you and walk in through the back if it's clear." He stopped at the corner and turned right. At the next corner, he turned right again. A quick trip down the street revealed nothing of note. When he reached the next intersection, he turned around and pulled into the apartment complex that butted up to her condo. He backed into a spot as close to the property line as he could get.

Sam shut the engine off and got out, opening the rear door to help Audra exit the car. She took his hand and sat up with a wince.

"You okay?"

"Yeah." She swung her legs out and let him tug her to her feet. "I just got a little stiff lying back there."

"Come on. Let's get out of the open." He kept hold of her hand and started for the tree line that separated the apartment complex from the private homes and condos on the other side. With a quick glance around, they slipped into the thicket.

Moments later, they reached the other side. Sticking to the shade, they walked twenty yards to their right, then paused.

"Does it look normal?" he asked.

"Yes. But let's wait a few minutes and make sure no one's watching."

Sam leaned against a tree and stared out at the yard. Birds chirped and leaves rustled. "This is nice. You don't see a lot of green space in Vegas."

"Yeah. I got lucky there was a unit for lease here. The other one I was looking at didn't have nearly as much shade."

Several minutes passed before Audra shifted and took a step toward her condo. "I think we're safe."

Eyes and ears open, Sam followed her through the back gate into her yard, wincing as the hinges squealed.

"How do you plan to get in? Did you have your keys with you?" He didn't remember seeing them, but it was possible she had it on her somewhere.

"No. But I don't need them," she said as they reached the back door.

"What? Why—" He stopped when she shifted a cover on the plate beneath the doorknob to reveal a keypad. "You have electronic locks?"

"Pretty neat, huh?"

"Aren't you afraid they'll get hacked?"

"No. I have a security system inside with a different code. Even if someone got through the door, they'd only have thirty seconds to enter the second code. It's not enough time for them to pop the panel off, connect their decoding device and get the correct code." She typed in the door code. The lock clicked and she opened the door. "This unit has a battery backup, so even if the power's cut to it, it'll still sound the house alarm." She walked to a beeping white box on the wall just feet from the door and typed in a second code. "There. All safe."

"Good. Let's get your stuff and get out of here. I don't want to be here any longer than necessary." He shut the back door and locked it.

"Me either." She walked through the kitchen and into the living room, then up the stairs. Sam followed close on her heels.

"Ignore the mess," she said as they entered the master bedroom.

Sam glanced around. The bed was rumpled and clothes littered part of the floor. He wouldn't call it a mess. It looked lived in.

She crossed to the closet and shoved a rack of dresses aside to reveal a panel on the wall. Audra grasped the small knob and opened it. Inside sat a small safe. She spun the dial back and forth, then turned the handle and opened the safe. His eyes widened as he caught sight of what was inside.

"Please tell me SIS gave you that money."

She took it out, along with a red passport book, then glanced at him. "Some of it. Most of it's mine. The op pays most of my living expenses. I've been withdrawing a portion of my paycheck every month and setting it aside for the last two years. Just in case."

He shook his head in disbelief and reached for a small suitcase stashed on a shelf. "You spy people are built different."

"It's common sense, Sam." She picked up several pairs of pants and followed him out into the bedroom to deposit the items on the bed.

He unzipped the case. "Go grab more clothes. I'll pack these up."

She nodded and walked away.

Sam stared at the cash. There had to be twenty grand or more there. He reached for her passport and opened it, surprised to see it was a British passport. "Angela *Brackley*?" He sat down on the bed, staring at the booklet. She'd used his last name for her secret alias?

She smiled at him as she returned with an armload of shirts. "I guess you could say you made an impact." She set the load of clothes down and sat next to him. "That passport means safety to me. I wanted a name that made me feel safe."

"My—" He stopped and clenched his teeth as the words stuck. "How—" He broke off again and growled. "Dammit." The words were right there, but they refused to come out.

Audra laid a hand on his thigh and squeezed. "Yes. You make me feel safe," she said, understanding what he was trying to say.

Sam closed his eyes and inhaled a breath through his nose, trying to calm his emotions. Being agitated or highly emotional always made the brain block worse. Staying calm was the key to being able to speak. Usually. Fatigue played a part too. But he wasn't tired. Just shocked.

He opened his eyes and looked at her. She stared back, a small, concerned frown putting a crinkle between her eyebrows. He smoothed it away with his thumb. "I'm glad." Leaning forward, he kissed the spot he'd just smoothed. Soft tendrils of her hair tickled his face. He let his touch linger for a moment, then pulled back. "I hope I can live up to that."

"You already have just by showing up. I didn't know where else to turn, so thank you."

Sam touched her temple and the fine, silky hair there. "You're welcome, Aud." He hoped fate wasn't done intervening in their lives. He wasn't ready to tell her goodbye.

A soft beep reached them. Audra's gaze sharpened, and she looked toward the door.

"What was that?"

She stood. "It sounded like the front door lock. It makes a beep like that when the wrong code is entered."

Sam cursed and got up. "Time to go." He grabbed the remainder of her clothes and threw them in the suitcase, zipping it shut.

Audra picked up her passport and the cash, stuffing them down inside the large purse she carried. She opened her nightstand and took out a handgun. "Let's go."

"You have another one of those for me?"

She handed him the forty-five she carried, then went to her closet and came back with a thirty-eight revolver. "I prefer this one, anyway."

Sam glanced at the weapon she held up. It was the same make and model as the gun she'd left in their hotel room. "Good deal." Hefting the suitcase off the bed, he trailed her to the door. She paused in the hall, listening.

"The door's still closed, I think." She glanced back at him.

That was good. They needed to go downstairs and pass through the living room—which was visible from the front door—to get to the back door.

On light feet, they descended the stairs. Sam kept the suitcase on his shoulder so the wheels wouldn't clack on the floor. Audra detoured to the coffee table and picked up her laptop, stuffing it inside her large handbag. At the back door, he put a hand on her arm. "Wait."

"What?"

"If someone's out there, I want you to take off for the

trees. Don't wait for me; just get to the car." He dug into his pocket for the key fob, then held it out.

"Sam—"

"Don't argue, Aud. I'm a better fighter than you, especially with your injuries."

Her mouth flattened, but she took the fob. "Fine." Stuffing it into her pocket, she moved toward the door and took up residence to its right.

Sam stationed himself on the left and peered through the window. The yard looked clear, but that didn't mean there wasn't someone up against the house he couldn't see or hiding behind the small garden shed. "I think it's as clear as it's going to get."

"Agreed."

He stowed the forty-five in his belt, then grasped the knob. "Ready?"

She nodded once, staring out at the yard.

Sam opened the door. She swung out, purse on her shoulder and gun at the ready. He fell in line behind her. Back to back, they walked toward the rear of the property. They were nearly at the gate when movement near the side of the condo caught his attention.

"Go!" He gave her a soft shove and turned to face the man coming toward them.

The stranger raised his arm, a matte black pistol in his hand. Sam feinted to the side as the man fired. He spared a glance over his shoulder to make sure Audra was in the clear. She'd made it through the gate and was moving through the brush. Sam turned back to the intruder and fired back. The man retreated to the side of the condo, and Sam ran for the property line.

Dashing through the gate and into the trees, he caught up to Audra. She ran, but not well. Still holding his weapon, he hooked an arm around her waist and lifted her off her feet.

She let out a squeak. "What are you doing?"

"I run faster too. Hold on."

Sam ran as fast as he dared. The woods weren't deep, so they quickly broke through the other side. He ran between the buildings and rounded the corner before heading straight again. They needed the cover.

He made it behind the first line of cars in the parking lot before he spotted the shooter.

"Put me down." Audra tapped his shoulder.

Sam set her on her feet. They were only yards from the car. Ducking low, they scampered toward it. "We're only going to have moments to get in and get away once we unlock it." The damn thing would beep when it was unlocked. He should have disabled that feature, but didn't think about it until now.

They circled the car, Sam at the driver's door and Audra beside him, ready to dive into the backseat.

"Ready?" she asked.

"Do it."

She pushed the unlock button, and the car beeped.

Sam yanked on the doorhandle and threw the suitcase inside onto the passenger seat. He dove in, smashed his foot onto the brake, and jammed the start button. With a quick look to make sure Audra was fully inside, he put the car in drive and sped out of his parking spot. A glance in the rearview mirror showed the shooter running through the lot after them, but falling behind.

"Do you recognize that man?"

Audra looked through the rear windshield. "Not specifically. But those tattoos—he's Irish mafia."

"You can tell that from this distance?"

"I saw them when he came around the house. Several of Liam's men have a similar design on their faces."

"Well, I guess this means we can trust your boss."

"Not necessarily. If there's a mole, Liam could have turned on him or her."

A deep frown marred Sam's face. He didn't like her logic. It made too much sense and meant they still couldn't trust anyone. "I guess that's true. We need—" His words stuck. Sam pulled in a breath, trying to slow his thoughts. "We need to get out of town. Quickly. The gunfire will have drawn attention." His gaze darted to his mirror and then to the road in front of them, then back again, looking for cops. In this area, the sound of gunfire wouldn't go unnoticed and the police would be quick to respond.

It wasn't just the immediate attention he was worried about, though. Someone had sent people looking for her. He knew she wanted to stay close, but he was thinking it would be better to fly down to Costa Rica now and circle the wagons.

She hummed a non-answer and stared out the window, watching for anyone following them. Sam wove through the streets, wanting to get away from cameras and people. He needed to call the team back and update them. Maybe Ezra could come pick them up. Though by the time Ezra flew to Las Vegas to get them, it would probably be quicker to just board a commercial flight. The only real benefit would be bypassing the TSA checkpoint.

He pulled into a quiet neighborhood and parked on a side street.

"What are we doing?"

"I'm calling the team. Asher might be able to get camera footage and identify the shooter." He opened his phone and found Asher's name in his contacts.

"Hey, Sam. I don't have anything yet on the files Audra sent over. I just opened them."

"That's not why I'm calling. Someone just shot at us at Audra's condo. She thinks it might be someone from Brogan's organization. Can you find any camera footage around the neighborhood and take a look?" He gave Asher the address.

"Are you guys okay?"

"We're fine. He missed."

"Well, that's good." The sound of furious typing came over the line. "There are cameras at a couple of the intersections near her building. Give me a description. I'll see what I can find. You two need to get out of town. Like, yesterday."

"Planning on it. The guy was about my height. Short dark hair. Face and arm tattoos. Navy blue t-shirt and jeans. There was a dark blue Audi sedan out front of the condo when we arrived. It was the only vehicle that was occupied. I don't know if the guy in the car is the same one who came at us. I didn't see the driver's face. He had short dark hair, though."

"Okay. I'll let you know what I find." Asher hung up.

"You know, I've been thinking."

Sam put the phone down and turned to look at Audra. "About?"

"I think we should stay here."

"What? Why?" That was the opposite of what they needed to do.

"Think about it. The trouble is here. I'm betting the mole is here, too, if there is one. We need to be close. Vegas is a big city. It shouldn't be that hard to hide."

Sam tapped his fingers on the steering wheel, considering her plan. "It'll be harder to stay off the police's radar."

"We can wear a hat and sunglasses when we're in public. I just think we'll accomplish more and get answers faster if we're where the action is."

Sam pinched the bridge of his nose. "Aud—"

"I'm right, and you know it."

He let out a soft growl. "I'm not sure what difference an hour away will make." That's really all he was asking for. He just wanted to be a city over, where they were away from all the major players.

"You know how fast these situations can change. It makes sense for us to be here."

She wasn't going to back down. He could see it in the set to her face. "Fine. But I want at least one of my team to come up and help. We need more eyes."

"If that's what you want, that's fine."

"Good. Because that part is non-negotiable." He picked up his phone again.

Thirteen

Audra stared at herself in the wide mirror over the sink in the hotel room they'd rented just off the Strip. She might have argued they should stay in the city, but that didn't mean she wanted to be somewhere Liam's men could stumble upon her. The airport hotels were too close, so they'd moved.

She tipped her head, examining her battered body. Dark purple bruises colored her hip and the top of her thigh. The area ached, but not as much as she thought it would. Mostly, it felt like a badly pulled muscle. The fogginess in her brain bothered her more than her hip. That would probably change as the days wore on. Once she didn't feel like she was swimming through a swamp, the ache would register more. The pain would increase as it healed too. She knew that from experience.

She touched her hair. Her dark brown, almost black tresses were a stark contrast against her pale skin. She didn't normally have a lot of color, but she was ghostly white. Her body was struggling right now.

Having had enough of staring at her bedraggled appearance, she turned and reached for her clothes. The room spun, and she lost her balance. Crashing into the counter, she slapped at it, trying to stay upright. Her hand hit the toiletries and sent them flying. They hit the floor with a clatter. Her lipstick rolled into the corner and her hairbrush skittered across the tile and banged into the toilet. Sam's deodorant ricocheted off the bathtub.

With a groan, Audra lowered herself to her knees and pressed her forehead against the cool granite, desperate for the room to stop spinning. The urge to puke hit her hard.

"Audra? Are you all right?" Sam's voice carried through the closed door.

Too busy holding last night's dinner down, she didn't answer.

"Aud? Answer me, or I'm coming in."

She opened her mouth to call out and immediately closed it again as her stomach rebelled further. She knew her injuries would catch up with her eventually. For the last two days, she'd been running on adrenaline. That was gone now.

The door opened.

"Oh my God. Audra." Sam sank down next to her, his warm hand landing on her bare back. "What happened?"

Audra swallowed and attempted to speak. "Dizzy." She knew she should feel some embarrassment over the fact she was naked, but it wasn't anything Sam hadn't seen before.

"Come on. Let's get you off the floor."

The hand on her back slid around her side. She hissed as he touched the bruise over her hip.

"Sorry." His hand rose, grazing the underside of her breast.

That sent different signals along her nerve-endings that weren't unpleasant. The zing didn't last, though. Her dizziness and the ache in her leg pushed it away.

Sam stood, bringing her with him. Audra sagged into his side as the world spun again. She clutched a handful of his black t-shirt and closed her eyes.

"I'm going to pick you up."

He shifted at her side. She felt his hand slide along the backs of her thighs, then lift at her knees. In seconds, she was cradled against his broad chest.

"Okay?" he asked.

"Yes," she croaked, not daring to nod. She stared at his jaw, hoping it would help her head to stare at a fixed point up close.

He carried her through the doorway and into the main part of the hotel room. A moment later, he laid her on her bed and tugged the comforter up over her body. Audra sank into the soft mattress, closing her eyes again, and let her muscles relax. After a minute of stillness flat on her back, some of her nausea eased.

"I think you need to rest today." The bed dipped as Sam sat down beside her.

She looked at him, her voice returning now that the spin cycle in her belly had slowed. "Your friends are coming. And we still have more data to go over." They'd spent a good portion of yesterday combing through the files she copied from Liam's computer. A lot of it was legitimate business accounting. So far, they didn't have much to go on.

"Asher's already on it. Dean and Max will rent a car and drive themselves here. You can greet them from bed."

She rolled her eyes. "That's such a great first impression. Let's make the female operative look even weaker than she's already perceived to be."

"You don't have to prove your toughness to them."

"You say that—"

"And I mean it. They know you're injured. They also know you've been undercover for two years. That alone would make anyone think you're tough."

He took her hand, holding her fingers and running his

thumb over her knuckles. "How's your head now that you're lying down?"

"Better." To her horror, tears formed in her eyes. She clenched her teeth and willed them away.

"Hey, what's wrong?" Sam touched her cheek, smoothing away the wetness she hadn't realized seeped out.

"Nothing." She batted his hand away and swiped at her face. "I'm fine."

"That's total crap, and you know it. You can talk to me, you know? I might not always find the right words anymore, but I'm still a good listener."

"How about we talk about that? Why do you have issues speaking now?"

"Nope. This is about you."

"Again, talking about other things distracts me."

"You haven't talked about what happened at all. It's been two days, Aud. You need to let your feelings out."

She grimaced, then glared at him. "I'd rather not." Feelings were messy. She didn't have the bandwidth to deal with messy right now.

He sighed and looked away. "Okay. How about you tell me more about this op? How close were you to the end?"

Audra lifted her free hand and massaged her forehead. A dull headache had replaced the dizziness. "Probably another month. Until I could leave, anyway. There's still all the follow-up. I was hoping that the hard drive and the pictures I took of that ledger I found would be enough to get some arrest warrants. It all has to be analyzed first."

"Well, now you not only have MI6 on it, but also Asher. He'll probably be faster."

A corner of her mouth lifted. "You sure do put a lot of stock in him. In all your friends, really."

"They never let me down."

"That's good. Having friends like that." Her brow wrinkled. She didn't have many people like that in her life. Sam was about the only one. And even then, the only reason she called him was because she ran into him in February. If it wasn't for that encounter, she never would have thought to contact him. She'd never forgotten their time together, but that didn't mean he was constantly in her thoughts. She pulled those nights out at times when she needed the endorphin boost. Thinking about him while she did—other things—always improved her mood.

Her face heated. She prayed he didn't notice. Or that he chalked it up to embarrassment over her last statement.

"I'm glad I do," he said. "And now you do too."

Her frown deepened. "What do you mean?"

"You're my friend, right?"

"I guess so."

"And you need help?"

"Yes."

"Then my friends are your friends. They'll do anything you need to stay safe."

Moisture pressed against the backs of her eyes again. She blinked and looked away. "Well, I'm not so sure it'll last, but be sure to thank them for me for helping."

Sam sighed. "I know you don't believe me, but you'll see." He squeezed her fingers. "This group—they're special."

They'd have to be to have Sam's loyalty. The man she'd known didn't bestow his friendship easily. But she'd gathered he'd been that way much of his life. He was an only child, raised by elderly grandparents after his mother abandoned him. He didn't know who his father was. They were alike in that respect. Her father was some guy her mother met on holiday. All Audra knew was he'd been an engineering student in Bristol and his first name was Steven. She didn't know much more about her mother, honestly. The woman hadn't been around much before she died.

"How did you meet them? You didn't know them when we were together, did you?"

"I knew Ford. We served together, though not on the same SEAL team. Not until later."

"And the others?"

"I met most of them when I moved down to Costa Rica. Dean's the only other one I knew before that. We were on the same team for a couple of years."

"What happened? What drove you to Costa Rica?"

He studied her for several moments. "You're really not going to let this go, are you?"

"Nope. I do not wish to talk about myself."

"What if I don't want to, either?"

"Then we're going to sit here and stare at each other. Though I'd rather not do that. Not while I'm naked under this duvet."

Fire lit in Sam's eyes. They flicked to the top of the blanket that was tucked under her arm, then back to her face.

Audra's cheeks heated again, but she didn't look away. It wasn't in her nature to back down. Even if meeting him head on wasn't wise. She couldn't do anything about the need he stirred in her right now. Not when simply sitting up made the room spin and her hip ache. "So, what's it going to be? Are you going to keep staring at me? Or will you finally answer my question?"

He stared at her for another moment, then shrugged. "It's not a secret. I got blown up. The Humvee I was in hit an—it hit a bomb. The blast—it tossed and flipped the truck. I got lucky and was sitting on the side it didn't land on. Shrapnel tore—" He broke off again and motioned to his legs. Taking a deep breath, he closed his eyes for a moment and then continued. "My biggest injury was to my head. I was in a coma for about a week. When I woke up, I couldn't talk. My coordination was off too."

"Geez, Sam." Audra stared at him with wide eyes, horrified at what he'd been through.

"It took a few months for me to regain my coordination. The speech took longer. I still struggle sometimes. The words get stuck. It's worse when I'm agitated. Or tired."

"And the deep breathing, that helps?"

"Usually. It's more about resetting my emotions. Keeping them under control. They can overwhelm my processing center and then the words get stuck."

"I'm sorry you had to go through that. That you still do." She couldn't imagine how drastically that changed things for him. He'd been quiet when they met, but also outgoing and gregarious at times. He wasn't as much anymore.

He lifted a shoulder. "It's life. Nothing I can do about it except accept it and move on."

"How long ago was this?"

"A few years. I was medically discharged from the Navy. Home—well, no one's there I care about anymore. Ford called me and asked if I wanted to come down and stay with him. How he heard about my injuries, I don't know. I've never asked. But I'm glad he did. It's the best decision I ever made."

"And now you work for him?" She'd looked Sam up after they ran into each other in February, but she hadn't done a deep dive, preferring not to get distracted from her mission. Seeing him had done enough of that. All she'd allowed herself to discover was that he was one of several Americans living in the Golfito area.

"No. I own a bar. Our team isn't official. We just help each other out—and some of our other military friends—when the need arises."

"Oh."

"That's why I say you can trust my friends. Why they'll treat you as a friend. No one's getting paid for this." He squeezed her fingers again.

That zing zipped through her once more. She knew she shouldn't—that she should pull away—but she turned her hand over and laced their fingers together. "Thank you for telling me."

A smile slashed over his handsome face, making his midnight blue eyes sparkle. "It's part of the friend code. Distraction. Do you feel better?"

To her surprise, she found he was right. She was less woozy. "Yes. My brain has stopped feeling like it's on a tilt-a-whirl."

"Good."

"So, tell me about this bar?" She smiled. "You weren't a big drinker, so why pick that?"

He shifted, coming up on the bed to sit beside her, stretching his long legs out as he took her hand again. "I decided I wanted to stay down there. But I needed a job to get a work visa. For a little while, I worked for Ford on his fishing charters, but the motion of the waves—my equilibrium can be unsteady, so it wasn't a good fit. I had disability payments coming in, and I'd been living with Ford, so I didn't have too many expenses. Tourism in our area was booming, so I looked into what would enhance the visitor experience. There wasn't a nice bar people could hang out at. So, I opened one."

"And you like it?"

"I do. Sometimes, the tourists get on my nerves, but I figured out that hiring bands for live music makes it harder for them to talk to me." He chuckled.

Audra laughed too. "It sounds nice. Less stressful than my life."

"Most anything is less stressful than being a spy. Especially an undercover one."

That was true. And for the first time, she was starting to rethink her career choice. Maybe if things hadn't gone sour with her op, she'd think differently, but she was ready to live at a slower pace.

"So, what have you been up to for the last ten years? Anything interesting, other than this case, since the one we met on?"

Audra smiled, remembering that op. A rebel faction in Africa had threatened U.S. and U.K. operations in the area. She'd been part of the intelligence arm gathering information. Sam had been the military attaché assigned to provide security for her and the other members of her joint team. She'd fallen fast and hard for him. When the op ended, they'd all been granted a couple weeks of leave. Oh so casually, she'd mentioned her intent to visit Rota, Spain after their debrief, hoping he would follow her there. He hadn't disappointed. Her first evening in the city, he plopped down in the wrought-iron chair across from her at a small café. That sexy smile on his face said it all. She'd enjoyed their time together, had been sad when it ended. But they both knew their lives were going in different directions.

"There have been one or two fun jobs. Not anything I can really talk about. This one has been the most grueling, though. And the most exciting."

He lifted their connected hands and put them in his lap. He traced circles on the back of her knuckles with his free hand and stared down. "I tried to keep track of you. First through official channels. When you disappeared off the radar, I worried you were dead. Even more so when even Asher couldn't track you down." He lifted his head to look at her. "I'm glad you're not."

That intense, dark blue gaze ensnared her. She'd always been captivated by his eyes. They were such a deep blue they verged on purple. For a long time, every time she looked at the twilight sky, she thought of him.

He shifted, turning onto his side, and leaned closer. His

free hand came up, skimming her cheek with the tips of his fingers. She knew he wanted to kiss her. She didn't intend to stop him.

The first touch of his mouth zapped her like a bolt of lightning. Memories flooded her head of how it felt to kiss him. To touch him. To have him hold her and make her lose her mind. The kiss they shared months ago had been so quick and so spontaneous, she hadn't done more than just react to how it felt.

This one, though. It was slow and deliberate. It felt like the kisses they used to share. The ones that led to them tangled in the bedsheets for hours on end.

Audra raised her hand to cup the side of his face. He'd shaved this morning, and the smooth skin of his jaw glided beneath her fingers.

Cool air whispered over her chest, tightening her nipples, as the duvet slipped. Some sanity crept back in. She was naked under the blanket. And while the wanton woman in her head screamed, "Hell yes!" her battered body couldn't handle much more than the kiss.

So, she did the prudent thing and pulled back.

He stared at her, his dark blue eyes almost black with desire. "I know you're hurt, but when you're all healed up—" he tugged the duvet down further and traced a circle around one nipple—"we're going to do much, much more than share a few kisses."

She swallowed hard. "What if I don't want to? Getting involved again probably isn't the best idea."

"Oh, you want to. You can't sit there and tell me your body isn't wet, ready for me." He leaned down again, his mouth just inches away.

Oh boy. She was in trouble.

"And I've learned life's too short for missed opportunities, Audra. I let you go once. I'm not doing that again."

A *lot* of trouble.

Sam pressed a firm kiss to her lips, then sat up. He swung his legs over the side of the bed and stood. "I'm going to get us some breakfast. And coffee. The caffeine will be good for your head."

Audra closed her eyes and pressed her lips together, struggling to corral her body. It didn't like being denied, even if it was too beaten up to participate in more than kissing. "Okay. Take your time. I'm not going anywhere."

FOURTEEN

Sam scrolled through the file of business memos Audra had emailed him and tried to pay attention to what he read. It wasn't easy. Not only was it dull and dry, he had to ignore her perched cross-legged on the bed just feet away. She'd piled her dark hair into a messy bun on top of her head and donned that sweatshirt he bought her. She looked cute and kissable. All he wanted to do was bury his face in her neck and breathe her in.

Kissing her this morning had been a mistake. He should have waited. His body wanted him to do something about his feelings, but she wasn't in any shape for that. It would be pure torture for the next couple of weeks, at least. And it was all dependent on whether she felt the same way. He knew he affected her, but it was her decision on whether they would act on it. He wouldn't pressure her.

Personally, he was in a place where he was ready for a relationship. He'd watched several of his closest friends fall in love lately. It had set off a yearning for the same kind of commitment. But he wasn't sure she was in the same place. That hadn't stopped him from declaring his intentions, though. Of all the times for his brain block to disappear, it had to pick that one. But he wouldn't take the words back. He'd meant what he'd said. Life was too short to let the good things go.

A soft knock on the door drew his attention. He clicked the button on his phone to turn off his screen and stood up, eager for a distraction. Dean and Max were here.

He checked the peephole to make sure it was them, then opened the door. "Hey, guys." Sam stepped back so they could enter.

"Hey." Dean grinned and walked in. Max said hello and followed. Sam closed the door, then trailed them from the entryway. They had stopped in front of the TV and faced the beds.

"Guys, this is Audra Ridley. Aud, Dean Adler and Max Carson." He pointed to each man as he said his name.

She smiled and lifted a hand. "Hello. Thank you for coming."

"Not a problem, ma'am," Max said. "It's kinda what we do."

"I appreciate it. And you don't need to call me ma'am. Audra will do." She wrinkled her nose and gave them a crooked smile. "Ma'am makes me feel like one of my primary school teachers. I'd rather not think about those dour-faced old biddies."

"No one could ever call you old or dour-faced." Max offered her a toothy smile, his blue eyes shining. The dimple in his cheek popped. He glanced at Sam. "Where did you find this one? And why didn't we know about her until now?"

"Long story."

"Yes," Audra said. "And one that isn't really relevant to why you're here."

Dean let out a low whistle and poked Max in the arm. "She shut you down good."

Max sent him a quick glare.

Sam decided to intervene before they escalated their banter any further. "How about we get to work? Have you two checked in?"

"Yes," Dean said. "We're just down the hall."

"What have you got?" Max asked. His flirty expression turned all business.

"A lot of paperwork." Audra turned her laptop around. "Most of what was on Liam's computer was for his legit businesses. There is one file, though..." She spun the computer around and clicked the screen several times before turning it back. "I found a folder full of images of myself."

Dean nodded. "Asher mentioned that. We haven't seen them, though."

She pushed the laptop toward him. "Have a look."

He walked forward and took the computer, then sat down on the other bed. Max sat next to him.

"Do you know when these were taken?" Max asked.

"Most of them. It was over a series of a few months."

"Did you establish a timeline for the photos?" Dean asked.

"They're pretty much in chronological order. Why?"

"It could tell us about the photographer's movements. If they're all at a particular time of day, it could mean he has a job or some other commitment."

"They're all over the place. I didn't really notice any pattern. I'm just thankful none of them show me meeting with Theo. They all seem fairly innocuous. It's pictures of me at home. A few of me shopping. Some at Byrne's and a few other restaurants."

"Except this one." Max's eyebrows rose. "Clicking away. Sorry."

Sam's mouth flattened. He knew which one Max meant and was thankful his friend didn't linger. No one except him needed to see Audra dressed like that.

"They got lucky. I don't often parade around in front of open windows in my knickers."

Sam growled. "Can we move on from your knickers?"

Max cleared his throat. "Okay, so, did anything unusual happen around the time of the first picture?"

"Not that I remember."

Dean's phone buzzed in his pocket, interrupting them. He fished it out, looking at it. "It's Asher." Sliding his thumb over the screen, he answered and held it out so they all could hear. "Hey, man. You're on speaker with Max, Sam, and Audra."

"Good. I got a screenshot of the guy in the car. I sent it to Sam's email. I also sent you an address. I got Audra's handler on video and followed him to his car."

"How?" Audra asked.

"There are cameras in that park you meet at. I found you two on camera on the footpath Friday night. He parked away from the cameras, but there's only two ways out of that neighborhood, and it was late, so there weren't many vehicles. I tracked the few I saw and found him. It's registered to a Ted Sanders."

Max snorted. "That's original."

"It's enough to throw someone off," Audra said. "I've used names that are similar to my own. They're easier to remember, and most people don't look too closely."

"She's right," Asher said. "But I'm not most people. It stuck out like a sore thumb. I found a driver's license in that name and the picture matched the one I found of Theo Anderson. The address on the license led me to a small house in North Vegas."

"Awesome," Dean said. "We'll check it out."

"Sam, did you two get anything out of the documents?"

"No." He looked at Audra.

"It's all about his legitimate businesses," Audra said. "The file with the pictures of the ledger, those are likely to be the numbers that deal with the illegal side of things."

"I've got that data running through a cryptology program. I need more info to feed it, though."

"What kind of info?" Max asked.

"Dates of meetings, illicit business partners. Even non-illicit ones. Locations."

"Okay," Audra said. "I have a lot of that written down already. I'll look it over and send it to you."

"Sounds good. You guys watch yourselves when you check out Anderson's house. We still don't know what we're dealing with."

"We will," Dean said. "I'll call you after we search it."

"Sounds good. Later." Asher hung up.

Dean turned off his phone screen. "It looks like we're going on a scavenger hunt."

FIFTEEN

Audra eyed the neighborhood cruising by outside the car window as Dean drove to Theo's house. They'd left the glitz and glam that characterized Las Vegas well behind and were now in a decent residential neighborhood full of two-story homes.

With about a block to go, Dean pulled over. Audra and Sam got out. Because there were four of them, and a large group of adults walking through the neighborhood would look strange to anyone who happened to glance outside, they were splitting up. Max had donned running gear and would jog to the house by himself after Dean dropped him off. Dean would park and arrive separately as a man out for a stroll.

"Does this look like a neighborhood where an SIS handler would live?" Sam asked as he took her hand.

She curled her fingers around his, welcoming the contact. "Maybe. He'd be less recognizable in an apartment setting, but it's easier to see if someone's following you here." She glanced around. There were few cars parked at the curb. Most of the homes had long driveways and two-car garages. It was more than enough space for families to keep their vehicles off the street.

They turned the corner and Theo's house came into view. Hand-in-hand, they marched up the walkway like they were meant to be there, and she knocked on the front door. It was only a ruse to make the neighbors think they were legit. While she watched the street, Sam picked the lock. In seconds, the knob turned.

"That was quick." Audra glanced at him.

He grinned. "I had a good teacher." He twisted the knob and opened the door.

Audra surveyed the entryway, then cautiously stepped inside. "Who?"

"Dean. He's the licensed private investigator of our group. He took learning the P.I. skills to heart." He followed her in and shut the door.

"Sounds like—Oh, boy."

Sam cursed as he came up behind her where she'd stopped and caught a glimpse of the living room. Someone had been here.

Stuffing littered the floor, and the ripped cushions were off the couch. Drawers were pulled out of the entertainment center and the television lay on the floor, the back torn off.

"Watch yourself." Sam grazed a hand over her shoulder as they waded deeper into the mess.

Audra nodded and picked her way over the carnage to the kitchen. In here, the damage was even worse. Every cabinet door hung open. Cans and open boxes covered the counters and the floor, some of them spilling their contents and leaving a fine powder coating the surface. The refrigerator and freezer doors were also open. She could hear the appliance humming as it worked fruitlessly to keep the items inside cold.

A knock on the back door drew their attention. She glanced up to see Dean's face in the window.

Sam was closer and opened it. "Someone beat us here."

Dean and Max stepped in, and Max let out a low whistle. "Damn."

"What are the chances we find anything now?" Dean asked.

"We still need to look." Audra walked around them and headed for the hallway. "I'm going to see if I can find his office."

Two doors down, she found what she was looking for. Grimacing, she stepped inside. This room was even worse than the kitchen. Theo had two monitors and both were lying smashed on the floor. Like the TV, their backs were ripped off. The computer case had been pried open. Wires hung from the bent metal. Audra peered closer and realized whoever had done this had taken the hard drive.

Walking around the desk, she noted the open drawers and the papers strewn over the carpet, interspersed with pens and paperclips. To her left, a filing cabinet had met a similar fate to the computer. Someone had taken a crowbar to the drawers, forcing the locks open. Manila file folders stuck out at odd angles. Some of them still contained papers.

Curious what the intruders could have left behind, Audra walked over. She pulled some nitrile gloves from her pocket and slipped them on, then leafed through the documents. It was the lease for the house and some utility bills.

After checking the other drawers, she dropped to her knees with a wince as the movement pulled at her hip, then started leafing through the papers on the floor. These, too, were just bills.

She brushed aside a water bill, then paused as she read the header. It was a bank statement. Picking up the page, she scanned it. It was a recent one. Several large deposits over the last month had inflated his balance to almost half a million dollars.

"Oh, Theo. What did you do?"

Audra set the statement on the desk and leafed through the rest of the papers. She found several more and gathered them up before going in search of Sam and his friends.

"Hey."

Sam glanced up from where he sat in the master bedroom closet, going through pockets. "Find something?"

"Yes." She waved the statements. "Theo received some large deposits over the last couple of months."

"How large?"

"Almost half a million dollars. I didn't do the exact math, but it's a lot."

A frown creased his forehead, and he got up, holding out a hand. She passed him the statements.

"Yeah, that's a lot," he said, leafing through the documents.

"Did you find anything?" she asked.

"No. I have a few more pairs of pants to check, then I think I'm done in here." He handed her back the statements.

"What else still needs checked?"

"I'm not sure. We split up. Dean took the spare bedroom. Max stayed in the living room. Outside? But I don't want you going out there alone."

She nodded. "Did anyone look in the garage?"

"Not sure."

"Okay. I'll go check."

"I'll find you when I'm done in here."

Audra nodded again and left him to finish the bedroom. In the living room, she found Max on his knees, checking the bottom of the entertainment center.

"Has anyone been in the garage?"

He glanced her way. "No."

Audra wandered into the kitchen and opened the door that led to the two-car garage. She stepped onto the concrete floor and glanced around. It was rather empty. A bicycle leaned against the wall to the left of the door, a helmet hanging off the handlebars. In the far corner across from the door, a broom and a rake sat propped against the wall near a door that led to the back garden. A small toolbox sat on the utility bench on the wall to her right.

She walked over and opened it. Poking through, she only saw basic tools. With a huff, she shut the lid. Bending down, she looked under the bench and ran her hand along the underside of the facing. It was clean. She gave the room another once over, but there was nowhere else to hide anything. She went back inside.

Sam emerged from the hallway, Dean following him, as she stepped inside. "Are you already done searching out there?"

She nodded. "It's pretty empty."

"There's nothing here," Max said. "Not anymore, at least."

"Audra found some bank statements." Sam gestured to her. "I think that's about all we're going to get."

"Okay," Dean said. "Let's get out of here, then. Same way we came in."

"Give me those papers, Aud." Sam held out a hand.

She passed them over, and he tucked them into his jeans pocket.

With a nod, he headed for the door. "Let's go."

Sixteen

The door snicked shut as the four of them piled into Dean and Max's room. Sam stopped in the doorway and stared. *Damn.*

"Bloody hell." Audra stopped next to him. "I didn't know this place had rooms this fancy."

Max grinned and walked around them. "It's nice being rich."

"I guess so." Audra shook her head and walked over to the couch. She grimaced as she sat. "It doesn't make the furniture any softer, though."

Dean barked a short laugh. "Nope. I tried to tell him he was wasting his money in a place like this, but he didn't care." He lifted a shoulder. "I got my own bedroom so I don't have to listen to him snore. I quit complaining once I found that out."

"I don't snore," Max retorted.

"Just like you don't flirt with every woman you meet?"

"I don't do that, either."

Audra chuckled. "The military really does make you all brothers, doesn't it?"

"Sometimes, yes," Sam said. "Can we knock off the arguing and dig into these bank statements?" He walked over to the desk and took the papers from his pocket, laying them out on the wooden surface.

"What's to look at?" Max asked. "There aren't any account numbers to tell us who sent him the money. Hell, we can't even see his account number."

"No, but it'll give Asher something to go on. And some of these, there might be enough in the name we can get something from a basic internet search." Sam rolled the chair out and sat down. He set his phone on the desk and opened his calculator app. "Can one of you read off the larger amounts? I want to add them up."

Dean walked over and started with the first statement. Sam typed in the numbers and watched as the total climbed ever higher. When Dean read the last one, he sat back and stared at the final tally.

"What did you get?" Max asked.

"Three hundred and fifty thousand."

"Wait," Audra said. "Exactly three hundred and fifty thousand? Not three hundred fifty thousand and ten dollars? Or two hundred and forty-two?"

He looked over. She had sat up and stared at him with an intense look. "Yes. It's exactly that." He held up his phone to show her. "Why? Does that matter?"

"It might. Can one of you pull up the images I took of Liam's ledger?"

Sam turned his phone around and logged into the server where she'd stored everything. "What am I looking for?"

"The final entry. What does it say?"

"350G TS DTC." He looked at her with a frown. She had her lip between her teeth as she stared off into space. Something was going on in her head. That was her 'puzzle it out' face.

Suddenly, her expression cleared, and she looked at him with wide eyes. "Liam paid off Theo."

"What?" Max said. "How do you figure?"

"Three hundred fifty grand to 'TS.' The 'TS' is Ted Sanders. Theo's alias."

Dean cursed. "Then what or who is 'DTC?'"

"I don't know," she said. "But why would Liam pay Theo? Wouldn't it be the other way around? If Liam knew who Theo was—who I was—why wouldn't Theo be the one paying to keep us both alive?"

"Unless Liam didn't know who Theo was and Theo was threatening to take something he had on Liam to the police to extort money out of him," Max said.

The room fell silent as they digested that. Sam stared at his phone, reading the other ledger entries. "There are other entries here that end with 'DTC.'" He looked at Audra again. "Do you know what it could be?"

"No. Are there other repeating initials?"

"Some, yes." He read them off. "Do you recognize any of those?"

"No. I don't know what they could be. It's possible they're someone's initials. Or it's code for places."

"I think you need to sit down and get that list together that Asher wants," Dean said. "We'll send him that and what we've discovered from this." He pointed at the statements. "Maybe he and his algorithm can figure it out."

SEVENTEEN

ot water beat down on Sam's back. He needed to get out of the shower and go to bed. But that meant returning to the same room as Audra and pretending she wasn't sleeping just feet away. When they were together in Spain, they'd never slept apart. He hadn't known what it was like to be in the same room at night, but not have her in his arms. He did now, and he didn't like it.

Their first night in Vegas, they'd both been exhausted, so it hadn't been a problem. He'd fallen asleep as soon as his head hit the pillow. But last night? He'd been well-rested and his brain had had a chance to catch up to the fact that she was real. Not some memory he'd conjured up to distract himself. It was a torture he didn't care to repeat. His body remembered holding her all night, and it wanted to do it again.

He reached for the water and shut it off. He couldn't stay in here all night.

After toweling off, he put on a t-shirt and running shorts and exited the bathroom. Audra sat much where he'd left her. Cross-legged in the middle of her bed. She was staring at the ledger photos.

"You need to get some sleep. And how does sitting like that not bother your hip?"

She glanced at him and lifted a shoulder. "It's fine. Mostly, it's only when I tip too far to that side."

"Well, that's good. How's your head?"

"Better since I rested earlier. I'm fine, Sam. Stop worrying about me."

He sat down on her bed and pushed the laptop closed with one finger. "I will always worry about you, Aud."

Her dark gaze met his. Electricity crackled between them. She looked away. "Don't. I'm fine."

"Maybe so, but I can't just turn it off because you tell me to."

She unfolded her legs with a wince and scooted toward the edge of the bed. "Try." She stood, paused for a moment, letting her sore body adjust to the new position, then walked to the desk and set the computer down.

Sam got up and stood in front of her. Words swirled in his mind, but not a single one wanted to form and come out. It wasn't his screwed-up brain stopping them this time, though. He wasn't sure what he wanted to say.

"What?" She frowned up at him. "Why are you staring at me like that?"

"Do you ever think about us?" Sam clenched his teeth. Of all the things that finally made their way out, that was it? Why couldn't it have been a simple, "I'm glad you're okay." Or, "We'll figure this out." But the words were out, and he couldn't take them back. It was like the missed opportunities speech from yesterday all over again.

Her expression closed off. "No."

He scoffed. "That's a lie." She only ever gave him the blank, secret agent face when she wanted to hide something from him.

"Believe whatever you want." She stepped around him.

Sam turned and snagged her hand, stopping her. Words burned in the back of his throat. He knew it wasn't wise, but he couldn't keep his feelings bottled up. Not with her. Something about her removed all his filters. Being around her the last couple of days, seeing her so vulnerable, had brought up a lot of old feelings. And some new ones. If he wanted a chance at what his friends had, he had to put himself out there with this woman. No one else had ever come close to making him feel the way she did.

"Sam…"

"I know you don't want to hear it, but I'm going to say it anyway. I meant what I said yesterday. I've missed you. I know at the time it was what we wanted and the only thing we could do, but walking away from you was one of the hardest things I've ever done."

That dark gaze held his for several beats before she squeezed his fingers. "Me too," she whispered. Letting go, she turned and walked into the bathroom.

He stared after her, stunned. What did that mean? He doubted she meant she was ready to give them another chance. She was probably just acknowledging how she'd felt all those years ago. But he'd be damned if he gave up on her now. He couldn't imagine going back to his normal life without her being a part of it.

Resolve filling him, Sam took off his shirt, then turned off all the lights except her bedside lamp and crawled into his bed. His mind whirled with plans for how he could convince her to give them a chance. A real one. Not just a fling.

He didn't want a fling. Not this time.

Light flooded the entryway as she opened the bathroom door. She extinguished it, then walked into the main room, pausing by the desk.

"Go to bed, Aud. The ledger will still be there in the morning."

She reached out and skimmed the edge of the desk with her fingers before she turned away. With a quick flick of her wrist, she flipped the covers back and got into bed, then turned off the light, plunging the room into darkness.

Fabric rustled as she shifted. Sam rolled over, hoping the inability to see her would stop some of the thoughts crossing his mind. It might have been ten years, but he still remembered how she looked sprawled over stark white sheets after they'd made love. That satisfied smile on her face and the slight sheen of sweat on her soft skin.

His body tightened.

She rolled again, and he bit back a groan. Sam scrunched his eyes closed and tried to think about other things. He needed to call Martina tomorrow. Make sure everything was running smoothly down there. He knew she could handle it, but he wanted her to know he was available if she needed anything and that he appreciated her jumping in when he'd effectively just dumped everything on her.

Audra turned again. Sam buried his head under a pillow. Tonight would be torture. Worse than last night. Absolute and utter torture. America's enemies could take notes from her on how to incapacitate their prisoners.

She shuffled again, but this time, he heard her get up. A moment later, she poked his shoulder. He moved the pillow covering his face to look at her in the darkness.

"Move over." She lifted the blankets and put a knee on the bed.

He rolled, then slid his hips back and grabbed his pillows, moving them. Hers landed in the empty space with a soft thump.

Sam propped his head on his hand, facing her as she settled in. "Not that I'm arguing, but why are you in my bed?"

"You just had to open your big mouth. Now all I can think about is Rota."

His body tensed as a shot of need blasted through his muscles.

"I'm in no shape for a repeat—not that it's wise—but neither of us will sleep well in separate beds. I'd rather not add zombie to the list of things wrong with me." She punched her pillow and stuffed it beneath her head as she rolled over. "Lie down and go to sleep."

Sam let his head drop to his pillow. She shifted again, her back still to him, and he heard her breath catch. She was on her bad hip. "Audra, roll over. I won't bite."

"I'm not worried about you." She rolled onto her back.

He wrapped an arm around her torso and tugged. "Come here. You want to sleep better? You know that will happen if I hold you."

She turned into him, resting a hand on his arm. Fingers skimmed his jaw. "You haven't lost your words in a while."

Sam tucked her closer. "I don't have to think when it comes to this. To us."

She sucked in a breath through her teeth. "You should."

"No. Some things are just meant to be."

"We're one of those things?"

"I think so, yes." He stretched his neck and placed a lingering kiss on her forehead. "Go to sleep, honey."

Her warm breath whispered against his face. She kissed his jaw. "Goodnight, Sam."

He brushed his fingers through the soft hair at her temple. His heart clenched with the need to make this woman his and to keep her. "Goodnight, Aud."

Eighteen

A sharp knock brought Audra awake. She sat up, then groaned as the muscles in her hip and thigh protested. Flopping back to the bed, she covered her face, waiting for the pain to subside.

Sam's hand landed on her belly. The warmth seeped into her, offering some comfort. "You okay?"

"Yeah. I moved too fast." Dropping her hands, she pointed toward the door. "Answer the door, would you?" To emphasize her words, whoever was on the other side knocked again.

He got up, treating her to a glimpse of his naked back. A tattoo decorated his left shoulder blade. She squinted, trying to get a better look. He hadn't had that in Spain.

Before she could contemplate it further, he opened the door, letting in Dean and Max.

"We have a problem," she heard Dean say a moment before he came into view.

The two men paused, taking in her position and the rumpled covers on both sides of the bed.

Max cleared his throat. "Sorry to barge in."

"You're fine," Sam said. He picked up his discarded t-shirt. "We were still asleep. It's early yet."

Audra glanced at the clock. It was just after seven. "What's up?" She pushed herself into a sitting position, but stayed in bed. She wasn't comfortable parading around in front of Dean and Max in her short shorts and silky pajama tee. The outfit left little to the imagination.

"This." Max took out his phone, then handed it to Sam.

"What is it?" Audra asked.

Sam groaned. "Trouble." He came over and sat down next to her to show her the screen.

"Hit play," Max said.

Sam touched the screen, and a newscaster began speaking.

"Police are looking for help identifying the body of a man found Sunday morning. He's described as approximately forty years old, dark hair and blue eyes." The newscast showed a composite sketch that looked exactly like Theo. "They're also looking for this woman." A grainy security image from the hospital appeared.

Audra let out a squeak and covered her mouth. "Shit."

"Authorities believe she may have information about his death. Anyone with information on her whereabouts or on the man's identity is urged to call Las Vegas PD."

Sam stopped the video. "Damn."

"Damn is right," Dean said. "We saw that on the television downstairs while we were getting breakfast."

"Dee was supposed to take care of my involvement." Audra ran a hand through her hair, her mind working over-time. This was not good. And not only because it thrust her into the spotlight. If Liam didn't suspect something, he would now. The entire Vegas branch of the Irish mafia could be on the lookout for her.

"She probably did until Theo showed up dead," Sam said.

He looked at Dean and Max. "We need to get out of this hotel and find a short-term rental."

"Honestly, I think we need to get out of town." Dean's gaze shifted between him and Audra. "I know you want to stay because the investigation is here, but you can't do anything when you can't even go out in public."

A thought struck Audra. "Let me see that." She pointed at Max's phone.

Sam handed it to her. "What are you doing?"

"I ditched my phones, but that doesn't mean the numbers are inactive. I wonder if Dee called and left a message." She dialed her burner phone's number.

"Can we trust anything she says?" Sam asked.

"I don't know, but in any case, it'll be information we didn't have." She touched the speaker button, and they listened to the line roll straight to voicemail. She punched in her code, then the automated voice told her she had two messages.

"Ridley, where are you? I don't know what you're doing, but you better be on a plane."

"She doesn't sound pleased," Max said.

"No." Audra saved the message and the next one played.

"Obviously, you weren't on a plane. I can't reach Theo, either. I don't know what's going on, but you need to call me. There's a lot riding on this operation and you need to debrief, so we can hopefully salvage some of it."

Audra saved the message and hung up.

"She didn't sound suspicious," Sam said. "Just concerned. Are you sure we can't trust her?"

"I don't know who to trust. Someone knows who I am. Why else would they try to kill me?"

"If the 'TS' in Brogan's ledger was Theo, then maybe he's the only bad actor." Dean crossed his arms.

"Possibly, but I'm not willing to put my life on the line and find out."

"I agree." Sam laid a hand on her leg. "We need to work this alone for now."

"What about your other phone?" Max said.

"My other phone?" Audra frowned.

"The one you used to be Alexandra. Have you checked that voicemail?"

Her face heated. "No."

"Do that. Maybe there will be something there."

She ducked her head. The phone screen swam as she punched in the number to Alexandra's phone. Some spy she was.

Sam squeezed her leg. She pressed her lips together, holding in the tears. She liked to pride herself on her independence and her ability to handle most any situation, but she didn't know how she would have gotten through the last few days without him. He'd not only been a safe space where she could let her guard down, but he helped settle her emotions so she could stay focused.

Her voicemail picked up, and she typed in the code to access her messages. When the robotic voice told her she had seven, she groaned. "What do you want to bet they're all angry ones from Liam?"

"Play them," Sam said.

The first message was from Liam's sister, asking her if she was free to go over more wedding details. So was the second one. The third one was from Siobhan, ordering her to call Hannah back.

"Are we sure she's not the one who's really in charge?" Max asked.

Audra let out a soft snort. "I've wondered that too. She has a lot of sway, but the final decisions come down to Liam. He usually does what she wants, though."

The fourth message played. It was from Liam.

"Alexandra, where are you? You missed dinner. And with no phone call. That is unlike you. Please, call me back."

"He actually sounds concerned," Dean said.

He did, but that didn't surprise her. She'd worked hard to endear herself to him and to earn his respect. It was how she'd kept him content with a sexless relationship.

The fifth message played. This one was again from Liam.

"Alexandra, I'm getting worried now. I went to your house, and you weren't there. I even called your father. He hasn't heard from you, either. Please call me."

Audra grimaced. "I hope dear old dad called his SIS contact about that and they put some extra people on him." Things could get dicey for Sean Burton if Liam thought he'd been double-crossed.

The sixth message began, also from Liam.

"You bitch. I saw the news. Who is he? Your lover? Is that why you always shut me down? Have you been fucking him behind my back? You better hope I don't find you, or you're going to end up just like him."

"Whoa," Max said.

Whoa was right. She'd never heard such vehemence in Liam's voice.

"What was the timestamp on that one?" Sam asked.

Audra played it again, listening to the AI voice read the timestamp. It was from last night.

Sam cursed. "We definitely need to get out of this hotel. The news must have aired that story yesterday, too, and we didn't see it."

"There's one more message," Audra said. "Let's listen to it, then we can make a plan." She hit the key to play it.

"Alexandra? It's Donny. Look, I don't know where you are or what you've done, but you need to call Liam and explain. I'm sure it's not what he's thinking. I know you love him.

Please call him. Even if you don't want to come back, please call. He's on the warpath, and I'm afraid someone's going to get hurt." The message ended.

"Who's Donny?" Dean asked.

"His number two."

"Is it normal for him to call you?" Sam asked.

Audra lifted a shoulder. "He has before. Usually it's at Liam's request. But that message—something like that is a first."

The three men looked at each other. Audra's gaze bounced between them. "What?"

Sam stared at his friends for a moment longer, then looked at her. "We definitely need to leave. It sounds like Brogan doesn't know who you are, but he's still angry. Spurned lover angry. That makes him doubly dangerous."

She tipped her head as a thought occurred to her. "If he doesn't know who I really am, and he doesn't know where I am and wasn't the one who tried to kill me, then who did?"

"I think we need to dig deeper into your handler," Max said. "The answers lie with him."

"I agree. What's the plan in the meantime? Where do we go? Because I can't stay in Las Vegas." That was now abundantly clear. Big city or not, she couldn't risk it. She glanced around the room at all three men.

"Maybe you should listen to your boss," Sam said, a contemplative expression settling on his face.

She frowned, tipping her head again, assessing his look. "What do you mean?"

"Brogan doesn't know who you are. He doesn't know who Theo is. The Irish mafia didn't try to kill you. That means it's someone inside your operation."

"Possibly, but that encompasses more than just SIS officers. This is a joint investigation."

"I know. And I also heard your boss's voice on those

messages. She sounded genuinely concerned. It could be she's just a really great actress. But it could be that she's not involved. We need to determine that, because we need an ally from within your agency that we can trust."

Audra chewed on her bottom lip. "Going to London would mean we could sus her out."

"Exactly."

"But how do we get there? I mean, I have my passport, but my face is all over the news."

A cheeky smile slid over Sam's face. He glanced at Dean and Max.

Max crossed his arms, grinning. "We might know a guy."

NINETEEN

The warm breeze whipped around her as Audra stepped out of the car onto the tarmac at the small regional airport just outside of Las Vegas. A small commuter plane sat in front of the hangar. The engines made a high-pitched rushing sound that made it hard to hear much else. The pilot was already in the cockpit, getting them ready to go.

"Ready?"

Audra looked at Sam, who'd come around the car to her side. She nodded, tipping her head closer to his so they could hear each other. "Who is this again?"

"His name is Jim. He's a friend of a friend."

"Ah. Yes. Ezra. The guy you all know. I'm still not convinced he exists." After they'd decided to go to London, Max and Dean had disappeared, only to come back an hour later with flight details to get her and Sam across the Atlantic that night. Every time one of them had a question about the trip, Max—or Dean—disappeared to call Ezra. She wasn't sure why they didn't just call in her presence.

"He does, I promise." With a hand on her back, Sam steered her toward the airplane.

Audra eyed the stairs to the cabin with trepidation. She hadn't tried more than a couple of steps since she injured her hip. It hadn't been a pleasant experience.

"Take your time." Sam gripped her hand, the other still on her back.

She squeezed his fingers, thankful once again that he was here with her.

Holding his hand, she started up the steps, clutching the railing with her other hand. Between him and the rail, she was able to take most of the pressure off her thigh muscle and make it to the top with little problem. Ducking through the doorway, she glanced at him with a smile. "That wasn't as bad as I thought it would be."

"I'm glad you're healing. I didn't think it would happen so quickly."

"Me either. A lot of what I have is muscle pain from getting tossed around. There isn't much actual damage, other than the massive bruise."

"Good."

They made their way into the cabin and sat down across from each other in the plush leather seats. Audra was thankful they weren't on a commercial jetliner. While she felt decent, thanks to the painkillers she'd been routinely downing, hours upon hours cramped into a tiny, stiff airplane seat would have been agony.

"Hello, folks."

The pilot emerged from the flight deck, smiling as he paused just inside the main cabin. "I'm Jim. We're about ready to take off. There are snacks and drinks here, if you want anything." He pointed to a set of cabinets to his left. "Help yourselves. Do you have any questions for me?"

Audra glanced at Sam, who shook his head at the pilot.

"No," he said. "We're good. Thank you for taking us on such short notice."

"Not a problem. I owed Ezra a favor, anyway. If you need anything during the flight, use the intercom there." He gestured to a panel beside their seats. "I'll try to make things as smooth as possible. There's a bit of rough air over the Rockies, but after that, it should be fine."

"Great, thank you."

Jim nodded. He moved to the door and pulled up the metal stairs, stowing them away, then pulled the door in and locked it. Once the plane was secure, he went back to the flight deck.

Audra got up and walked to the mini-fridge, taking out a bottle of water. She glanced at Sam. "Do you want one?"

"Sure."

She grabbed another and walked back to her seat, handing it to him as she sat down. The plane rocked as Jim released the brake. They slowly rolled forward. She buckled her seatbelt. "This is a nice plane." She cracked open her water and took a drink.

"It is. The one we'll be in on the flight to London has an actual bedroom, so we'll be able to sleep."

She raised an eyebrow, slowly lowering the bottle. "Who is this guy?"

Sam grinned. "Ezra was a Night Stalker. An Army Special Forces pilot. He retired and went to work for Appalachia Resorts. Brooke—the woman who was on the group call and Ford's fiancée?" He paused. It only took her a moment to recognize the name, and she nodded. He continued. "Her family owns the resort chain. Ezra now works for them, flying her and the other executives for the chain around the world. It's her plane we'll be on."

"She just lends it out? All willy-nilly? What if someone in the company needs it?"

"They have more than one plane and more than one pilot.

And yes. Brooke will be the first one to offer assistance. It's just the way she is. I think she also feels a need to repay us for helping her."

"Helping her? What did you do?"

"It's a long story."

"We have a wee bit of time." Audra gestured to their surroundings.

Sam grinned. "I guess so." He propped his ankle on his knee, settling in. "Last year, she got into a bit of trouble with her ex-fiancé. He was a real piece of work." He waved a hand. "Anyway, Ezra—" He stopped, his jaw working, then glanced away. Inhaling a breath, he looked at her. "Sorry. My brain is— it's moving too fast."

Audra wished they weren't seated across from each other. She wanted to hold his hand.

After a moment, he continued. "Ezra knew she needed help, so he brought her down to Costa Rica and asked Ford to keep her safe until Johnathan—her ex—could be arrested. She and Ford fell in love in the process."

"And you all had a hand in keeping her safe?" She glanced out the window as they turned. The runway was close.

"Yes. Johnathan found her. Max and I helped get her and Ford to safety."

"What about Dean?"

"He went to the U.S. to dig into Johnathan's business dealings to get more evidence to take to the authorities. He met his fiancée on that case too."

"Really?"

"Yep. Her name is Annabeth." A bemused smile crossed his face. "It's also what led to Edie marrying Jordan. I think it will lead to Max getting married too."

"How so?"

"Edie went to the U.S. to help Dean when what he dug up

turned dangerous. Jordan is his best friend—Dean brought him in on the case. When he needed—a"—he stopped again, clenching his fist—"when he needed help earlier this year with an unrelated issue, Dean asked Edie to step in. As for Max, well, he's not attached yet, but Annabeth has a friend. Margot's husband left her and their twin daughters abruptly last year. Those girls have Max wrapped around their little fingers."

Audra frowned. "How are they involved in all of this?"

"Oh, sorry. Annabeth and Margot are doctors. The problems with Margot's marriage cropped up while Dean was investigating Johnathan's background. She's just—she's sort of been pulled in as Dean and Annabeth's relationship took off. With all the uncertainty about her own future, she came down to Costa Rica with Annabeth to regroup. They've decided to open a clinic down there together. It's part of the resort Brooke's building."

"Brooke's building a resort?"

"Yes. In fact, Ezra and his family are coming down as well." A gentle smile formed on his handsome face. "It's nice. Having them all close. When my grandparents died, all I had was the military and my buddies there. I don't know what I would have done without Ford and our other friends when my injury happened. Having that place to go—that—support —family—it probably saved my life." He held her gaze, the look in his eyes turning intense. "Them and thoughts of you."

Audra blinked twice. "Me?"

"Yeah." He paused as the engines revved.

The plane lurched forward as they took off down the runway. A few seconds later, her stomach dipped and rolled as they left the ground. Once they were steadily climbing, Sam unbuckled and came to sit next to her. "I know now is not the time for us to think about where we go from here. But when this is all over—and it *will* end in our favor—we need to have a long chat."

She nodded and leaned forward, tipping her head into his. Emotion clogged her throat. She hardly knew what she felt right now. But one thing was certain. She didn't think she could walk away from this man again. This time, walking away might break her heart beyond repair.

TWENTY

Their flight touched down with a soft bounce in Richmond several hours later. The engines roared as the pilot reversed the thrust, slowing them. In moments, they were taxiing off the main runway toward another private hangar, where Ezra waited.

Sam glanced out the window, looking for the jet. He was eager to get in the air, so he hoped Ezra was ready.

Jim steered them along the line of steel buildings and brought the plane to a halt next to a gleaming white plane with black and gold stripes down the side and on the tail. The emblem for Appalachia Resorts was on the door.

The engines wound down, and Jim came out of the cockpit to open the door. He unfolded the stairs, then stepped back. "You're all set. I hope you have a good trip and everything works out for you."

Sam offered him a hand. "Thank you."

"You're welcome."

Audra smiled at him and echoed Sam's thanks.

With her hand tucked into his, Sam walked down the stairs, making sure she made it down all right. Her gait was a little stiff, but she made it without incident. Jim followed them down and retrieved their luggage from the compartment beneath the main cabin.

"I hope you didn't get bounced around too much. Jim likes his stunts."

Sam looked to his left and smiled as he saw Ezra coming toward them. "It was fine. Smoother than the last time I flew with you."

Ezra scoffed. "Lies." He grinned and held out a hand. "Good to see you, Sam."

"You too." Sam shook his hand, then Ezra reached past him and shook Jim's hand.

"Glad you kept it under control."

Jim smiled. "This bird's not as maneuverable as our helos."

"True. That thing's a tank." Ezra pointed at his plane. He turned to Audra. "You must be Audra. It's nice to meet you. I'm sorry it isn't under better circumstances."

She smiled and shook his hand. "You too."

Sam nudged her shoulder. "See? He does exist."

Ezra's eyebrow raised. "You doubted my existence?"

"I think I would doubt most of your groups' existence if I hadn't heard their voices on the phone. Especially Asher's."

Ezra laughed. "Understandable. We do some crazy things. Are you two ready to go?"

"Could I use the loo first?" Audra nodded toward the hangar.

"Of course. It's through the door and to your right."

"Thank you."

Sam watched her walk away. She was loosening up the more she moved, but he could tell she was still stiff. The bed on the plane would be good for her. She needed to stretch her legs out and relax.

"Damn, Dean was right," Ezra said.

"About what?" Sam turned to him.

"Asher and Max—and really just Asher—are going to be the only single ones left."

Sam glanced toward Audra again just as she disappeared inside the hangar. "If I can get her on board with that, yeah."

"She doesn't want to get back together with you?"

"It's not that. Things are"—several words vied for dominance in his mind—"complicated."

"They always are. Until they aren't." Ezra laid a hand on his shoulder and squeezed. "I'll get your bags loaded up. Come on board whenever you're ready."

"Okay. Thanks, Ezra."

"Anytime." The man nodded, then picked up the luggage and walked away.

Sam wandered closer to the hangar to wait on Audra. He'd used the restroom on the plane. She hadn't. He was sure it was because the tight space was difficult for her to move around in right now. She'd have more room on Brooke's jet.

The outer hangar door opened. Audra spotted him and smiled. His breath stuck in his chest. Would she ever not do that to him?

He cleared his throat and held out a hand. "You ready?"

"Yes." She took his hand, and he led her toward the plane.

"I'm looking forward to that bed."

He brought their hands up and kissed the back of hers. "Me too. It's been a long day."

On board the aircraft, they took seats in the main cabin for takeoff. Ezra climbed in and stowed the stairs, then shut the door.

"I'll use the intercom to tell you when we've reached cruising altitude. You're welcome to get some shuteye at that point."

Sam nodded. "Okay, thanks."

"Yep." Ezra turned, then disappeared into the cockpit.

Audra wrapped an arm around Sam's and leaned into him, yawning. "I hate jetlag."

Sam chuckled and kissed the top of her head. "Everyone does. But at least we're sleeping close to when people in London are."

"Not nearly enough, though."

Definitely not. But it would do for now.

The engines spun up, and they were soon moving away from the hangar. Within minutes, Ezra had sent the plane rocketing down the runway and they were in the air. Twenty minutes into the flight, he came over the intercom to tell them they were at cruising altitude.

Sam unbuckled his seatbelt and stood up, extending a hand to her. "Come on. Let's get some sleep."

She unbuckled and let him help her to her feet. They wandered into the back of the aircraft and through a door.

"Whoa."

"No kidding." Sam shook his head. He hadn't been to the back of the plane when he'd flown in it before. A queen-size bed sat against the far wall, tufted headboard and all. Stacks of pillows were piled on the gray comforter. On either side of the bed was a nightstand with a lamp.

"When you said bed, I was envisioning a cot that folds down from the wall." Audra walked toward the bed. "This is amazing. I might actually sleep soundly."

"Well, let's find out." Sam snapped on the bedside lamp, then slapped the light switch on the wall and toed off his shoes on the other side of the bed. He pulled the covers back.

She hesitated, a slight scowl on her face.

"What?" He frowned.

"I wish I hadn't packed my pajamas in my suitcase. I hate sleeping in my clothes."

A wicked smile erupted on Sam's face. "Don't stay dressed on my account."

Red stained her cheeks. "I'm not giving up any shows tonight. Sorry." She lifted the blankets on her side and climbed into bed.

He joined her, turning off the light, then pulled the blankets up as he moved closer. "That's all right. I remember the details quite well."

She smacked lightly at his shoulder and chuckled. "You're awful."

He chuckled with her and bent his head to capture her lips. "Nah. Just stating facts." He kissed her. He knew they risked getting carried away and ending things frustrated, but he wanted to feel her mouth move beneath his. To taste her. And to just hold her close.

She moaned, wiggling closer. Sam tunneled a hand beneath her top and spanned her ribcage. She nipped at his bottom lip, and he kissed her more deeply. Need spiraled upward, rapidly choking out the rational side of his mind. With a superhuman effort, he brought his hand up and palmed the side of her face, gentling the kiss.

Audra ran her fingers along his jaw and into his hair. Sam's eyes rolled back, and he had to exert every ounce of willpower he had not to kiss her again. If he did, pulling back the next time would not be so easy. They'd both end up well past frustrated, and he was afraid it might cause her concussion symptoms to flare up.

"Sam... why do you do this to me?" she whispered.

He could tell by the tone of her voice she meant something far deeper than why she was attracted to him. But he didn't have an answer for her. He couldn't explain it, either, except to think they were meant to be.

"Go to sleep, Aud." He tucked her head beneath his chin.

She wrapped an arm around his torso and snuggled closer.

Need still coursed through him. He couldn't even use his

trick of picturing her face to settle his mind. She was the reason he was out of sorts.

Instead, he turned it on its head and used the way he felt to hone in on her in the hopes his reaction would provide its own distraction. He listened to her breathing, taking in every breath, listening to them gradually grow slower and deeper as she fell asleep. He felt her muscles grow slack until she sank into his body and the mattress beneath them.

He lifted his head to peer at her in the near-darkness. In the low light, he could just see the glimmer of her porcelain skin. He touched her face with one finger, tracing her cheekbone. Bending his head, he pressed a soft kiss to the spot he just touched.

Sam laid his head on the pillow and closed his eyes as sleep finally pulled at his mind.

Twenty-One

S tifling a yawn, Sam led Audra through Heathrow. Their nap on the plane hadn't been nearly long enough. But with a strong cup of coffee, it would keep them running close to full capacity.

After they said goodbye to Ezra, they'd quickly headed for customs. Surprisingly, they made it through with ease. Audra had presented her fake passport without batting an eye. He'd tried to match her energy. Apparently, he'd done so well enough, because the border agent bought their story that they were married and waved them through after checking their documents.

"So, you gonna tell me how you got that passport into their system?" Sam asked, keeping his voice low as they headed for the exit.

She sent him a coy smile. "You aren't the only one with resources."

Sam chuckled. "Touché, my dear."

She grinned. "So, I've been thinking. About those resources, actually. Mine, not yours."

"Oh?" The doors swished open, and they stepped outside.

A soft drizzle fell, giving the air a hazy appearance. He was glad he didn't have to drive in it.

"On the flight over, I was running a list of people I know through my head and sorting them into two categories. People I can possibly trust and those whom I either don't know well enough to determine that or those who I could see going behind my back and contacting Dee."

"How many trustworthy people did you come up with?" He lifted a hand, waving down a taxi.

"Only a couple. One of them is the guy who made my passport. I'm not sure what he can do for us now, but if it becomes necessary, I know I can get us some excellent travel documents."

"Who are the others?"

"A couple of friends who are unrelated to the Secret Intelligence Service."

"Is there no one inside the service you trust?"

"Not yet. I'm hoping I can trust Dee. We'll see."

The cab pulled up, and Sam opened the door for her. She slid inside while he helped the driver load their bags into the trunk.

"Where to?" The man asked as they got in.

Audra gave him the name of a hotel in Westminster. Sam laid an arm over the back of the seat and tipped her into his chest. Even though they'd slept some, Audra still needed more. He knew she'd push herself as far as her body would allow—likely even beyond—but for now, she could rest.

The cab wove through the narrow London streets. Sam held his breath a few times as they narrowly missed sideswiping a bus or another car. This city was not built for modern vehicles. But Londoners were determined not to let that stop them. Eventually, he laid his cheek atop Audra's head and closed his eyes, preferring not to know if they were about to crash.

To his surprise, he dozed off. The next thing he knew, the cabbie announced they'd arrived.

Sam blinked the sleep from his eyes and gave Audra a nudge. "Honey, we're here."

She came awake with a quick inhale and sat up. "Oh." Yawning, she covered her mouth and looked outside. "After we check in, we need to get some coffee."

"Definitely." Sam pulled on the door handle and climbed out. Once they had their luggage, he paid the driver, and they went inside the hotel.

They booked a room for several nights, paying the extra fee to check in early, and stowed their belongings before heading back out into the mist. At least it was relatively warm, since it was May. "Where to?" he asked.

"Coffee. And I need a phone. We've put it off long enough."

He nodded. "Sounds good. Let's find a coffee shop, then we'll see about getting you a burner." He took her hand and set off down the sidewalk. They didn't have to wander far before they found a small bakery.

The scent of fresh bread and pastries hit him as they stepped inside. His stomach growled. They hadn't eaten much on the plane, so he was starving.

"I'm going to get a sausage roll and a *pain au chocolat*. I might even get a yogurt. I could eat a horse, I'm so hungry." Audra rocked onto the balls of her feet, then back down, crossing her arms as they took their place in line.

"I've got you beat because I plan to eat two sausage rolls and an éclair. They look fabulous." He could see them in the case just a few feet away. His mouth watered at the thought. He hadn't had a decent éclair in years. Not since he was last in Europe.

The person in front of them completed their order and stepped to the side. Sam motioned Audra forward. They gave their order to the young woman behind the counter and paid. Luckily, the wait for the barista to make their drinks and heat their sausage rolls was a short one. Food in hand, they found a table and sat down.

Audra moaned as she bit into her sausage roll.

Sam chuckled. "That good, huh?"

"You have no idea how much I've missed this. It's been almost two years since I've been back. Even before I fully became Alexandra, I was in the U.S., setting up her back story, making sure any current pictures were of me and not the actual Alexandra Burton. I couldn't come back here. It was too risky." She glanced around. "Even now, I don't like being out in the open. But my cover's already blown, so..." She shrugged.

Sam bit into his sausage roll. The savory taste of sausage warred with the buttery, flaky pastry, setting off a firestorm of flavor in his mouth. Most people would argue British food was bland. But no one could argue they didn't have amazing sausage.

"So, what do you want to do after we get you a phone?" He took another bite.

She sipped her coffee, a thoughtful look on her face. "I'd like to stake out headquarters and Dee's flat. Following her from HQ really isn't the best option, but we might get lucky. Normally, she takes the Tube to and from work, but sometimes she leaves for a meeting at Westminster in a hired car. And she doesn't always return to the office before she goes home. I don't know if we'd be able to see her in the back of a car if she left that way. But on a normal day, we'll catch her coming and going. And I know we can stake out her flat. There's a coffeeshop across the street."

Sam grimaced. "Great."

Audra tossed him a smile. "Spy work isn't always glamorous. In fact, most of the time it's spent sitting around trying to look inconspicuous while you watch your target. At least with you along this time, I won't have random men stopping to chat with me." She rolled her eyes.

He laughed. "It won't stop the bold ones."

She chuckled. "True. Some people just don't care. And that will work both ways too. I'm sure there will be a few women who take a chance at you."

"They can try." He sipped his coffee. "But I only have eyes for one woman." He sent her a heated look.

She met his stare for a moment before looking down at the remnants of her meal. A soft chuckle escaped. "I don't remember eating all this already."

Sam grinned, stuffing the last of his croissant into his mouth. He chewed and swallowed, then picked up his coffee and pushed his chair back. "Come on. Let's go get you a phone and get this stakeout rolling."

Twenty-Two

Grittiness made Sam's eyes itch. Too much sitting and staring the last few days. He rubbed at them and yawned. And not much to show for all their work.

A quick glance at his watch told him they needed to head out soon. "You about ready to go?" He glanced at Audra, who sat across from him at the little table outside the coffeeshop in Dee Thompson's neighborhood.

"Yeah, I guess." She blew out a frustrated breath.

He knew how she felt. They'd been at this for several days now and nothing had happened. "We need a new plan," he said as he got up.

She winced as she got out of her chair. "Yeah. Can we try Asher when we get back to the hotel? The last time we talked, he said his program was nearly done with its analysis."

Sam nodded. He held out a hand to her. She laced her fingers with his. They tossed their coffee cups in the trash and headed for the Tube station. A quick trip under the river to the stop by their hotel, and they were soon back in their room.

Audra sat on the bed, her legs outstretched. Sam pulled up the desk chair and sat as he dialed Asher.

"Yo. How's the surveillance?" Asher asked when he picked up.

"Dull. Do you have anything? We need a lead," Sam said.

"Not exactly."

Sam glanced at Audra. Her frown matched his.

"What does that mean?" he asked.

"My program is nearly done. I know it's taking forever, but I had to do some research. I fed it virtually every map out there, as well as the names of every known Irish mafia associate I could find. Another couple of days and I think I'll have some results. Once it's done analyzing all the data, I'll feed it some more parameters to narrow down the options. We're getting close. But I have a source for you. Someone who can hopefully get you some info."

"Oh?" Sam sat a little straighter.

"Yeah. And don't be mad—I've known this woman awhile. I didn't tell you about her because I didn't want to put her in an awkward position. But you're right; we're running out of options."

"Who is it?" Audra asked.

"Her name is Jocelyn Richardson. She's a cybersecurity specialist with SIS."

Audra scooted forward, the expression on her face turning incredulous. "You know someone in SIS—someone trustworthy—and are just now telling us? We've been sitting here for four days waiting for my boss to do something!"

"I know. But like I said, involving Jocelyn puts her at risk. I didn't want to do that unless we didn't have another choice. You guys can't stakeout Ms. Thompson forever. Jocelyn will understand."

Audra huffed. Sam met her gaze. He didn't like it either that Asher had sat on this, but he understood. He could see in her eyes that she did too.

"How do we contact this woman?" Audra asked.

"You don't. I talked to her earlier today. She's gathering intel on Thompson and your handler. When she has something, she'll contact you. I gave her Sam's number."

Audra pressed her lips together.

Sam covered her hand with his. "Okay. We'll continue with the status quo until then."

"Sounds good. I'll let you know as soon as this program spits something useful out. Keep me in the loop with what you hear from Jocelyn."

"Will do. Thanks, Ash."

"Yep." Asher hung up.

Audra groaned and flopped onto her back on the bed. She covered her face. "If we'd known about her when we landed, we could have already moved on this. Instead, we've spent the last four days twiddling our thumbs."

"His reasoning makes sense, Aud." Sam laid a hand on her belly. "This woman is probably putting her career on the line to help us."

She brought her hands down to cover his. "I know." She sighed. "I'm just frustrated. I want answers!" She sat up and climbed off the bed to pace to the window.

He walked up behind her and wrapped his arms around her waist. "How about we relax tonight? No internet searches, no talk of the case. Let's go to dinner. For a real date." His heart thumped as he said the last few words. He wasn't sure how she'd feel about making their relationship official. They'd shared a few kisses the last few days; she knew how he felt about her. And he'd slept with her in his arms every night. But they hadn't talked about what it all meant for them as a couple.

She turned in his arms, resting her hands on his chest. He palmed her hips, holding her in a loose embrace. "Dating is not wise. Not at this stage," she said.

"I don't think it ever will be with us. But I don't care

anymore. It—we—are worth whatever struggles we have to go through to make this work. The way we feel—it hasn't changed in ten years. That has to mean something. Right?"

She sighed and pressed her forehead against his chest. Lifting her head, she looked at him. "It does. But I—" She broke off with a quick headshake. "I don't want you to get hurt."

Sam frowned, tipping his head as he wondered why she'd think that. "Why would I get hurt? You planning to break my heart?"

A slight smile crossed her face. "No. I meant physically. Being with me could be dangerous."

He arched an eyebrow. "You do remember what I used to do for a living, yes?"

"And it almost got you killed. I don't want that to happen again."

Sam let out a soft exhale. "Audra, whether I put myself in harm's way or not is my decision to make. I'd rather run the risk and have you by my side than go back to Costa Rica and try to forget that you're out in the world without me. I'm done doing that. Fate's given us a second chance, and I don't intend to squander it."

She searched his gaze. He let her. He had nothing to hide. Almost from the moment he showed up to help, he'd been all-in on being together. He wasn't about to return the gift fate had given him.

"It won't be easy," she said, her fingers drifting higher to toy with the ridge of his collarbone.

Heat traveled over his shoulder and raced up his neck, sparking a need that made his scalp tingle. "Probably not."

"There will be times we won't be able to contact each other. Sometimes for weeks or months."

"I know." Though with the friends they both had, he

figured there would be a way around that. He leaned closer, ready to end this conversation.

"I've been single a long time, and I'm pretty stuck in my ways." She tipped her face up.

"Me too." He dipped his head, an invisible force pulling him in.

"We might—"

"Stop talking." He closed the gap and fused his mouth to hers, unable to hold back any longer.

A soft whimper escaped her as he delved into her mouth. Her hands skated up over his shoulders to wrap around his neck, turning the tingle racing over his skin into a steady hum. Sam shifted his hold, drawing her into his body. A wash of need flooded him, heating his muscles and making him want to lay her down on the bed and peel off her clothing.

But his mind knew her body wasn't ready for that, so he ignored the hum vibrating him down to his bones and forced his body to heel. Gentling their kiss, he lifted his head.

Her lashes fluttered for a moment before she turned her liquid chocolate eyes on him. A slight wrinkle formed between her eyes. "I know why you stopped, but it doesn't make it any easier."

He offered her a crooked smile and dropped a quick kiss on her forehead. "No. But one day, you won't be all beaten up." His gaze heated. "Then there will be no stopping."

She pulled his head down and kissed him again, then just as swiftly pulled back and pushed him away. "Let's go eat. We both need the distraction."

Twenty-Three

The words on the laptop screen blurred, and Audra blinked, stifling a yawn. She was so tired of being cooped up, going over Liam's files. They'd read, reread, then reread them again. At this point, she doubted they'd see anything, even if there was something there to see. They were too close to it.

What they really needed was for that cybersecurity specialist to contact them. It had been a couple of days since Asher dropped his bombshell, and they'd heard nothing so far. Audra had expected the delay, but it didn't mean she liked it. Hopefully, the wait would be worth it.

She glanced at Sam over the top of the laptop. He'd perched in the reading chair by the window, his phone in his hand. He was looking at the files too. And probably wishing he'd grabbed his laptop when he hopped on a plane out of Costa Rica. She knew she would be if she was forced to do all her work on a tiny phone screen.

With a huff, she closed the laptop. "I need some air. Do you feel like taking a walk?"

Sam glanced up. "Sure. It's not like we're getting anywhere." He got up and slipped his phone into his pocket.

Audra climbed off the bed and slipped on her shoes, then they were out the door. Sam took her hand, as he had every other time they'd gone somewhere. She glanced away to hide her smile. She quite liked the feeling of holding his hand.

Outside their hotel, they headed for a row of shops nearby. They were near Buckingham Palace, so the place was awash with tourists. That was fine with her. They could blend in.

Audra's hip had begun to heal nicely, so they strolled along for a few minutes, looking at the architecture. She pointed out several things to him, proud to show off her city. Eventually, they stopped at a small café with a little seating area. It wasn't quite teatime yet, so the place wasn't too crowded. They could sit and sip a coffee without feeling pressured to leave.

"So, tell me..." Sam leaned forward on his elbows after they placed their order. "Why isn't it raining?" He grinned.

Audra laughed. "It doesn't always rain in England. Especially in the summer. Now if it were winter..." She trailed off and tipped her head.

He wrinkled his nose. "I thoroughly dislike cold rain."

She lifted a shoulder, still smiling. "You get used to it."

"No. Never." Laughing, he glanced away. "I have to admit, though, I like the milder temperatures. Costa Rica is hot."

"You could always move back home."

"It's hot there, too, in the summer." He looked at her. "Perhaps I should move here."

Audra caught her bottom lip between her teeth at the completely serious look on his face. "I think I'd like that."

Chair legs scraped the ground to her left. "Whew!" A young woman with her blonde hair piled in a bun on top of her head pulled the chair to their table and sat down. "You two sure can move." Her black-framed glasses slid down her nose.

Crossing her eyes and letting out a soft huff, she pushed them back up.

Audra sat straighter and glanced at Sam. His intense frown matched the one she could feel on her own face. She turned to the woman. "Excuse me?"

The woman smiled. "Hi. Sorry. I should introduce myself. I'm Jo."

"Is that supposed to mean something to us?" Sam asked.

"I would hope so. Asher sent me."

"You're Jocelyn Richardson?" Sam said.

The woman nodded. "Yes. But call me Jo."

"It's nice to meet you." Sam offered her a smile.

"You have something for us, I'm guessing?" Audra said, forgoing the pleasantries. "Since you tracked us down."

"I do." She glanced toward the café's interior. "Your drinks are coming."

Audra turned, and sure enough, the same server who'd taken their order was headed back out with a tray. He smiled as he set the two black coffees on the table. "There you are." He looked at Jo. "Would you like to order?"

Jo waved a hand. "No, thank you. I'm fine."

With a nod, he disappeared.

Audra fiddled with the handle on her cup. Her heart thumped in her chest. She took a deep breath, trying to force it to calm down. "What did you find out?"

"Quite a bit, actually. I logged into your boss's computer. Both the one in her office and her personal one. She's been doing some digging on you and on your handler."

"Oh?" Audra set down the cup she'd just picked up.

"Yep. Finances, internet history, even some camera surveillance she pulled from Las Vegas CCTV. She had a file with notes about what she'd found. The only thing she noted about you was how you'd withdraw cash from your personal account every month. She wondered what you were doing with it."

Audra caught Sam's quick glance her way and knew he was remembering her stash of money in her safe. "What about Theo?"

"She found the bank account that goes with the statements you all found at his house—Asher mentioned that. I'm not some psychic—but she couldn't access it to see how much money was in it. She traced it through a shell corporation he set up called TS Holdings."

"That goes with the code from Liam Brogan's ledger that Audra found."

Jo frowned. "What ledger?"

"Asher told you about the bank statements, but didn't tell you about the ledger?" Sam's eyebrow shot up.

She shook her head. "All I got were copies of the bank statements and the two names he wanted me to dig into." She shrugged. "He was CIA. They compartmentalize information like no one else."

Audra snorted. That was the truth.

"Oh. Well, Audra found a ledger with what looks like code for business transactions. One of them was 350G TS DTC. We figure 'TS' refers to Theo's alias. The 350G is how much he received. Asher's still working on the 'DTC' part."

She nodded thoughtfully. "I got into his email. I don't remember seeing anything that would refer to that, but I'll look again."

"Were you able to tell where the deposits came from?" Audra asked.

"A shell company. It's buried under so many layers it'll take me more than the couple of days I've had to figure it out. I did find something interesting, though. Not about his bank records." She waved a hand. "About something else. I got into his phone's GPS data, and he visited a house in Enterprise,

Nevada, multiple times in the last few months. Around the same time the first payment came in."

"Do you have an address?" This could be the break they needed to find out what Theo was up to. To find his killer.

Jo grinned. "I do." She reached into her pocket and pulled out a slip of paper. "I have a name too." She nodded to the little scrap as she slid it over to Audra.

With a quick glance at Sam, Audra picked it up, her heart racing. Her eyes widened as she read the name. "Bloody hell."

Twenty-Four

A dark frown overtook Sam's face. "What? Who is it?" He reached for the slip of paper in Audra's hand. She let go, and he read the name and address. "Who's Patrick Callahan?"

"He works for Liam. Actually, he works more for Siobhan. The guy who left the voicemail on Alexandra's phone—Donny?"

Sam nodded, remembering the name.

"Patrick is his brother. He does for Siobhan what Donny does for Liam, basically. He's like her assistant. Their father, Sean, was Liam's father's assistant. He died in the same attack that killed Liam's father, Derek. For a while Siobhan and Liam shared the leadership responsibilities, so instead of just Donny taking over for his father, Patrick stepped in to help."

"Siobhan didn't already have her own assistant?"

"She did, but before Derek's death, her role was as the mafia boss's wife, so her assistant did more with parties and household organization than with the business side of things. Both of Sean's children were involved in his work. Donny more so because he was slated to take over for his father when he retired. Just like Liam took over for Derek."

"Okay." Jo propped her chin on her hand and leaned forward. "Why would your handler go see Patrick?"

"I don't know. He would have no reason to. They weren't supposed to know he existed."

Sam frowned as a thought occurred to him. "Liam didn't know about Theo. Not until he saw your face on the news when the police asked for help with his case. Why would his number two know, but not the boss?"

"A double cross?" Jo said. "Maybe Theo was trying to convince them to overthrow their boss."

"But what could he offer that Patrick would be willing to pay that kind of money?" Audra asked.

"The truth?" Sam suggested. "Think about it. What if Theo laid out who he was—who you were—and told them how terrible it would be for Brogan when the news got out that he let an undercover operative into their inner circle? That he could help bring Brogan down, and they could take over. It would make them easy to control. He holds the cards because he knows who they are and has the credentials to keep them out of harm's way. So long as they do what he wants."

"Could they be the ones who paid him off?" Jo asked.

Audra jolted. Sam looked at her, frowning. "What?"

"DTC—DC—Donny Callahan. I don't know his middle name, but his first and last initial match. Maybe they convinced Liam they had a source worth paying. Or told him they were buying a service of some sort. I'm not sure which."

His mind whirled as he mulled that over. "Three hundred fifty-thousand dollars is a lot of money, though, for not knowing what you're getting," Sam argued.

"Right, but Liam would trust Donny. He could make up something plausible and Liam wouldn't question it." She pursed her lips. "I wonder how many other entries in that ledger were ones Donny made up?" She looked at Jo. "Did you discover anything else?"

"No, that was all."

"And there wasn't anything that would make you think I couldn't trust my boss?"

Jo shook her head. "I think she was aware there was a problem. I don't know what set off her radar, but something did."

"Okay." Audra looked at Sam. "I think we need to talk to Dee now."

He tapped his fingers on the table once. "I agree. I just hope she sees things our way."

Twenty-Five

Nerves fluttered through Audra's belly. She shouldn't be nervous. She was a bloody spy. She didn't do nerves. But everything she'd worked toward the last couple of years was on the line with this conversation. If Dee didn't hear them out, if she decided to arrest them and not listen, all her hard work was for naught.

"You ready?"

Audra drew in a deep breath and looked at Sam. "As I'll ever be. Let's do this." They'd decided the direct approach was best. Dee was home, so they were just going to walk up and knock.

Hand-in-hand, they approached the door. Sam rang the bell, then squeezed her hand.

"It'll be okay." He leaned down and kissed the top of her head.

Audra closed her eyes briefly, wondering how he always seemed to know what was on her mind. Though right now, it probably wasn't hard to tell. A fine tremor coursed through her as they waited.

Movement flickered in the light coming from the side

windows beside the door. Audra could see the silhouette of a woman pause for a moment before the door swung open.

She smiled at her boss and waved. "Hi. I'm home."

Dee's surprised expression quickly morphed. Her eyebrows slammed together. She raked her gaze over Sam, then speared Audra with a hot glare. "It's about damn time. And who is this?" She eyed their clasped hands, sighing. "I'm not going to like what you have to say, am I?"

"Could we come in?" Audra asked.

Dee stepped back, opening the door wider, and motioned them inside. "My husband is still at work, but he won't be for long. We need to make this quick."

Sam hesitated in the doorway, and Audra glanced back.

"Maybe we should take this elsewhere, then. I'm not sure how long it'll take."

"It'll be fine," Dee said. "You can slip out the back, if necessary. There's an exterior door to the block's shared court-yard in my office."

Audra tugged on Sam's hand, and he followed her into the ground-floor flat.

Dee led them through the small foyer to a room behind the stairs. Audra glimpsed a kitchen to her left and a living room to her right as they passed. Both were good size rooms for a London flat. It looked like there was a dining room beyond the kitchen as well.

Flipping on the light, Dee breezed into the room. She walked behind the desk and grabbed her chair, wheeling it around to the other side. "Sit." She pointed to the brown leather sofa.

Audra perched on the edge, hanging on to Sam's hand for strength.

"Explain, Ridley." Dee pierced her with a look, then flicked her gaze to Sam. "And who's your friend?"

Sam and Audra shared a glance. He nodded slightly, and she inhaled a breath to steady herself before she jumped in.

"So, you know that nine days ago, someone ran me down near the park by my condo."

Dee nodded once.

"Sunday morning, they found Theo's body in the park."

Her boss let out a string of curses and stood. She paced to the bookshelves and stared at them for a long moment before turning back. "You're sure it was him? How did I not know this?"

"Yes." Audra waved a hand. "As for how you didn't know, I'm not sure. His image was plastered all over the news stations there. Someone dropped the ball, I guess. I haven't talked to Moran, so I'm not sure what happened. Anyway, I should back up. When I woke up after being hit, something bothered me about the incident. It was the shoes."

"The shoes?" Dee frowned. "What shoes?"

"The black trainers I told you about. A man walked up to me as I laid there, and he had on black trainers. The same ones Theo had on the night before. When I woke up and tried to remember what happened, I couldn't shake the feeling that Theo—or someone from within our organization—was involved."

"Why?" Dee's gaze turned sharp. "What happened?"

"Nothing major. It was just a bunch of small things. Like the shoes. And the fact that someone followed us to the park that night. Someone had been following *me*." Audra stabbed her index finger into her chest. "Taking my picture. And I didn't know. Then, when you ordered me back to London, that feeling got stronger. I couldn't understand why you would want to remove me from the investigation. Even with my cover blown, I had information the people in Las Vegas could use. It made me wonder if Theo was the only one involved and whether you could be too."

"You thought I was a traitor?" The indignation in Dee's voice rang clear.

Audra shrugged. "I didn't know what to think. So, I called Sam, because I knew I could trust him, and that he could help."

Dee looked at him. "You're Sam?"

"Yes."

She looked at Audra. "How do you know him? And why would you call him?"

"Sam and I worked together ten years ago, before I came to your unit. And full disclosure, we were also lovers. Long story short, we parted amicably and lost touch. Until we ran into each other in Las Vegas in February."

Dee's eyes widened. "Did Brogan—"

Audra shook her head, cutting off her words. She already knew where Dee's mind had gone. "No. I was alone. He stopped me in the street while I was walking. I basically told him to bugger off." She glanced at him, a slight upward curve to her lips.

He smirked. "I didn't listen, though. I went back later to the area where I saw her, hoping to see her again. I was curious about—what she was—up to."

Audra squeezed his hand, seeing his mind struggling. "Relax. She won't bite." She grinned. "Much."

Her attempt at levity worked, and his shoulders relaxed.

"What did I miss just now?" Dee waved a finger between them.

"A few years ago, I suffered a traumatic brain injury on a mission. Words get stuck in my head sometimes. Stress and anxiety make it worse," Sam said.

"I stress you out?" Dee raised an eyebrow.

"Anxious," he corrected. "I know what power you hold over Audra, and I don't want to see her suffer because she chose to trust me."

Dee's eyes narrowed. "What did you do?"

"I involved some friends."

"What kind of friends? Who are you, exactly?"

"I'm a former SEAL. Audra called me from the hospital. I met her in Vegas later the same day. She filled me in on what happened and what her suspicions were. We took the information she'd gathered and I gave it to a friend of mine. He built some program to analyze it all and has been running things through it."

Dee blinked and sat back. "Okay." She pinned Audra with a hard stare. "You gave mission critical information to a civilian?"

"Yes."

"And let him give it to someone else?"

"Yes."

"We have answers, though," Sam said.

"What? Why didn't you lead with that?" A deep vee formed between her eyebrows. "Bloody hell... Okay, what did you find out?"

"Theo's been playing both sides," Audra replied. "Do you have access to the most recent information I gathered from Liam's office?"

"What information?"

Audra's eyes widened, and she glanced at Sam for a moment before turning back to Dee. "Theo didn't pass along the information I copied from Liam's computer? Or the pictures I took of the ledger I found in his desk?"

Twin pops of red broke out on Dee's cheeks. Her silvery eyes darkened with anger. "No. What did you find?"

"Get your laptop." Audra gestured to the desk.

Dee rolled back and grabbed it. After logging in, she passed it to Audra.

"I know it's against agency policy, but I put too much time and too much of my life into this operation to leave everything in someone else's hands. I bought a private server, and I've been backing up information." Audra pulled up the server and logged in.

"Audra..." Dee sighed and pinched the bridge of her nose.

"You can pretend you didn't hear that." Audra turned the laptop around. "I copied the thumb drive and all the pictures. Sam sent everything to his friend. We think Liam's number two—Donny Callahan—has been paying Theo to keep quiet. And that his brother Patrick could possibly be involved as well."

"What?" Dee took the computer and started scrolling. "That doesn't make sense. Why wouldn't he rat Theo out to his boss?"

"To take over. It gave him leverage with everyone else. Theo would be long gone—forsaking me—when Donny made his bid to take over. He could use me as proof that Liam was inept as a leader. Who brings the enemy into his family circle?"

Dee rubbed her forehead as she continued to scroll. "All right. So, what brought you to me? Why did you decide you could trust me again?"

Audra glanced at Sam. She didn't want to expose Jo. So, she threw Asher under the bus. "His friend discovered you've been doing some digging of your own." She tipped her head toward Sam.

Dee narrowed her eyes again. "Who's your friend?"

"No one you need to worry about." Sam's smile dropped, his expression turning serious.

"You realize I can ruin your life just as easily as I can ruin hers, right?"

Sam offered her an artificial smile. "But you won't. Not with what we've brought you. And not with what you still need from us."

"I have dozens of operatives I can put on this. I don't need either of you."

"That is a load of tosh, and you know it." Audra glared at her boss. "Who else knows this op like me? Sure, you've got the files now, but I've got the key." She pointed to the side of her head.

"I could lock you up. Right now. And keep you there until you give us everything."

"You could. But why? I'm offering it to you."

"With strings."

"To protect the people who have helped me. Sam's only here because he wouldn't let me come alone."

For several seconds, Dee stared at them. Audra forced her lungs to inhale and to maintain a relaxed posture while she watched the indecision war in her boss's eyes.

Finally, Dee huffed. "Fine. But let's not give out anymore sensitive information, all right?"

Audra started to reply, but Sam cut her off before she could do more than open her mouth.

"Let's get something clear. I'm here for Audra. I don't care about your rules or your agenda. If I think it will benefit her and keep her safe, I will give whatever I want to whomever I want. That said—" He stopped, taking a breath. "We're on the same side. We want the same thing. Mostly."

Dee tipped her head. "You're either a brave man or a foolish one."

"I'm probably a bit of both."

A sudden smile spread over Dee's face and crinkled the corners of her eyes. "Yes, I think you are. Hopefully, you're also a sane one."

Twenty-Six

Sam concentrated on the feel of Audra's hand in his, keeping his emotions in check—mostly—while they talked to her boss. They'd gotten past the highest hurdle, convincing her they'd done what they had for the greater good. His anxiety level was lower now that he knew she wouldn't call the cavalry to hunt them down and throw them in jail.

"Have you uncovered anything on Theo?" Audra asked. "About why he did it? Because all we have is speculation."

Sam focused on Dee, waiting to see if she'd tell them the truth. They knew she knew about the large deposits to Theo's bank account.

"No. I uncovered some large financial transactions—the same ones you found, most likely—but I haven't made any inquiries with his colleagues. I wanted more proof before I started asking questions. I didn't want it to get back to him and chase him underground."

"No need to worry about that now," Sam said.

"I suppose not, no. Audra, do you know who he might talk to?"

"No. Like I told Sam, Theo and I didn't have a personal relationship. We met to pass along information. That was it. I knew the basics about him that I would know about any co-worker."

"That doesn't give us much to go on. I didn't hire him. He was here when I took over. I'll reach out to my predecessor. See what he can tell me. And I'd like to tell you to stay here, out of sight, but I doubt you'll listen to me." Dee pinned Audra with a look.

"Probably not," she admitted. "I'm happy we can trust you, but there's too much riding on this for me to sit idle."

"So, what's your plan?"

Sam met Audra's gaze when she glanced his way. They hadn't talked about what their next steps were.

"I think we need to go back to Las Vegas," Audra said.

Sam's stomach sank. He didn't like the idea, but she was right; all the answers were there. His mouth flattened, and he nodded. "We need to find out why Donny paid Theo, if the other Callahan brother is involved and to what extent, and what other secrets Theo may have sold."

Dee let out a soft groan. "This could be a nightmare. He's been with you for the last couple of years, but there have been other ops before this one. Plus, his clearance level gives him access to most everything."

"We'll find out what we can."

The older woman's gaze bounced between them again before they landed on Sam. "I don't like that you're involved. Don't make me regret not doing anything about it."

"No, ma'am."

"Make sure your friends are aware of that as well."

Sam clenched his teeth, this time to hold back the words that wanted to come out. He didn't like being threatened. Instead, he nodded once, then stood, pulling Audra to her feet. "We'll be in touch." He headed for the door.

"Ridley." Dee's voice stopped them. "I don't think I need to tell you what would happen to your career if news of Theo's betrayal leaks out before our solicitors can develop a damage control plan?"

Sam turned, stepping between the two women at the woman's blatant threat.

"Sam, it's okay." Audra laid a hand in the middle of his back.

He tempered the urge to really lay into Dee. But he couldn't stay completely silent. "I might not have the same direct political sway you do, but I have some powerful friends. It would be wise for you to remember that." He held the older woman's gaze with a long look, then stepped toward the door. "Come on, Aud. We're done here."

They reached the door, but Audra caught the doorjamb, glancing back.

"Oh, Dee? Las Vegas PD wants to question me about Theo's death."

Dee balled her fists and gave a short nod. "I'll take care of it."

TWENTY-SEVEN

"Welcome back." Dean opened the hotel room door with a grin. "Did you miss us?"

Sam rolled his eyes and motioned Audra to precede him inside. "Not really."

Dean pouted. "That's a knife to the heart."

Audra tossed him a smile. "Ignore him. He's being grumpy. We got stuck in middle seats on the plane." She would have preferred they flew back on the same plane they took to London, but they'd have lost a full day waiting for Ezra to come get them. And her body had healed significantly while they were abroad. She could handle the cramped flight back to Vegas much better than the week before.

"You didn't have to cram your six-foot-two-inch, two hundred-fifteen-pound frame into that tiny space for eleven hours. My back hurts." He pressed a hand to the small of his back.

She wrinkled her nose. "I'm sorry." Her journey hadn't exactly been comfortable; the seatbelt bit into her hip for most of the trip. But she hadn't been squished like he was.

He flashed her a smile. "You can rub it later."

Her cheeks flushed as an image of his bare backside wandered through her mind. More and more, she wanted to touch him. She wanted him to touch her. It was no longer a question of if it would happen. It would. As soon as her body was well enough—and it was close—she wouldn't be able to stop herself from climbing his tall, muscular body and begging him to take her.

Disguising the need flooding her veins, she rolled her eyes, then turned away. She looked at Dean and Max. "What have you two been up to while we've been gone?"

"Plenty," Max said, taking the hint to change the subject. "But we don't have much to show for it. We've been tailing Donny and Patrick Callahan. It doesn't seem as though they're doing anything out of the ordinary. Except, did you know they live in the same house?"

"Really?" Audra frowned thoughtfully. "No, I didn't." Maybe Patrick wasn't involved at all. It was Donny's initials on the ledger. And Donny was the one to call her, concerned.

"Maybe they're lying low right now. Until things die down a bit." Sam sank into the desk chair.

"That's what we were thinking," Dean said. "If we're going to get anything on them, we're going to need to flush them out. Make them make a mistake."

She pushed the thoughts of whether one or both brothers were involved aside for now. "So, while we were waiting on our plane, I called the FBI agent in charge of the case against the Brogans. Dominick Moran." Audra perched on one of the beds. "Dee told us Theo never turned over the USB drive I gave him. I figured Dom was unaware as well, so I wanted to catch him up. He said Liam's been in a tizzy since I left. The few informants they have that have any dealings with the Irish mob said Liam put out a bounty on me. He wants me brought to him alive."

"Well, that's something, at least," Max said.

Sam snorted. "It doesn't make it any better. Alive doesn't mean unharmed."

"No," she said. "But it gives us an opening."

"What do you mean?" Dean frowned.

"So, I had a lot of time to think on the trip over here. What if I went back voluntarily?"

"Hell no." Sam leaned forward, the fierce look of a warrior on his face.

She held up a hand. "Hear me out. He still doesn't know who I am. He thinks Theo was my lover. What if I go back and tell him I'd lost my memory? That I left the hospital because I was scared and not thinking clearly."

Sam got up and paced to the window. "Aud—" He stopped and ran a hand through his dark hair.

"I know it's risky. But we need to get to the Callahans. I don't know if we can do that outside of the organization. I know I can't. They'll recognize me."

"What about the guy who saw us running from your condo? You thought he was Irish mafia. He'd have gone back to Brogan and reported what he saw. How do we explain your association with me?"

She bit her lip. "Bodyguard my father hired. I can say that he heard about what happened to me and hired someone to find me. You tracked me down and took me to my condo to get clothes, then we saw that guy and got spooked."

Sam sighed, and she could see in his eyes that he didn't like the plan.

"Look, I know it's not perfect, but it doesn't need to be. It just needs to get me back into the fold. And only long enough to plant some trackers and maybe a couple of bugs on Donny and Patrick."

"I can get that stuff," Dean said.

"Not helping," Sam growled. "And what if they know your true identity? That was one of our theories, remember?

That Theo was offering info to them in exchange for a payout."

"Right, but we don't know for sure. It's a chance we need to take. You guys can wire me all up and stick close. If things go ass over teakettle, you can bail me out."

"Hold up." Max waved his hands. "What if there's a better way?"

Three sets of eyes turned on him.

"How so?" Dean asked.

A corner of Max's mouth lifted, and a speculative glint entered his eyes. "I'm a wealthy man. What if I'm looking for something only Brogan can offer? Audra, I'm sure you can help me figure out what would pique his interest. We could put me there in your place."

She tipped her head. Aspects of Liam's business ran through her mind. One particular part stuck. Something she hadn't given much thought to before now, but it might work. "There were two men. The night I got hit. I went to a business dinner with Liam. We met with the Powell brothers. Simon and Geoffrey. Simon gave me the willies. Anyway, they run a distribution network in Vegas. I didn't get much out of them at dinner. It felt more like Liam was feeling them out. At home, later, I looked them up. They have several wholesale warehouses in the city. Like a mini Amazon."

Sam crossed his arms; a curious frown settled on his face. "You think they're running stolen goods?"

"It's possible. If they want Liam's business, it's highly unlikely they're legit."

"So, we need to dig deeper into the Powells," Max said. "Find out why they want to partner with Brogan."

"Or why Brogan wants to partner with them," Dean said.

Max tipped a finger toward him and nodded.

"I can go back through all the intelligence I've gathered on Liam's organization. See if I can find a hole they could fill."

"Sounds good," Dean said. "I'll call Asher and have him run background on the Powells. Can you bring that intel here? If we all go through it, it'll happen faster."

"I already have it. I stored everything on my private server. My laptop is in my bag." She pointed at her suitcase.

"Well, let's start digging, then." Dean glanced at Max. "You want to call Asher?"

"On it." Max already had his phone in his hand.

Sam crossed to her bag and unearthed her laptop, then handed it to her. Audra logged in.

"Ash, you're on speaker." Max set his phone on the table between the two beds.

"What's up?"

"We think we've come up with a plan to get to the Callahans. We're going to go through everything Audra has on Brogan and find a way to get me into the fold. She thinks maybe somewhere in distribution. The night things went sideways, they met with two men. Simon and Geoffrey Powell."

"Okay." The sound of Asher typing came over the line. "Audra, what can you tell me about them? I need something to narrow the search."

She blew out a breath, ruffling her bangs, thinking. "Not much. They own some wholesale warehouses in Vegas. They didn't actually talk much business at dinner. They had some lady friends with them. One was named Celine. I don't know about the other one. No one introduced us. She was high as a kite, though."

"Hmm..."

"What?" Dean asked. "That didn't sound like a speculative hum. That was a, you've got something hum."

"I typed as Audra talked and found them, I think. They popped up in a law enforcement database. Let's see here..." He paused for several moments, then let out a soft whistle.

"They've both been arrested for drugs. Years ago. Does Brogan run meth?"

Audra's heart rate quickened. This could be what they needed. "Yes."

"I think there's your answer."

"So, it's not stolen goods they're running out of their warehouses," Sam said. "It's drugs."

"It might be goods too," Asher said. "I doubt they limit themselves. I'll keep digging. Audra, can you talk to your team there and find out if the Powells are on anyone's radar? From before, I mean. Not since you made contact with them."

"I can ask my boss. And maybe the FBI agent in charge here." Though she was a little hesitant to give him too much. They still didn't know if Theo had been working alone.

"What about that friend of Brooke's?" Max asked. "We could come at this from multiple sources. I think we've all learned over the years that the talking heads don't necessarily all talk to each other."

Asher snorted. "That's the truth. And are you talking about her friend Finn?"

"Him, too, but I meant that sheriff who's married to her friend. Wasn't he FBI?"

"He was. I'll talk to Brooke; have her talk to them. I'm not sure he or Finn will want to get involved, but it doesn't hurt to ask. We need information. Max, I'm going to start building a fictitious background for you. We'll fill in what kind of crime you're into once we get a better picture of how to approach Brogan and his organization."

"Sounds good. Give me a good name. Not something weird, please."

Asher let out an evil laugh. "I have all ze power," he said in an exaggerated German accent. "We'll talk again tomorrow and compare notes."

Max rolled his eyes. "I swear, if I end up as Boris Smelzer

or something equally awful, I'm going to murder you when I get home."

"You can try." Asher chuckled, then hung up.

With a groan, Max scooped up his phone. "Y'all are going to have to help me come up with a nickname, I think."

Dean chuckled. "I'm not sure what we come up with will be any better."

"It won't," Sam said, coming to sit next to Audra. "Let's start digging into Audra's intelligence. Give Asher a guide for his name choices."

Max and Dean grabbed their laptops.

Sam leaned closer as Audra opened her computer and logged in. "I'd log in on my phone, but the screen's too tiny for me to do much."

She agreed, remembering what a nightmare that had been.

"Can you give us your login info?" Dean asked. "It'll be easier than you emailing us files."

She bit her lip. It bothered her to give out that information, but she knew he was right. "Fine." She gave them the IP address, then walked them through logging in. Once their computers were connected, she split the files between them.

Two hours later, Audra pushed the computer onto Sam's lap and scooted toward the edge of the bed. "I need to move around." Her hip still ached from the long flight and from sitting on the bed, not moving, for so long. Plus, she was thirsty. "Anyone want a drink?" There was a small store in the lobby of their hotel. She'd meander down there and get a soda or something. The break would let her mull over all the stuff she and Sam had looked through. There was something there. A pattern she was missing. There had to be.

"I'll go with you." Sam got up.

They left the room and wandered down to the elevator.

"How're you doing?" Sam asked as he stabbed the down button.

"I'm fine."

He let out a snort. "No. I can hear your mind working. And I saw your limp."

"So my hip hurts? Sue me. I got hit by a car." She didn't know why she was so snippy all of a sudden. Exhaustion was part of it. And frustration, if she was honest.

"Hey." He laid a hand on her shoulder and turned her, a frown on his face. "Talk to me, Aud."

"I'm fine, Sam. Tired and ready for this to be over." She forced her mind onto the files they'd poured over for the last couple of hours. "What are we missing? Liam's got his fingers in a lot of pies, but I don't see any holes in his distribution network. Why would he need the Powells?"

Sam's frown deepened for a moment. She could see in his eyes that he wanted to keep talking about her and how she was doing. But he let it go with a sigh. "Let's go over what we know."

The elevator dinged, and they stepped into the empty car.

"He launders money through the restaurant and several other legitimate businesses." She held up a hand and ticked things off as she went. "Drugs—of all kinds—flow through the restaurant as well. And through his nightclub. There have been a few people to disappear in the year I've been here, so they're likely at the bottom of Lake Mead or some other deep body of water. Hell, he might have dumped them out in the desert too. Nevada's a great place to dump a body."

"Maybe he's looking to expand."

"To where? And into what? I didn't get deep enough into the Powells' business to find out their major shipping hubs. They have several warehouses in the city, so it's not a small operation."

"No. Hopefully, Asher can find us something there. It might be the missing piece."

Audra sighed and leaned back against the wall, crossing

her arms. "Yeah." She raised a hand and rubbed at the ache between her eyes.

Sam stepped closer. He framed her face in his hands. "We'll figure it out, Aud. The Wagner Brigade—we haven't failed yet."

She raised an eyebrow. "The Wagner Brigade?"

He grinned. "It's a nickname Edie gave us. We all ended up together down in Costa Rica one way or another because of Ford."

She smiled back. "I like it. It's catchy."

"Tell that to Ford. He rolls his eyes every time she says it."

Audra chuckled and laid her hands on his chest. "You should make t-shirts."

Sam laughed. "He'd love that," he said with an eye roll.

The elevator dinged again, and the door swished open. Audra pushed on his chest, but he didn't move. "Sam. The doors are open."

"I know." He brushed a hand through her hair and leaned into her. "I want to know you believe me. I won't let you down, Audra."

The doors closed.

Her heart squeezed. She skimmed her fingers over his jaw, her own working as emotions she wasn't ready to name flowed through her. "Even if we don't solve this case, I know you'll be there."

"I meant what I said in London. I'll move if I have to. I'm not giving up the second chance we've been given."

The squeeze let go so her heart could soar. Before she could respond, he kissed her, sending her heart even higher. She was glad he wanted to stay. While they'd been gone, she'd done a lot of thinking. She was done being alone.

The doors opened again.

"Oh, sorry."

Sam lifted his head, and Audra hid her face in his neck.

Getting caught necking in an elevator was not something spies did. But Sam threw all her sensibilities out the window. He always had.

"It's all right," Sam said. "We're getting off."

Head down as she fought a smile, she followed him into the lobby. They headed for the small store adjacent to the check-in desk.

A young woman smiled as they approached. "Hello. What can I get for you?"

"I'd like a lemonade, please." Audra pointed to the case behind the girl. "And a bag of crisps." Prawn cocktail crisps would be preferable, but the regular salty kind would do too. She probably should get some protein of some kind, but she really didn't care. She wanted comfort food.

"Make that two of each," Sam said.

Audra glanced around the lobby while he paid. It was surprisingly busy. There were a couple of families with young children, several couples, some teenagers, and a handful of businessmen passing through. Las Vegas was hopping even off the Strip.

"Aud." Sam touched her shoulder with the cold lemonade.

She turned and took the bottle and the bag of crisps. "Cheers."

"Do you want to stay down here or go upstairs?"

"Let's walk around a bit. I'm still stiff from the plane."

They headed outside. Even though it was close to a hundred degrees, the sun felt nice. She tipped her face to the sky and soaked in the warmth.

Hand-in-hand, they wandered the perimeter of the hotel. A plane roared overhead to land at the airport just a few miles away. A child's shriek, then a splash, drew her attention. She glanced over to see several kids playing in the hotel's outdoor pool.

Sam used his keycard and let them into the courtyard

enclosure. They found a table in the shade and sat down. Audra opened her crisps and watched the kids play. A woman laughed and clapped at one child's cannonball skills.

A lump formed in her chest. Would she ever have that? A family? Would she ever take a family vacation with her kids and watch them play in the water? Get splashed by them as they jumped off the side?

Her gaze flicked to Sam. He watched the kids too.

"Do you ever think about having a family?" Her eyes widened as the words left her mouth. *What?* The question was out before she could stop it.

He sat up, surprise flickering in his blue eyes as he looked at her. "In a general sense, sure. Who hasn't?"

She swallowed and nodded, then ate a crisp as she tried to sort through her thoughts. "Do you want a family?" Her heart thumped. She desperately wanted him to say yes. Why, she didn't know. She had never particularly wanted a family before. It's what made her so good at her job. Why she was so committed. It was all she had. All she wanted.

But not anymore.

"I guess that depends on who it's with. Do *you* want a family?"

"Depends on who it's with." She echoed his words back at him, then popped another crisp in her mouth. Cracking open her lemonade, she took a drink. "Family has never meant much to me. I'm a foster kid, and I bounced around every few years. I wasn't one of the lucky ones who found a family that wanted me to be a true part of theirs. It made me a good fit for my line of work. I didn't have any attachments. Didn't want any." She stopped, watching the kids again.

"And now?"

She lifted a shoulder. "I didn't give it much thought until you showed up again." She looked at him. "I'm still not sure what I want. But that possibility is definitely circling now. So is leaving SIS."

He studied her for a long moment. "I will support whatever you decide, Aud. But just know, you're stuck with me. I'm not going anywhere. Not this time. You want me gone? You'll have to pry me out of your life with a crowbar."

The thought made her smile. "I want you to stay. That much I'm sure of."

He wrapped an arm around her shoulders and kissed the side of her head. "How about—" he paused, taking a breath. "How about we figure out the rest as we go? No promises. Not for now, anyway."

Audra tucked her face into his shoulder, inhaling the spicy scent that was all Sam. "I like that. I do need one promise from you right now, though."

"Oh?" He looked at her, a question bringing his eyebrows down over his eyes.

She lifted her crisp bag. "Find me some prawn cocktail crisps. I need them in my life."

He laughed. "I'll see what I can do."

Twenty-Eight

Soft music filtered through Audra's mind, drawing her from sleep. She shifted, reaching out an arm to slap at the nightstand. Her hand connected with Sam's phone. Lifting the device, she pressed the snooze button, then set it down. She drew in a deep breath, then yawned it out and scrubbed at her face.

"I don't want to get up." Sam's sleep-roughened deep voice filled her ear.

She bit back a shiver. That sound would never not send a jolt of need through her. "Me, either."

He hooked a hand over her side and tugged, rolling her into his body. "Then let's stay here a little longer." He buried his nose in the space behind her ear.

Gooseflesh erupted down her neck and pricked her scalp. "I hit snooze."

"Good." His low growl was her only warning before he nipped at her neck, then smoothed the bite with his tongue.

Her eyes rolled back, and she let out a soft whimper. "Sam." His name came out on a breathy whisper.

"Sam, what? Do that again?" He nipped her neck and

smoothed the sting with his tongue. He moved up her jaw and pressed a kiss to the underside.

Audra tangled her fingers in his hair.

"Sam, please find that spot that makes my body weep?" He licked the hollow at the base of her neck.

Moisture flooded Audra's core. How he still knew all the places that drove her wild, she didn't understand. Though she shouldn't be surprised. She remembered how to work him into a frenzy as well.

She brought a knee up, then hooked her leg over his. He put his hand on her hip and ran it down her thigh, curving over the back side to hold her there.

He tipped his hips forward, teasing her with his hard shaft. "Or, how about, Sam, please make me scream your name?"

She moaned and grasped his face, bringing it in alignment with hers. "Sam, shut up and kiss me."

One corner of his mouth lifted on a naughty smile. "Yes, ma'am." He latched onto her lips.

Fire exploded in Audra's mind, and the room spun. She clutched his head, closing her eyes against the sensation, and moved her leg further around his, ignoring the ache in her hip. It was mostly healed. It certainly wasn't enough to stop her from enjoying this.

Sam broke away from her to rain soft kisses along her jaw and down her neck. He nuzzled the neckline of her sleep shirt with his nose, dipping his tongue into the crevasse between her breasts. Audra's nipples beaded painfully. They remembered what it was like to have his mouth on them. She grabbed his hand from her thigh and put it on her breast.

He took the hint and gently caressed her through her shirt. She moaned. It wasn't enough. She needed his hand on her bare skin.

"More."

He nudged her onto her back, raising up on one arm, and

slid his other hand under the hem of her shirt. His calloused fingers skimmed her belly. She sucked in a breath as his touch tickled. The air escaped her on a low moan as he reached her bare breasts. One flick of his finger over her tight nipple sent a pulse of need through her core. For long moments, he toyed with her flesh; massaging the soft globes and plucking at her sensitive flesh until she thought she'd come without him touching anywhere else.

She'd missed this. Missed him. No one could make her body burn like Sam. He knew exactly what she needed to build the fire.

His hand reversed direction, moving down her abdomen and burrowing beneath the waistline of her sleep shorts and panties. Her breath caught, her body anticipating his touch. When it did come, it was better than she remembered. Perhaps because it had been so long. The first glide of his fingers through the wetness coating her was enough to send her hips toward the ceiling and pull a keening cry from her throat. The fire burning in her veins flared, sparking a wildfire. Memories of their past encounters flashed through her mind on a reel. Her body responded like they'd never been apart. But at the same time, it yearned for something she hadn't had in a decade. Sam. Just Sam.

She reached up, hooking a hand around his neck, and fused their mouths. The stubble on his face rasped beneath her fingers, loud in the quiet room. Her moan drowned it out, though, as he slid his hand lower, probing her entrance.

Abruptly, he pulled away. Audra blinked, trying to process the shift.

"We need to—to slow down."

Body still humming, she frowned. "Why?"

"Your head. Concussion?"

"I'm fine."

"Now. But what will the blood rush from an orgasm do?"

"I think I'll be fine. It's been almost two weeks, and I weathered the plane ride and change in air pressure all right." She sat up and pushed him onto his back. Straddling him, she pressed her hands to his chest as she settled against him. "You can't work me up like that, then leave me flapping in the breeze." She circled her hips over the hard ridge beneath her. The friction sent a zing of pleasure through her, and she caught her lip between her teeth.

"Dammit, woman." He grabbed her hips to hold her still.

"I'll be fine. We can go slow to limit the exertion." She was getting off whether he did it to her or not. She refused to go about her day in a perpetual state of arousal because he worked her to the brink and didn't finish her. "My blood pressure is probably already high."

He growled, and she could see the indecision in his eyes still.

Time to play dirty. She whipped her top off.

Sam groaned and reached for her breasts.

The alarm on his phone went off again. Audra leaned forward, silencing it for good. Her eyes rolled back as Sam sucked the tip of her breast into his mouth.

"That better mean you intend to finish me."

"I intend to finish us both."

Thank heavens. Audra sank down again. Reaching under her hips, she dragged his boxer briefs down, setting him free. She grasped his length, running her fingers along the velvety skin. Her mouth watered, wanting to taste him. Another time. He was needed elsewhere more urgently.

"Baby, you play much more and I'll be finishing you another way."

"Promises, promises." She gave him a squeeze.

He let go of her hips and slid his fingers inside one leg of her shorts. Tugging the silky fabric and her panties to the side, he pushed his fingers into her channel.

Her grip on him faltered. All her brain cells redirected to her core and the pleasure his touch created. It wasn't just euphoria she felt, though. Being with him filled a part of her soul she hadn't realized she'd left behind all those years ago.

An explosion of ecstasy went off in her brain, blinding her to her surroundings. Her body clamped down on his fingers, and she let out a sharp cry, unable to contain the pleasure.

"Lift your hips."

On autopilot as she rode the wave, she did as he asked. A moment later, she felt the head of his shaft push against her entrance. Her body took over, and she sank down. "Oh!" She sucked in a sharp breath as he filled her.

"You okay?" he asked, a host of tension in his voice as he held himself still.

"I'm fine. Don't you dare stop."

"No, ma'am." He grasped her hips and rolled his own.

The friction reignited the flames that had cooled to an ember only moments before. Her world tilted and the room spun. It took her a second to realize he'd pulled out and changed their positions. Now he sat back on his knees. In the dark, she could just make out his form in the strip of light coming in between the curtain panels.

"Sam?" She propped herself up on her elbows. "Is everything all right?"

"It's fine. I'm letting the moment sink in." His hands fluttered up her thighs until he reached the waistband of her shorts. Hooking his fingers over the top, he tugged, peeling them and her panties down. "I decided I wanted you completely naked."

She raised her hips, wincing a bit as the one hitched. She'd be sore later, but she didn't care.

When the last of her clothes were off, he crawled toward her, spreading her thighs wide as he got closer. His hands cradled her calves. He pushed, tipping her feet toward her shoulders. "You tell me if you need me to change position. I don't want to hurt you."

"Okay." The word came out with a quaver to it. She knew what he planned to do. They'd made love in the same position many times when they were together before. It was one of her favorites. No one else had ever tried to make love to her the same way. She didn't want them to. This was theirs.

He shuffled closer on his knees and tipped her feet back further, raising her hips. Then he leaned forward and impaled her with one long stroke.

She flopped back and moaned, loud and long, as he hit all the right spots on his way in. He didn't give her a chance to recover before he withdrew and did it again. Powerless to do anything but hold on for the ride, she threw her arms over her head and grasped the headboard. In moments, he sent her riding high in the clouds again.

"Sam!" She writhed, as much as his grip would let her, as wave after wave broke, timed to each thrust. As the waves gradually faded, she caught her breath and realized he wasn't done. A third orgasm built, but she refused to give in. Not until she could take him with her. "Let me go." She knew what he needed.

Immediately, he released her. "You okay?"

"I'm fine." She put her feet on the bed and sat up, pushing him back. He moved away, and she reached over to turn on the bedside lamp. Her breath hitched as she took him in. Muscles shifted beneath his golden skin, the layer of sweat dampening him enhanced the effect. Her gaze strayed to his erect shaft, and again, she wanted to taste him. But she wanted the connection of their bodies more.

His gaze took in her surely disheveled appearance. Sleep always did crazy things to her hair. She wasn't one of those women who could go to bed with perfect hair and wake up the same way. Sex hadn't helped her problem.

He crooked a finger at her, beckoning her closer. Audra didn't waste time. She walked forward on her knees and wrapped her arms around his neck and her legs around his waist, sinking down onto him as she did so. He moaned against her mouth and shifted them toward the edge of the bed. He'd always been a close contact kind of lover. Nothing set him off faster than holding her close while she rode him hard.

So, that's what she did. Pressed against him, she tangled their tongues and rolled her hips, faster with every second. She raked her nails along the powerful muscles of his back, eliciting gooseflesh and a deep moan. A second later, he broke away with a harsh cry. His fingers dug into her hips, biting into the fading bruises. She barely felt it. Her third climax had hit, taking her away from reality.

Sam buried his face in her neck. She could feel his warm breath wash over her heated skin. Her body clenched around his again. He lightly bit her neck, then lifted his head.

A satisfied smile tipped his lips up. "So, you up for a shower?"

Audra laughed. "We need one."

Fire licked at his eyes. He palmed her hips and stood, their bodies still connected. "I know I said once you got me off it would be a bit before we could do it again, but apparently, I was wrong. My body missed you and has other ideas."

She felt him stir within her. Every step he took toward the bathroom rubbed him against her sensitive flesh. She bit her lip. "I'm okay with that."

TWENTY-NINE

The white paper bag crinkled in Sam's hand as he knocked on Dean and Max's door. He glanced at Audra. She still had a healthy flush to her cheeks from their exercise earlier.

A smirk crossed his face. He intended for her to wear that for the next few decades, at least.

Dean opened the door. "You're late. We said eight. It's eight-thirty."

"We were tired." Audra breezed inside with her laptop tucked under her arm, lying through her teeth with ease.

Sam bit back a smile, not wanting to contradict the master spy at work. "Sorry. Hit snooze one too many times. And she gets hangry, so we stopped for breakfast." He lifted the bag. "Don't worry. We brought you some."

Audra speared him with a glare. "Whatever. You're the one who hauled me out of the shower to quell your grumbling tummy."

His eyes widened a fraction at her words. The quick flare of her nostrils was the only indication she gave that she realized her faux pas.

He quickly moved the conversation along. "I wasn't about to wait for you to use all the hotel's hot water before I got to eat." He crossed to the desk and set the bag down. Opening it, he took out a bear claw and passed it to Max, who sat in the desk chair.

"Thanks."

"You could have brought us coffee too," Dean grumbled, accepting a pastry.

"We figured you'd have that in spades," Sam said. He tipped his head toward the cup next to Max.

"We can always use more," Dean replied.

"We'll get it later," Audra said. "I'm sure we'll all need it. Can we call Asher now?"

Max opened his laptop without a word and pulled up a video call screen.

"We're video calling today?" Sam took a third pastry out of the bag and passed it to Audra.

She smiled her thanks and sat on the bed behind Max.

"Yep. Better audio than speakerphone."

Sam tipped his head. Max had a point.

With the last pastry in the bag in his hand, Sam sat next to Audra. The call connected, and Asher's face filled the screen. Ford sat next to him.

"Uh-oh," Dean said. "Boss man's here. What did you find?"

"Some crazy shit," Asher said. He sighed. "So, the Powells are on the FBI's radar and have been for some time. Brooke talked to her friend's husband. But I need to back up. I ran a correlation search on their names, their business, and criminal activity in the areas where they've lived or worked, and I found something... well, interesting. And not in a good way. Do any of you remember the serial killer case in Colorado a few years back? Ryan Marsters?"

"Wasn't he the guy who went out in dramatic fashion after he kidnapped the local sheriff's girlfriend?" Max said.

"That's the one." Asher nodded. "When I ran the Powells, it turns out they're from the same area as Marsters. Elko County, Nevada."

"Brooke also talked to Ben—her friend's husband?" Ford arched an eyebrow, making sure they understood before he went on.

Dean's head bobbed once, and Ford continued.

"He put in a call to his former partner and asked him to do a quick search. The brothers are under investigation for drug activity. I guess they got put on the FBI's radar during their investigation into Marsters. There were some drugs involved in that case somehow. I'm not really clear on that point. But Ben's partner gave him the name of a guy you can contact for more information. Sebastian Archer. He's the sheriff of the county where this all went down. He's a former fed too."

"I'll email the info to you guys," Asher said.

"Okay," Sam said. "We'll give him a call."

"Sounds good. Did you guys come up with anything in Audra's files?"

Audra scrunched her face, clearly annoyed by their lack of progress. Sam agreed with the sentiment. There was a lot of information to sift through. It all pointed to Brogan being guilty of many things, but nothing about who would have motive to kill her—besides the obvious—or why Theo was involved.

"From what we can tell, most of the case against him comes from what I've observed. It's the people I've seen him meet with. Some of their discussions I've overheard. The ledger is the best physical evidence we have against him. Have you made any headway into decoding it?"

"Possibly. My program spit out many combinations for the

initials from the info I fed it. I need some background on the names and businesses you gave me to get any further. How about while Sam calls that sheriff, Max and Dean can continue to comb through your evidence files and you and I can talk? I think with your insight, we can put together a pretty accurate list."

"Sure."

"On that note, I'll leave you guys to it," Ford said. "If there's anything else you need from me, just ask."

"We will," Sam said. "Thanks, Ford. And tell Brooke we said thanks."

"Will do." He got up and left.

Asher leaned closer to the camera. "You three—scram. The nice English lady and I need to chat."

Sam rolled his eyes, but moved away from the computer. Max chuckled and Dean gave him a half smile.

"Audra, is it okay if I use your computer while you're on mine?" Max asked.

She glanced at him and nodded.

"Thanks." He picked it up from where she'd set it when they came in, then sat down in the corner chair.

Dean grabbed his laptop and stretched out on one of the beds.

"I'm going to make that call outside." Sam pointed at the door, already moving that way.

Max and Dean acknowledged him. Audra sat down in the desk chair to talk with Asher.

Leaving the room, Sam rode the elevator down to the lobby and went outside. He didn't want anyone overhearing the conversation—accidentally or not. Once he was well away from the other guests, he took out his phone and opened his email. The message Asher sent was at the top. He clicked on it and scanned it quickly, grinning at the man's foresight. He'd given him the sheriff's direct line. He wouldn't have to convince whoever manned the phones to put him through.

Sam dialed the number. It rang twice before a man picked up, sounding distracted.

"Sheriff Archer."

"Hi, Sheriff. My name is Sam Brackley. I have some questions for you about a serial murder case you worked a few years ago. Do—"

"I don't talk to reporters, sorry."

"I'm not—" The line clicked in his ear. Sam huffed and dialed again.

"Sheriff Archer."

"I'm not a reporter." Sam figured it was best to start with that, so he at least had a chance of not being hung up on again.

"Tenacious like one, though. So, who are you?"

"Like I said, my name is Sam Brackley. I'm a former Navy Senior Chief with the SEALs."

A beat of silence passed.

"You have my attention. What do you want with the Marsters case?"

Sam let out a short, huffed laugh. "Um, well, how much time do you have?"

"How about you give me the cliff notes version?"

"All right. My"—Sam paused for a second, debating how to categorize Audra, then just went for it—"girlfriend is an SIS officer undercover with the Irish mafia in Las Vegas. Someone tried to kill her two weeks ago. Through our investigation, we found a couple of individuals who have a link to Marsters."

Another long pause came over the line. Then, "Well, shit. I have questions." The sheriff sighed. "But not a lot of time right now. Um, okay. Can I call you back? Around, say, twelve-thirty? I need to rearrange some things and there are a few other people who should probably be on the call. And can you do a Zoom meeting?"

Sam blinked, an amused smile forming on his face as he listened to the sheriff's rapid-fire questions. "Sure. There are some people here who should probably be part of the conversation as well."

"Great. What's your email? I'll send you the meeting link."

Sam gave it to him.

"Okay. We'll talk soon."

"Sounds good."

THIRTY

"Everyone ready?" Sam glanced side-to-side at the others as they gathered around the computer. The four of them were scrunched together on the end of the bed, facing the computer on the desk.

"Hit it," Dean said.

Sam reached out and clicked on the icon to join the meeting. A moment later, a window opened, showing over half a dozen people sitting around a conference table.

"Hello." A dark-haired man in a police polo raised a hand and offered them a polite smile. "I'm Sheriff Archer. Call me Seb. Let's do a quick round of introductions, yes?"

Sam nodded. "I'm Sam. This is Audra Ridley, Dean Adler, and Max Carson." He pointed to each of them in turn.

"Nice to meet you all," Seb said. "I'm just going to go around the room." He started on his left. "My wife, London; my chief deputy, Jace Travers; our medical examiner, Dr. Alex Randall; our chief forensic scientist, Katie Mitchum-Randall; my brother, Thomas Archer and his wife, Rayna; and finally their son, Mason."

"That's quite the party," Max said. "I don't think we were

expecting so many people." He glanced at the others, a brow raised.

Sam agreed. Especially the family members. He understood why the sheriff's wife was there. If she was the girlfriend, she was one of Marsters' victims. But the others?

"Yes, well, this case had far-reaching implications for our area," Seb said. "Can you elaborate more on why you're asking about Marsters?"

"Sheriff, Sam told me he gave you a basic overview of what's going on," Audra said. "I've been undercover with Liam Brogan's operation for almost two years, in one capacity or another. We were on the cusp of taking him down when someone tried to kill me and killed my handler, Theo Anderson. Long story short, I lost trust in him and in my agency, so I contacted an old friend." She gestured to Sam.

"He said he's your boyfriend."

Sam's neck reddened. He probably should have gone with friend. He glanced at her and shrugged.

Her mouth lifted and a light entered her eyes. She looked at the camera. "I suppose he is now. But that's immaterial. I trust him, and that's what I needed. What I didn't know was he had deep resources. With those, we've figured out that whoever murdered Theo and tried to kill me didn't do so because I was too close to bringing Brogan down. It's mafia adjacent, if you will."

"Okay." The blond man named Jace sat forward. "What does that have to do with our serial killer?"

"Honestly? Maybe nothing."

The group on the screen all looked at each other.

"We need an in for a new operative—me—into Brogan's organization, since Audra's been compromised," Max said. "Over the course of the last few days, we think we might have found an opening, but we need more information."

Audra took over for him. "The evening of the attempt on

my life, Brogan and I met with Simon and Geoffrey Powell. They run a wholesale company here in Las Vegas. The purpose of the meeting was to discuss them becoming a distributor for Liam's businesses. We didn't do much discussing, though. It was an informal dinner meeting. I think he was feeling them out. What we've discovered about the brothers since is that they have some drug convictions and are from the same area of Nevada as Ryan Marsters."

"Which is what led you to us," Seb surmised.

"Yes," Audra said. "One of Sam's contacts has a contact with someone in the FBI. The Powells are under investigation for drug trafficking, but what put them on the feds' radar was their association with Marsters. Do you know anything about them that we can use to get Max in? The idea is to put him into competition with the Powells."

Seb and his group all shared a look.

A pit formed in Sam's stomach. It was a heavy look that went through that room.

"What do you know about the Marsters case?" Seb asked.

"Basically, what we heard on the news," Dean said. "We checked out a few news articles this morning after Sam talked to you."

"Did you read the ones about the human trafficking ring?" Thomas Archer spoke up, a hardness to his voice.

Sam sat straighter, the pit getting deeper. "It was mentioned, yes."

"I remember the Powells' names," Seb said. "The initial case was just Marsters. He killed several women in our area and kidnapped London. It wasn't until later that we found out he had ties to a child trafficking ring. The Powells came up in conjunction with that investigation."

"How so?" Audra asked. "Were they trafficking children?" Her face hardened.

"We're not sure," Seb said. "The Paulsons—the traffickers

—had some documentation of their connections with other businesses and individuals. We found the Powells' names listed with a phone number. The FBI wasn't able to find anything else to connect them to the case, though. Based on their past history, we think they supplied the Paulsons with drugs to keep the kids compliant, but we could never prove it."

"What if they took the kids away too?" The young blond man named Mason asked. All eyes in the conference room swung toward him. He glanced at Rayna, uncertainty in his eyes.

She laid a hand on his forearm.

"What do you mean?" Thomas asked.

"The kids who were too old for the Paulsons' clientele. They didn't just vanish. And Seb, you never found their bodies. So, what happened to them?"

Seb stared at him for a long moment, a crease between his eyebrows. "You think the Powells took them?"

Mason lifted a shoulder. "It makes sense. What if they gave the Paulsons drugs, and the Paulsons gave them to those of us who had served our purpose?"

Sam sucked in a breath, his eyes widening at the man's phrasing.

"Well, damn," Seb said. He looked at the camera. "Ms. Ridley, you might have stumbled on something worse than the mafia."

She pursed her lips and looked at Sam. He raised a brow, seeing in her eyes that she didn't like that idea. He didn't either. Human traffickers were the worst scum out there. "Aud, is it possible Brogan was dealing in the flesh trade?"

She drew in a breath and tipped her head, chewing on the corner of her mouth. "Regular, run-of-the-mill prostitution, sure. But the kind of human trafficking they're talking about? Buying and selling sex slaves? I'm not sure. I never saw evidence of it."

"Okay," Seb said. "Let me reach out to a few of my FBI contacts in the Vegas area. See if I can get more information on their investigation."

"Is Special Agent Dominick Moran on that list?"

"He is. Why?"

"Do you trust him?"

Seb leaned forward. "There a reason I shouldn't?"

"No. I'm just asking. After Theo's betrayal, I didn't know if there were others involved. It took over a week before I decided to trust my boss. I contacted Moran once about the new evidence. I haven't spoken to him since."

"Moran is solid," Seb said. "We went to the academy together, and we've worked on several cases. So, I would say, yes. Trust him."

"Okay. We'll loop him in."

"Good. I'll talk to my other federal contacts. See if they know anything useful."

"Seb." Dr. Randall interrupted them. "Whoever you talk to, you might want to tell them to dig deeper into the Powells' lives before they moved to Vegas. If they're dealing in people, it might have started in Elko County."

"Ryan mentioned his father abused his stepsister," London said. "Maybe there were others before her."

"I'm so glad that man is dead," Katie said. "And that the Paulsons will never see the light of day again."

"We all are," Thomas said. His gaze flicked to his son.

Sam agreed. The world was a better place without people like Ryan Marsters.

Seb turned back to the camera. "Keep us informed on what you find. We'll do the same."

Sam nodded once. "We will. Thank you for the information." He glanced at his friends. "I think we have a place to start now."

"You're welcome. I hope you get what you're after."

Thirty-One

Audra chewed on her lip as Sam ended the call. That was not at all what she'd been expecting. From what they'd learned about the Powells, drugs seemed like the most likely entry point into Brogan's operation. But now she wasn't so sure.

"Well, that was... unexpected," Dean said.

Sam snorted.

"We need to talk to your FBI friend, Audra," Max said.

She nodded. "Let's give him a call." She took out her phone and dialed the number, putting the call on speaker.

It took several rings, but he finally picked up. "Moran."

"Hi, Dom. It's Audra."

A short pause came over the line. "It's good to hear your voice. Thompson called. Your boss had a lot to say."

"Yes, well, we have more."

"We?"

"I'm here with some friends."

"Good friends?"

"Yes. You can trust them. Dee knows about them."

"All right, then. What's up?"

"So, we just had an interesting conversation with Sebastian Archer."

"Seb? Why were you talking to him? How do you even know him? He hasn't been a fed in years."

Audra quickly gave him a rundown of their conversation and why they'd talked to him.

Dom let out a low whistle. "That—that's some heavy stuff. But Audra, I can't let your friend go in undercover."

"Let me?" Max said, indignation coloring his tone.

Audra sent him a sharp look. He stared back at her. She sighed and shook her head. Sam's friends were as stubborn as he was.

"I'm done playing nice with this whole thing," Audra told Dom. "Someone tried to kill me. It wasn't Theo, because he's dead. Official channels take too long. And we have a solid plan. Trust me, Max will be able to charm his way in. We just need the info to get him there. What do you know about the Powells' criminal activity?"

It was Dom's turn to sigh. "You're going rogue no matter what I say, aren't you?"

"Yes."

"Fine. I haven't had time to do much digging into them. I only talked to Dee a few days ago. You're right that there is an open investigation into the Powells. It's for drug trafficking."

"We knew that. Is it just drugs?" Sam asked.

"Yes. But after what you just told me, I'm going to call him back and ask if unofficially, they're looking into whether there's any human trafficking going on."

"Good, you do that," Audra said. "We'll wait."

"What? You want me to do that now?"

"Yes."

He let out a growling sigh. "I think I liked you better when you didn't trust me."

"What would you do if someone tried to kill you? If you knew that someone might be dealing *children*?"

There was a short pause. "You're right. Give me a few minutes." He hung up.

Audra's shoulders slumped. She was tired of waiting. Now that things were moving, she wanted to execute their plan ASAP. She looked at Max. "You need to go shopping. No matter what criminal enterprise your alias undertakes, you need to look like a savvy businessman."

"I actually went to a tailor not long after we landed on this plan and commissioned a few suits. They should be ready tomorrow."

She grinned. "I like you."

A quick laugh burst from his chest. "That's good. I think we'll be seeing a lot of each other."

Her smile widened. "You will."

The next few minutes passed with excruciating slowness. Audra willed the phone to ring again, but knew it could be some time before Dom called her back. It all depended on how quickly the other agent picked up and what he knew.

She got up and finished the pastry she'd set aside and sipped her coffee. Sam, Max, and Dean made idle chitchat while they waited. They were planning a cookout for when they got back to Costa Rica. Audra hoped she'd be able to join them.

The phone rang. Dean pounced on it, putting it on speaker.

"Dom?" Audra said, walking closer.

"Yeah. So Pierce wants to talk to you now. I told him maybe."

"Did he tell you anything?"

"Yes. Your suspicions aren't baseless. He's heard rumors the Powells deal in the skin trade, but they don't have anything concrete. I think before you proceed, you need to find out more about why they met with Brogan. It could be drugs or people at this point."

"Yeah, but the question is how?" Dean said.

An inkling of an idea struck Audra. Sam wouldn't like it, but they were running out of options. "So, I think I have a plan."

Thirty-Two

"You got him?"

Audra leaned over her drink and looked up through her lashes. The blonde wig she'd donned cascaded around her shoulders, hiding the small earpiece tucked into her ear. They were taking a huge risk, but if it worked, it would pay off in an even bigger way. "Yep," she answered Dean. "I see both of them and their lady friends."

"Everyone stay sharp. Aud, we've got your back." Sam's voice sounded in her ear.

She smiled, hiding it with her straw. Sam hadn't liked her plan. He'd adamantly tried to talk her out of it. But once he figured out she wouldn't be dissuaded, he'd stepped up and become wholly involved. The mission was still dangerous. One of Liam's people could be around and recognize her despite her disguise. But she felt safer with Sam at her back.

She tossed a strand of her blonde wig over her shoulder and glanced around the room. She didn't see anyone she knew, but that didn't mean someone wouldn't recognize her. In the year she'd been here, she'd risen in status as people came to know her as Brogan's fiancée. She'd been paraded around like a prized possession at party after party. There were bound to be people who would recognize her that she wouldn't give a second look to.

Hence her current disguise. They'd found her a passable blonde wig and some outrageous eyelashes. She'd changed her makeup too, making it much more dramatic. Alexandra was more demure. A lady. This new woman was not.

"Hi."

Audra ground her teeth together and looked at the man who'd sidled up next to her at the high table. "I'm not the woman you want. Move along." He wasn't the first one she'd sent packing this evening. She knew there would be more too.

The man's smile died. Red tinged his cheeks, but he picked up his drink and left.

She huffed after he disappeared into the crowd. "Why do men always think a woman alone is looking for a hookup?" she muttered.

Max chuckled in her ear. "They don't. But it is what *they* want. Especially when that lone woman is as beautiful as you are."

"Quit hitting on my woman, Carson."

Audra fought another smile. "Relax, Sam. You're the only one for me."

"Good."

She picked up her drink and moved away from her table, hoping that mingling would discourage others from talking to her. They'd debated sending her with Sam, but were afraid someone might recognize him if they were together. They didn't know if the man who'd chased them away from her condo got a good look at either of them, and it was harder to change Sam's appearance. The chances were slim, but they wanted to play it safe.

That left Max and Dean. Max needed to stay in the wings for now, so he could go in to Brogan's operation clean, which left only Dean. In the end, they decided it was better for her to go alone in case they needed to use him for something later where she had to have a partner. They were all in the club; just staying in the shadows.

"Your woman's on the move," Max said.

"Restroom?" Audra asked.

"Looks like it."

Audra changed directions, putting her on a collision course with Simon's lady friend. "Let's do this."

"The other woman's going with her," Dean said.

Dammit. She needed the blonde alone. The plan was to slip a bug onto the woman. Audra needed to get close and was afraid she couldn't if she wasn't alone.

"I'm on it," Sam said.

Audra kept walking, not worrying about Geoffrey's lady friend Celine, now. Sam was a quiet soul, but he could turn on the charm when he wanted to. All he had to do was smile and that woman would simper at his feet. It certainly worked on her.

Weaving her way through the crowd, she followed Simon's girlfriend down the dim corridor toward the bathroom. A single light hung in the long hallway, casting deep shadows. An exit sign glowed in the darkness at the far end of the hall. The woman disappeared into the bathroom. Audra entered in time to see a stall door swing shut and lock. Audra stepped into the one next to hers and shut the door. While she waited, she took the listening device from her clutch and rolled it in her hand to warm the small bit of plastic. After a minute or so, she heard the toilet flush next door. Quickly flushing her own, she stepped out. The woman emerged from her stall and crossed in front of Audra.

"Hi, there! I didn't expect to see you out tonight." Audra grabbed the woman and gave her a quick hug, laying the surprise on thick. She didn't bother to hide her accent.

The woman seemed frozen in her arms, but also limp. Anger simmered in Audra's gut. The girl was high again.

Audra slipped the small bug under the strap of the woman's dress over her shoulder blade, then pulled back to look at her. "How are you doing, love?" She injected some heavy sympathy into her voice.

The woman blinked up at her with dull blue eyes. "Um, do I know you?"

"Sure you do. We met at that party a few months back. You were with that dark-haired guy. What was his name... Sean? Seth? Simon! That's it, isn't it? Simon?"

The woman nodded. "Yes. I'm sorry. I don't remember you. What's your name?"

"Amber."

Someone else entered the bathroom. Audra wrapped a hand around her arm and moved her to the side. The woman stumbled.

"Oh! Careful there." Audra helped steady her.

"Sorry. I must have had too much to drink."

She'd had too much of something, but it wasn't alcohol. A new plan formed in Audra's head. One the boys really wouldn't like. "Are you here with him? Let me help you back. I wouldn't want you to get knocked over. It's a crush out there."

"I'll be okay."

"Aud, what are you doing?" Sam's voice growled in her ear. "Plant the bug and let her go. Her friend is on her way to you now."

She ignored him. "Love, I insist." She took the woman's hand and looped it through her arm, then laid her other hand on top, securing her grip on the girl. And she was a girl. Up close, Audra could see through the heavy makeup. If this woman was twenty, she'd be astonished.

Hoping the drugs made her compliant for everyone and

not just Simon, Audra led her toward the door. They needed to hurry. She had no intention of taking her back to Simon. If her friend showed up, she'd never get the girl out.

They stepped into the hall, and she had to hold back a triumphant grin. No one was in sight. She turned right, toward the blazing red exit sign.

"Where are we going?" the girl asked after they'd taken several steps. "The club is the other way."

"I'm getting you out of here."

Sam cursed in her ear. "Max, Dean, go outside. I'll create a distraction, then follow her through the exit."

"Copy," Dean said.

"On it," Max replied.

The girl twisted her head to look Audra in the eye. She didn't try to stop, though, and Audra continued to haul her toward the door.

"You look familiar now. Who are you?"

"A friend, love. You can trust me."

The girl snorted. "I've heard that before."

"Well, with me, it's true." They reached the door. Audra prayed it wasn't alarmed—or locked. She pushed on the bar. It swung open with a soft protest of the hinges.

Warm night air blasted her in the face, and the bright lights of the Strip made her squint. "Phew! It's warm out here. I thought the desert was supposed to be chilly at night. How about we hit up the Paris for some air-conditioning? And some of their crepes? That sounds good. I'm starving." She needed to get the woman away from the club and some place safe. Liam's band of merry men usually stayed away from the Paris. It was one of the reasons she'd met Sam there.

"I hear you loud and clear, babe. We'll see you there," Sam said in her earpiece.

"I'm not very hungry," the girl said. "I think I'd like to just go home. Can you take me there?"

"Where's home?"

"Aud, no," Sam said.

"I live with Simon."

"No. We're not going there. And I don't think you really want to go back there. Do you?"

"No," the young woman whispered.

"Then we're getting crepes."

THIRTY-THREE

Sam met Dean and Max out back of the club. Audra was nowhere in sight.

"You know where she went, right?" Dean asked.

"I do. Let's go." He jogged around the side of the building to the street, signaling a taxi. The three of them squished into the backseat.

"Paris Hotel." Sam leaned forward. "Quick as you can. There'll be a good tip in it for you."

"Yes, sir." The driver pulled into traffic.

"What the hell was she thinking?" Max asked. "This isn't the plan."

"I don't know." Sam swiped a hand down his face. "She's always liked to go her own way. It's part of what makes her so good at undercover work. She can think on her feet. But this —" His words hadn't stuck this time. They'd just left. He didn't know what to say. They'd agreed to bugging the girlfriend in the hopes Simon and Geoffrey would talk in front of her. No one had ever mentioned absconding with the woman.

"Moran's going to be really unhappy now," Dean muttered.

That was no lie.

The cab driver wove in and out of traffic, making the little Focus's engine whine as he accelerated. Sam was impressed, though. The guy had some skills behind the wheel. In less than ten minutes, they were pulling up to the Paris entrance. He handed the man a wad of bills and patted him on the shoulder. "Thanks, man."

The man took the cash, a look of surprise on his face. His gaze met Sam's. "You need a ride elsewhere, you call Denton." He picked up a card from the cupholder and gave it to him. "I take you anywhere, man."

Sam took the card and offered him a smile. "Thanks." He slid out of the car, pocketing the card.

"Where are we going?" Dean asked.

"The connector between Paris and Horseshoe. There's a creperie there. It's where I met Audra when I came to town." He jogged past his friend and went inside.

They waded through the smoky casino and hurried past the crowded restaurants. In the corridor, it was quieter. Sam saw the sign for the restaurant. "There." He glanced into the seating area. At the back sat two blonde women.

His heart rate slowed. They were safe.

Anger at what she'd done took over. He marched into the café. "What were you—"

Her hand in the air and the pleading look in her eyes stopped him. His gaze flicked to the woman across the table from her. She held a plastic fork and was busy cutting off a chunk of the ham and cheese crepe.

Sam's anger died. Woman was stretching it. Beneath the makeup, there was a softness about her features that said she was just a girl.

He glanced at Max and Dean. Their faces held much the same realization.

Gathering chairs, they pulled them up to the table,

flanking Audra. Sam didn't want to scare the girl by surrounding her.

She lifted her head, her eyes going wide as she took them in. "Um, Amber? Who are these guys?"

Audra offered her a soft smile. "These are my friends. They're here to help too."

The girl set her fork down. "I think I should go."

"Please stay." Audra touched her hand. "Let us explain? I promise we're not here to hurt you. You're safe."

Indecision and a hint of fear lit the girl's eyes. Sam tried not to look intimidating, but wasn't sure if he succeeded. He wanted to know what was going on, and those thoughts made him frown.

"Please?" Audra said again.

After a moment, the girl nodded. "Okay. It's not like I have anywhere else to go." Despair colored her voice. Sam saw tears gather in her eyes.

"Love, look at me." Audra's voice was soft, but firm.

The girl lifted her head to look Audra in the eye.

"You said I looked familiar."

The girl nodded. "You do, but I can't place you. My brain's all fuzzy. I can't think straight."

Sam fought to keep the glower off his face. He wanted to strangle Simon Powell with both hands.

"How about if I talk like this?" Audra slipped into her American accent. "And tell you to imagine me with dark hair. We had dinner about two weeks ago. With Simon, his brother, that woman you were with tonight, and Liam Brogan."

It only took a second for recognition to light the young woman's face. "You're Liam Brogan's fiancée." She glanced at Sam, Dean, and Max, then frowned. "I don't understand."

"I'm not really Liam's fiancée." Audra slid back into her normal voice. "Well, technically, I was, but I never intended to marry him. My name is Audra. I'm an undercover operative.

These men are friends of mine, helping me to clean up the mess my op has become."

The young woman blinked twice, slowly, then laughed. "You? You're a cop? Get real."

"Actually, I'm a spy."

The woman laughed harder. "Oh, come on. Seriously?"

Audra just stared at her. Sam didn't blame the girl. It all sounded rather far-fetched.

Slowly, the woman's laughter died, and her eyes widened as she took in Audra's serious expression.

"Wait. You're serious? Like double-oh-seven stuff?"

Audra cracked a smile. "Not quite, but yes, I'm telling the truth. What's your name?"

The girl frowned. "You said you knew me."

"I do, but no one introduced us that night."

"Oh. I'm Poppy."

Audra's smile widened. "It's nice to meet you, Poppy."

"Um, you too, I guess. So, what do you want with me?"

"We need your help." Audra glanced at Sam. He gave her a quick nod, and she turned to Poppy. "Does Simon ever talk business around you?"

Poppy's expression closed, and she shrank in on herself, looking even more like a scared child. "I try not to listen. He thinks I don't understand but—" She stopped, shaking her head. "It's hard not to when you yourself were forced to do things you didn't want to do." She picked up her fork and toyed with her food. "I try not to think about that."

Max muttered something under his breath Sam couldn't understand. By the dark look on his face, though, he agreed with whatever it was.

"That's okay." Audra laid her hand over Poppy's again. "We won't ask you about any of that. We need to know what Simon and Geoffrey are up to. We know they traffic drugs. Is there more than that?"

Poppy speared a piece of ham, then pushed it around in the sauce on her plate. "Yeah. They get girls. About once a month. Simon doesn't like to leave me at home. I go pretty much everywhere with him. Even if I just stay in the car." Her face crumpled. "I was one of those girls. He—he decided to keep me." She burst into tears.

Audra looked at Sam, anger simmering in her eyes as she got up and moved around to Poppy's side. She draped an arm around the girl. "I'm so sorry, love. I know it doesn't make up for the past, but you're safe now. We won't take you back there."

"We should probably get out of here." Dean glanced around.

Sam concurred. They hadn't drawn much attention, but that could change. The creperie wasn't all that busy. A woman sobbing, even in Las Vegas, would make people concerned.

"Come on, Poppy. Let us take you somewhere you can get cleaned up and get a good night's rest, okay?" Audra stood, tugging on the girl to bring her to her feet.

Poppy nodded against Audra's chest. "Okay."

They walked toward the main corridor, Dean and Max at the lead. Sam trailed behind Audra and Poppy.

"I need you to lift your chin up and try to act as normal as possible, love. We don't want to attract unwanted attention. Can you do that for me?"

Poppy sniffed. "I'll try."

"Good. We'll get you safe and warm and you can have a good cryfest in the shower, okay?"

Poppy cracked a smile. "Okay."

The group traipsed back through the casino. Sam fished out the card the cab driver gave him. "Guys, let's find a secluded corner for a minute. I need to make a call."

Audra frowned, but didn't question him.

He dialed the driver.

"This is Denton."

"Denton, this is the guy you just dropped off at the Paris. Can you come back? And with a bigger car?"

"Yes, sir. Give me twenty minutes."

"Make it fifteen and you'll get a bigger tip."

"I'll see you in twelve."

The line clicked in Sam's ear, and he chuckled. Someone needed to put that guy on the racing circuit.

<h1 style="text-align:center">Thirty-Four</h1>

A soft tap sounded on Audra's hotel room door. She shot a quick glance at the bed by the window, where Poppy slept soundly. They'd come back to the hotel and quickly decided that Sam would move in with Dean and Max for the night. Poppy didn't need the worry about whether the strange man in the room would use her the way Simon did.

After a shower—and the long cry Audra promised her—the girl had fallen into a deep sleep. She didn't want to disturb that.

Tiptoeing across the room, she checked the peephole and saw Sam. She figured he'd show up sooner or later. She'd jumped royally off-script tonight. Unlocking the door, she cracked it open. "Hi."

"Hey. How's she doing?"

"Sleeping soundly."

"Can I come in? I won't stay long."

Audra stepped back and let him inside, then rebolted the door. She drew him into the bathroom and closed them in.

The door barely clicked shut before she was in his arms, their mouths fused together. Audra sank her fingers into his hair and held on as his hands roamed her body. She knew this wouldn't go anywhere tonight, that it was a response to the danger earlier, but she didn't care. She needed the connection as much as he did.

When they broke apart, their heavy breathing echoed in the tiled room.

"You scared the shit out of me tonight, Aud. This was not the plan."

"I know. I'm sorry. I couldn't leave her in that situation. Not once I got a good look at how young she was. I haven't asked her yet, but I'm betting she's only nineteen or twenty."

Sam grimaced. "We need to find out how she got into this situation. And make sure she has the resources not to fall back into it."

"Yeah. I plan to talk to Moran in the morning. With what I think she knows, they'll put her into protective custody. And I plan to stay on top of things and not let them just cut her loose with nothing once they're done with her."

"My team can help too. I'm sure Brooke could set her up with a job and help her get back on her feet."

She took his hands and stood on her toes to kiss his lips. Emotion washed over her. "Thank you for understanding. And for not being too angry."

"Never. You may not always do what I want you to, but you always have your reasons." A half smile tipped his mouth. "And they're usually good ones."

She grinned.

He leaned in and kissed her again, then rested his forehead on hers, still holding her hands. "I'm going to miss sleeping beside you tonight."

"Me too. But it's one night. I think we'll survive the sleep deprivation."

He smiled. "Hopefully." He straightened. "I should go. The guys and I set up a rotation to keep an eye on you two. To make sure she doesn't slip out while you're sleeping. There's a sitting area at the end of the hall. One of us will be there all night."

"Okay." She'd been a little worried about that very thing. She should have known Sam would have a plan. He'd been on top of everything so far.

"Tomorrow, we need to sit her down and pick her brain about those monthly deliveries. And on what she knows about why Brogan and Powell were brokering a deal."

"We will." She put her hands on his chest. "For now, give me one more goodnight kiss, then scram."

His mouth curved up, and he wrapped his arms around her waist. "Yes, ma'am."

THIRTY-FIVE

Audra led Poppy out of the room the next morning on their way to a meeting with the guys. She didn't want the girl to feel trapped, so she'd suggested they set up by the pool. Early in the morning, there wouldn't be too many guests out there.

Poppy huddled into the blue sweatshirt Audra let her borrow. She smiled, glad to see it offered the girl the same kind of comfort it offered her. Sometimes, all you needed was a little warmth and something soft.

They swung by the breakfast buffet on their way outside, where they each filled a plate. Audra only wanted fruit and some eggs, but Poppy seemed to have regained her appetite. She filled her plate high with a waffle, eggs, a biscuit, and three strips of bacon.

She caught Audra eyeing the stack and gave her a sheepish smile. "Sorry. I don't normally get to eat like this. Simon keeps me on a strict regimen of protein shakes, lean meat, and vegetables. I haven't had a waffle or bacon in the eight months I've been with him."

"I'm not judging. Eat whatever you want." Audra reached

for a coffee cup and filled it. Poppy poured a cup of orange juice and they headed for the pool.

Sam, Dean, and Max were already there with plates of their own.

"Good morning." She smiled as they approached the table.

The men smiled back and echoed her greeting.

Audra let Poppy sit at the end of the table, then took the empty seat next to Sam. Dean was at the other end and Max sat next to him, leaving the other seat next to Poppy open. The girl opened her syrup packet and poured it over her waffle.

"It's nice to see you have an appetite today," Sam said. "You only picked at that crepe last night."

Poppy cast him a quick look and lifted a shoulder. Audra turned and gave him a quick headshake. Food was a sensitive subject for the girl.

"Did you sleep well?" he asked, catching her point and changing the subject.

"I did. I wasn't sure I would, but I guess my mind felt safe enough to sleep." Poppy cut off a bite of her waffle and popped it in her mouth.

"And how are you feeling?" Max asked. "You were on some pretty heavy drugs."

Poppy's movements paused for half a second before she resumed cutting another bite. "I feel okay. A little anxious. And like I need a hit. But I'll manage. I feel more like myself than I have in a long time." Her chin wobbled. "As much as I don't want to confront what's happened, I don't want to go back there." Her words ended on a choked whisper.

"That won't happen." Audra laid a hand on her shoulder. "I'll make sure of that."

Poppy pressed her lips together and nodded.

"What did he give you?" Max asked. "Some drugs can have nasty withdrawal effects."

"Um, mostly ketamine. How much depended on—on

what he, um, wanted to—to do." She looked down at her plate. "He didn't like it when I screamed," she whispered.

Audra reached for Sam's hand and squeezed. It was preferable to crumpling her coffee cup and burning her hand. Sam held tight to her fingers.

"How old are you, Poppy?" Max asked.

She looked at him through her lashes. "Nineteen."

Audra forced herself to calm down. "Can you tell us what happened? How you ended up the way you did?"

Poppy lifted one shoulder. "Like anybody else, I guess. I was a foster kid. My mom OD'd when I was ten. My dad was in prison for armed robbery. His parents were too old to take me in, and my mom's parents washed their hands of her when she got hooked on drugs. I moved around for the first couple of years, then I thought I'd found a place I'd never have to leave." A soft smile lit her face, making her look much younger than nineteen.

"The Osterman's were nice. They had a daughter my age, and we got along great. It was like having a real sister, you know?" Her smile faded. "Alex—the dad—he got offered a big promotion. Out of state. Like, really big. He couldn't pass it up. So, they left. And I had to stay. My dad wouldn't relinquish his rights or allow them to take me with them." The piece of bacon she'd picked up crumbled as she made a fist. She let the pieces fall back to her plate. "I ended up in a group home. It was—not nice. Nobody hurt me; not physically. But nobody cared, either. I was bullied. All the way up until I aged out of the system."

She glanced up. "After I finished high school, I got a job in one of the clubs. Dancing. I was too young, but the owner— he didn't care. It wasn't the nicest establishment. But it paid well enough I could afford my own place." She pushed at the crumbled bacon, piling it on one side of her plate.

"One night, I walked out the back door, on my way to

catch the monorail home. I didn't even make it to the corner. An SUV turned down the alley and a man jumped out. I was in the backseat before I knew what happened. I don't remember much after that. They drugged me and took me to a warehouse. I woke up in a large cage with several other women."

"This was one of those 'deliveries' you mentioned, wasn't it?" Audra asked.

Poppy nodded, eyes downcast. "Yeah. Someone snatches the women and brings them to the warehouse on Coleman. I don't know who. I just see them when they're paraded in front of Simon and Geoffrey."

"They make you watch?" Dean said.

"I'm in the room, yeah. It's this area of the warehouse that's been converted to a large lounge. There are couches and a bar. I sit there and listen to Simon, Geoffrey, and Celine rate each of the women."

"Wait." Audra frowned. "The woman with Geoffrey at dinner the other week? She participates in that?"

Poppy nodded. "She's a piece of work. She told me she was one of those girls once too. And like Simon did with me, Geoffrey took a shine to her. Except she embraced it and turned it around to work in her favor. She's an active participant in all their criminal activity. I think that's what Simon was hoping for with me. Celine even told me I just needed to change my thinking. That I'd be much happier if I acted like her. But I just couldn't. It's just so... so... *wrong*."

Audra agreed. "Did you ever see the people who bought these women?"

"Every time. They held the auctions in the lounge." Tears welled in her eyes. "I hated it," she whispered. "I'd beg Simon to drug me so I'd forget seeing those women look at me with pleading in their eyes. But he always laughed and said no. That he wanted me to remember what would happen to me if I didn't cooperate. He said he'd sell me and that there was no guarantee my buyer would be as kind as he was." She sniffed. "In many ways, I'm actually thankful I ended up with Simon when I was snatched. He likes a—a pliant lover and not a fighting one. I've learned if I make enough noise, he gives me more drugs, and then I don't remember any of it."

Audra's heart broke for the girl. She shouldn't be thankful for any of it.

"I'm not dumb, you know. I know that some of those men like to inflict pain. If I ran, and Simon caught me, I knew he'd hand me over to one of them. Living a life high as a kite was preferable to one filled with pain."

"I think you're very brave, Poppy." Audra's voice rasped with unshed tears. This girl had lived a nightmare few could comprehend. "You did all the right things to keep yourself alive."

Poppy gave a jerky nod. She picked up her orange juice and took a drink.

"Do you know when the next auction is?" Sam asked.

Audra sent him a quick glance. His gaze met hers. She could tell he was thinking what she was. They could bring the entire operation down if they raided one of these events.

"Next weekend. Their buyers come to town on Fridays. They look through the 'merchandise,'"—she air-quoted—"eat a lot, and drink even more. The auction is always Saturday night. Some of them elect to stay until Sunday. Others take the women they bought and leave."

"Do you think they'll still hold it with you missing?" Max asked.

"I think they'll have to. They've sent out the invites and already have several women to sell."

"Invites?" Max sat straighter. "How does someone get an invite?"

"The website."

"They have a website?" Sam's eyebrows shot up. He shook his head. "I shouldn't be surprised. The dark web is a horrible place."

"How do you know all this?" Audra asked. "Does he really not care if you hear it?"

"Some of it, no. Celine talks too." A bit of a smirk toyed with her lips. "I've done some snooping too. Just on the out chance that I'd end up with the police. I wanted a bargaining chip, so I never had to go back."

"Well, I think you've got a good one," Sam said. He turned to Audra. "You need to call Moran. We don't have the power to arrest anyone."

"I think we should call Asher too," Max said. "See if he can find that site and wrangle us an invitation so we can get someone inside. If we can get Simon and Geoffrey in custody, we have a real chance at finding out if they wanted to distribute drugs or people for Brogan."

"They didn't know what he wanted," Poppy chimed in.

Four sets of eyes turned on her.

"What do you mean?" Audra asked.

"He called them. Brogan, I mean. Simon didn't know what he wanted. He just said that the head of the Irish mafia in town wanted to have dinner to discuss business."

"They didn't talk much business that night." Audra frowned, running the evening back through her mind.

"I don't remember much of it. That was a day when Simon wanted... more. I was pretty high at dinner."

Audra's mouth flattened as she reined in her temper. Simon was going to pay for all he'd done, one way or another. She looked at the others. "That's rather odd. Why would he call a meeting and then not talk about business? Especially when he didn't tell them what it was about?"

"You're sure they didn't talk details?" Dean asked.

"Not in front of me, no. But I was late to dinner." She turned to Poppy. "You don't remember anything?"

"Not much, no. I remember you. Sort of. It's your eyes. They were kind. Until you looked at Simon. I remember that. You looked like you wanted to rip his throat out."

"I did. I still do. Is there anything else?"

Poppy glanced away, a far off look on her face. After several moments, she shook her head. "No. I'm sorry. I get vague snatches of the restaurant. There's an image of the salad I had for dinner. You. That's it. I'm sorry." A crestfallen look took over her pretty face.

"Don't be sorry," Audra said. "You've been a tremendous help."

"She's right, Poppy," Sam said. "Now, how about you—eat more of your—food?"

Audra laid a hand on his thigh. He'd been good lately with the stuttering. Hearing Poppy's account of what she'd been through was horrifying, so she wasn't surprised his emotions were high.

"We'll take things from here," Max said. "You'll have to talk to the authorities, but you have our word you'll be safe."

Poppy's chin wobbled again. "You're sure? What if—" She broke off and sniffed. "What if there are cops on Simon's payroll?"

"Poppy, you stumbled into the right people, okay?" Dean leaned forward. "No one's going to hurt you with us involved."

The girl smiled, her eyes watery. "Okay," she whispered.

Thirty-Six

An ache twinged in Audra's hip and back. Grimacing, she flopped onto her other side with a huff. This hotel bed was infinitely worse than the previous one. They'd changed hotels after they turned Poppy over to Moran. Not only because they didn't want anyone at the previous hotel to associate them with her if someone should come asking about the girl. They simply didn't want to stay anywhere more than a week. It made them more memorable with the staff the longer they stayed. They'd also wanted to be closer to the warehouse where the auction would be. It made staking the place out easier.

She rolled again, still uncomfortable. She wished they'd picked a hotel with better beds, though. This was night five here. Audra was thankful they were nearing the end of this part of their mission. After Saturday, she intended to move to a different hotel whether the guys came with her or not.

"Do you want to use me as your mattress?" Sam's low voice rumbled over the sound of the air-conditioner humming under the window.

"No," she huffed. "I'm fine."

"That's bullshit, and you know it, Aud." His strong hands wrapped around her waist and pulled. She slid over his side to sprawl across his chest and abdomen on her belly.

Stacking her fists, she propped her chin on top and stared at him in the near-darkness. "It's not just the bed keeping me awake."

His hands rubbed the small of her back in soothing circles. "Worried about tomorrow?"

"Yeah. We need this to go well. For Simon and Geoffrey to be arrested and to cooperate. I don't want to look over my shoulder for the rest of my life."

He hummed a non-answer and continued his soothing circles. "You said you were contemplating leaving the spy game. Are you still thinking that?"

"More now than ever. It doesn't hold the same appeal anymore. I mean, there have been a few close calls, but this one —" She stopped and sighed. "It just hit harder. I've never not been able to trust my team. If I hadn't run into you in February—" She stopped again as emotions clogged her throat, forming a hard lump. "I don't want to think about where I'd be or what could have happened."

"You'd have figured it out, honey. Don't second guess yourself. It doesn't do any good."

"I know. Doesn't make it any easier, though." She sniffed and waved a hand. "Let's talk about something else."

"Like what?"

"Why did you come running when I asked for help?"

"You know why."

"I know what you said. That I'm important to you, blah, blah, blah. But *why* am I important to you? It's been ten years, Sam."

He sat up, scooting back to sit against the headboard. She moved with him, still resting on his chest. His hands resumed their circles on her back.

"Remember on the plane when I mentioned how it was my friends and thoughts of you that kept me going after my brain injury?"

A furrow dug into her forehead. "Yeah."

"When I was—injured, after I woke up, I was in a lot of pain. My brain wasn't firing right, so I'd get a lot of nerve pain. In my legs, especially. There wasn't much the doctors could do except medicate me into oblivion, and I didn't like that. I also had a lot of trouble organizing my thoughts enough to get words to come out. It was a lot of noise going on in my head. One of the therapists I worked with—she suggested retraining my brain. That when I felt the pain or when my thoughts were jumbling up and tripping over each other, to picture something that could drown everything thing else out. Something—good."

He skimmed his thumb over her cheek, turning her face so he could look into her eyes. Audra's breath caught at the intense look that glittered in his eyes. Even in the barely lit room, she could see it.

"I used memories of you—of us—to banish the pain and to calm my mind. When I thought about us, everything stood still. My mind cleared; the pain receded. Eventually, I got to a point where I could silence things without even thinking about it. But it all started with you. You—memories of you— got me through some of the darkest days of my life, Audra. There isn't anything I wouldn't do for you."

Audra's heart cracked open in that moment. All the feelings she'd been shoving to the side to deal with at a later date rushed out, overwhelming her. She turned her head, pressing a kiss to his palm, as she tried to sort through them. They'd offhandedly talked about staying together. He'd been adamant he wasn't leaving her again. But she'd kept pushing thoughts of what she wanted away, trying to focus on this mission. She couldn't do that anymore.

She loved him.

"Aud? You all right?"

"Yeah." She sat up, then leaned in to align her mouth with his. "I love you, Sam Brackley. I think I always have."

The hand stroking her back stilled. His entire body froze beneath her. Then it was like she'd flipped a switch. The hand on her face threaded into her hair, and he pulled her in, kissing her with more passion than she'd ever felt. It was like he wanted to consume her.

She knew the feeling. Holding his head in her hands, she kissed him back. Her body grew warm as desire flooded her veins. She needed this man like she needed air to breathe.

Still naked from their bout of lovemaking when they went to bed, it was easy for Audra to lift her hips and slide back down over his erect shaft. Seated deep inside her, she felt like he'd touched her soul.

And he had. Not with their lovemaking, but with his words. His beautiful, broken words that he'd fought so hard to be able to say. Words she had a hand in making possible. She'd never been someone's inspiration before. That she was his was humbling. He was so strong and kind. The sort of man many men wanted to be.

And he was all hers. She was his. Wholly and completely. She understood what all the books and movies were about now. What it meant to find your person.

He pulled back from their kiss to look into her eyes. With one hand on her hip, guiding her as she rode him, he cradled her face with the other. "I love you, Audra. You're stuck with me."

She gave a jerky nod, words failing her as the heat created by the friction of their bodies consumed her. "I'm—I'm all right with that."

He kissed her again, holding her close as their bodies

moved together. When she broke, he swallowed her cry, his own mixing in a moment later.

Ears ringing from the most intense orgasm of her life, she flopped against him. Their chests heaved in unison, and she could taste the salt from his skin when she pressed a light kiss to his collarbone.

His hand landed on her back, resuming the slow circles from earlier. Audra's eyelids drifted closed. Sleep finally tugged at the edges of her mind, growing heavier with each stroke of his hand. He slipped out of bed as her muscles turned to jelly, then came back a moment later with a damp cloth. She murmured a thank you as he cleaned her up. The last thing she noted before sleep fully cloaked her brain was Sam snuggling up to her back and the soft press of his lips to her hair as he whispered, "I love you so much."

Thirty-Seven

Sam snapped another picture as a car pulled up to the gate at the Powells' warehouse. He and the others, plus Moran and a tech from his unit, were in a utility van parked in the visitor's parking at the scrapyard next door. This was the tenth car he'd photographed. He glanced back at the technician, Jessica Dorset. "Did that one come through okay? He was speeding." The fancy camera Moran put in his hands earlier was a marvel of modern technology. It uploaded the images as soon as he took them. Jessica was running license plates in real time.

"It's fine. A little blurry, but the software will clean it up."

"There's another one coming," Moran said.

Sam aimed the camera out the back window and started snapping as the luxury sports car drove by.

Max whistled. "That's a nice car. Nicest we've seen so far."

"For sure." Sam took several shots as the car slowed to turn into the Powells' drive, giving him a perfect view of the rear license plate. "Let's hope we can catch them red-handed tomorrow and Moran can seize that car and whatever cash the guy has. It'd go a long way toward stopping more of this kind of activity." He turned to Audra. "You getting anything from the license plates, babe?"

She let out a soft snort. "It's a bloody goldmine. A lot of the vehicles are coming back to corporations, but they're ones we know about that are fronts for illegal activity. What I'm not seeing, though, are ones tied to the Irish mafia."

"Maybe they didn't get that far in their relationship," Dean said. "You did say you thought their meeting was just a feel each other out type of thing."

"I know. But I missed the beginning, so..." She trailed off and shrugged.

Max's phone dinged. He looked at the screen. "It's an email from Asher. He's done with my new identity." Opening it, he skimmed it. "Oh, come on, man!"

Sam chuckled. "Let me guess. He gave you a shitty name?"

"Heinrich von Ribbentrop."

Audra chuckled. "Well, that seems fitting."

"Why? Do I look like a Heinrich von Ribbentrop?"

"No. I just meant the name is fitting for the op. Joachim von Ribbentrop was a bad dude. He was instrumental in making Hitler the German Chancellor. The man was one of his closest confidantes during World War II. And a filthy rich businessman."

"How do you know this?" Moran asked.

She shrugged. "I'm English. We know our war history."

"Wonderful." Max rolled his eyes. "I'm a Nazi."

"Better brush up on your German accent," Dean said with a chuckle.

"Stuff it, Adler. I'm going to be his American cousin."

"Got another car." Moran sat forward, peering through the tinted window. "An SUV."

Sam took more pictures.

"I still don't know how your guy swung that invitation." Moran glanced at Max. "Who is he again?"

Max snorted. "Nice try. You don't get more than his first name."

Sam frowned at the FBI agent. They'd all agreed that the less the feds knew about them, the better. It was bad enough Moran knew their identities. He'd be able to figure out who the rest of their group was if he really tried. He was hoping they would prove helpful enough—and that Audra had enough sway—that the man would leave it alone, though.

Suddenly, Max laughed. "Oh, this is great." He had his phone in his hand and looked up from it at Dean. "You're going with me. As Bernard Almendinger." He turned to Moran. "You too. As Manfred Ulrich."

"What?" Dean snatched the phone from his hand and read the email. He groaned. "Ford thinks it's too dangerous for Max to go in alone, so he made Asher create two more identities." He thrust the phone back at Max. "That's just fricking fantastic. Just what I wanted to do. Watch a bunch of sorry excuses for men salivate over scared, traumatized women."

"Look at it this way," Audra said. "You'll get to be one of the first to liberate them."

Dean grunted an acknowledgment. "I'd rather be a sniper on a neighboring rooftop, taking all the assholes out one-by-one."

"I can probably get my hands on some explosives," Sam said, watching out the window. "We could round the fuckers up after we get the girls out and blow up the place. Moran, you should probably turn your ears off for a minute. You, too, Dorset."

Moran chuckled. "No dice, man. I like that plan, but we can't."

Sam sighed. It was a shame they couldn't. The world wouldn't miss men like that. "I know."

Over the next couple of hours, they catalogued close to

thirty cars arriving at the compound. It made Sam sick to think how many women were inside, waiting to be sold to some depraved human being. How many had already been sold. It would all end tomorrow, though. The Powells were finished robbing women of their lives.

THIRTY-EIGHT

"Man, these are some fancy threads." Moran smoothed a hand down the sleeve of his suit jacket. "I still can't believe that tailor worked so fast."

"Gotta dress the part to fool the Powells and their goons." Max strapped a Rolex to his wrist. "It helped that I'd already bought three suits from him. He was more than willing to work overtime to make two more for you and Dean."

Sam handed an in-ear earpiece to Moran. "We'll be on comms the entire time."

"So long as they haven't scrambled communications." Dean took an earpiece and put it in his ear.

"Hopefully, they still think they're flying under the radar." Sam handed the last one to Max. "You each have a camera, though, so at least we'll have footage of the event Moran can use in court later." They'd opted for some small tie-tack cameras with a built in micro-SD backup. It would transmit real-time video as well as record it on the card in case the signal was cut.

Moran adjusted his tie tack, straightening it. "Poppy said she doesn't think they scan for bugs, and that the men use their phones throughout the auction. It's only weapons they look for. We should be good."

"Are we ready?" Dean tugged on his jacket. Straightening it over his broad shoulders.

"I think so." Audra glanced at Jessica. "Are you picking up signals from all of their equipment?"

Dorset nodded. "Yep. We're good." She closed her laptop. "Let's roll."

They left their hotel through a side entrance and piled into Max's rented SUV. They'd left the utility truck parked around the corner from the warehouse. Max would drop Sam, Audra, and Jessica off there, then continue to the auction site with Dean and Dominick. Another FBI surveillance van and several undercover state trooper units were waiting in the area, ready to swoop in to make arrests once their team had all the evidence needed to shut down the ring. Moran had done his best to limit who knew about the plan to people he trusted.

The drive to the van was a short one. In minutes, they were installed inside. Jessica hooked up the camera and audio feeds to her monitors, and they each took a seat in front of one.

"Here we go," Sam muttered as Max pulled up to the gate. Mentally, he crossed his fingers and toes that the invitation Asher stole from their system would hold up.

Max flashed his phone screen at the guard.

The man took the phone and glanced at it, then peered into the car. "Who are your friends? This invitation is for you."

"No one said I couldn't bring my buddies. We all have certain... tastes, shall we say? And deep pockets. Your bosses won't be disappointed that I brought them."

The guard studied them once more, then handed the phone back. He stepped back and waved at someone out of view. Max rolled up the window and drove through.

"Bleck," Max said. "I feel dirty having uttered those words."

"Yeah, well, we're about to feel even dirtier." Dean took off his seatbelt as Max pulled up to the entrance.

Putting the car in park, they all got out. Max handed the keys to a valet and approached the door. Another guard scanned them for weapons, then waved them in. They entered into a long hallway that had been constructed with heavy black cloth and metal poles. Fairy lights lined the corridor, leading them down to the lounge Poppy mentioned. Inside, men in expensive suits milled around, sipping cocktails and champagne. Women in barely there dresses wandered the room with trays of drinks and hors d'oeuvres.

Sam heard Audra gasp as they saw one of the guests snake a hand under one of the server's skirts and palm her butt. The woman let out a tinkling giggle, but the pinched expression on her face told him what she really thought of the move. He couldn't help but wonder how many of these women were stolen ones whom Simon and Geoffrey "rescued" for their own gain.

"Split up and mingle," Moran said. "Get as many faces on camera as you can." He lifted a glass from one of the server's trays and walked away.

Max and Dean did the same.

"Good evening, Mr. von Ribbentrop."

Sam leaned forward as a man approached Max.

"Hello."

The man extended a hand. "I'm Geoffrey Powell."

Max shook his hand. "Hi. Heinrich. You can call me Rich."

Sam snorted. Leave it to Max to find a way around a false name he didn't like.

"Thanks for the last-minute invitation. Our latest business

trip was grueling. The next one doesn't look like it'll be much better. It'll be nice to have a way to unwind right on hand."

"Yes, my guards told me you brought a couple of friends along. For future reference, we don't normally allow that sort of thing without advance notice. Security protocol. You understand?"

"Of course. My apologies. I appreciate that you let them in this time."

"Yes, well, I did my due diligence on you. You have deep pockets, so I'm expecting you to bid often and well."

"I pay for quality merchandise, Mr. Powell."

"We have that, I assure you."

"I don't suppose you'd let me take a peek, would you? Since I missed the preview night?"

Geoffrey tipped his head. "I suppose we could do that. Gather your friends and meet me by the bar." He walked away.

"Yuck," Max muttered.

"Yuck, indeed," Jessica said.

"I do not want to watch this." Audra pressed her fingers to her eyes, then blinked several times. "Human trafficking was not what I signed up for with this op. Liam's never been in the flesh trade, from what our intel said."

"I guess he's branching out," Jessica replied.

"I still haven't seen anyone I recognize."

"The night's still young." Sam shifted in his seat. "It doesn't look like everyone is there yet."

"No. It's cocktail hour." Audra wrinkled her nose, disgust dripping off her words.

Max walked up to Dean and poked him in the shoulder. "Come on." He led him away, and together, they found Dominick.

"What are we doing?" Moran asked.

"Geoffrey offered us a tour of the merchandise."

"Great," Dean grumbled.

"Quit your bitching, *Bernard*. It gives us a lay of the land for the raid," Max said.

"I'm going to kill Asher when we get back."

"I'll help you."

They reached the bar, where Geoffrey was waiting.

The older man smiled. "Introduce me to your friends."

"Of course. This is Bernie and Manny."

"It's nice to meet you both. I'm Geoffrey. This way." He turned and led them through a door in the wall behind the bar.

The music and chatter from the party faded as they entered the darkened warehouse.

"Excuse the mess. We run a legitimate business out of here as well. Have to keep up the front to keep the cops away." Geoffrey chuckled. "Though a few well-placed bribes help with that as well."

Jessica shook her head. "So many people are going down. I can't wait."

"So you have a fairly sophisticated operation, then?" Max asked. "Your location leaves something to be desired, but your refreshments and entertainment are nice. Tell me, are your servers part of the sale?"

Geoffrey tipped his head, glancing back as he stopped at a door. "I'm sure we could come to an arrangement." He produced a set of keys from his pocket and inserted one into the lock. Before he turned the handle, he looked at them. "This is strictly a look-only preview. You cannot test the merchandise before purchase. And all the ladies are dressed for the auction, so please don't ask them to disrobe. I think you will find their outfits satisfactory, though. We try to put their best assets on display. My fiancée has a keen eye for fashion and what looks good on the female form." He pushed the door open.

"Oh my God." Audra covered her mouth as the image on their screens changed.

Sam clenched his teeth, disgust churning in his gut at what he saw. The men had stepped into a room that was about thirty-by-thirty in size. A prison cell took up most of it, leaving only a six-foot strip along the front, outside of the bars. Inside the cage, dozens of women sat huddled in groups, staring at them with wide eyes.

"All of you on your feet." Geoffrey motioned for them to stand. "Line up."

With a sluggishness born of being drugged, the women got up and did as he asked.

"Oh my." Jessica squinted at the screen. "Some of them look really young."

"They do, yeah." Sam pushed the button on the panel in front of him that would let him talk to Max. "Max, tell him you like the young ones. Let's see how young they go." They could be looking at heftier charges if some of the girls were underage.

"You've got some nice girls. I prefer young ones. Like that one, maybe." He pointed at a young, dark-haired girl in a pink dress. "Virgins, preferably."

"Many of our clientele are the same way, though not all of our girls are virgins. Sometimes, there's something to be said for a woman with experience."

"That's true. I have one of those at home, though, so I'm really on the lookout for a young, nubile little thing."

Geoffrey nodded. "I understand that. My fiancée is a tigress in bed, but sometimes you just need that virgin under you to feel like a man."

Sam felt bile work up his throat.

"The one you pointed at is a good choice. She's sixteen." Geoffrey walked down the line and pointed out several more who were between sixteen and nineteen. "We don't tend to deal in girls younger than sixteen. It gets too messy. The authorities look harder for the younger ones."

"I'm going to nail his arse to the wall and make sure he ends up with a group of murderers who hate pedophiles." Audra shook her head.

"I'll help you," Jessica said.

The four men spent a few more minutes discussing the women, then Geoffrey led them back to the party. It was more crowded now.

"Aud, you see anyone you recognize now?" Sam kept his eyes on the screen, cataloguing new faces.

"I'm looking. So far no—wait." She tipped her head, then reached for the panel to talk to Dean, whose camera she monitored. "Dean. The guy in the silver suit and blue tie. Get closer."

Dean walked toward one of the servers holding an hors d'oeuvres tray who was in the man's path.

"Shit." Audra leaned in. "That's Donny."

THIRTY-NINE

Audra kept her gaze on the screen, watching Donny interact with another man she didn't recognize. "Stay with him, Dean." She scanned what she could see of the room, looking for Patrick. She didn't see him, but she couldn't see everything.

"You got it," he muttered. Munching on his hors d'oeuvres, he walked around, getting into conversations with several people, but keeping his camera aimed at Donny.

She saw Simon approach and hit the intercom. "That's Simon. Can you get close enough to hear their conversation?"

Dean excused himself from his current conversation and walked to an empty table nearby, snagging another drink from a server as he went. The last one had ended up on a table still full. They'd all pretended to sip the expensive liquor, getting new drinks on occasion to eliminate suspicion.

"Nice crowd, Simon," Donny said.

"Thanks. We got... blood." The audio cut out as Simon turned his head.

"I noticed. Quite a few new faces."

"We had a good-sized crop of girls this time, thanks to you.

I don't know how you did it with Brogan breathing down your neck."

Donny scoffed and took a sip of his drink. "Liam's an idiot who can't see the forest for the trees. With the cut I get from tonight's sales, I'll have the backing to take over. I've got the hits lined up on him, his bitch of a mother, and my annoying brother. I just need the cash."

Simon slapped him on the shoulder. "I still can't believe you want to take out your own flesh and blood."

"He's too far up Siobhan Brogan's ancient ass. He'd never follow me, and that makes him a liability." He lifted a shoulder, then raised his drink to his lips. "It's just business."

"That answers whether Patrick's involved." Audra shook her head.

Someone called Simon's name.

"If you'll excuse me?" Simon backed away.

"Of course. We'll talk again later." A smirk graced Donny's face. "I might negotiate a slightly lower fee for one of those girls back there."

Simon grinned. "Take your pick."

Dean lifted his drink. "I'm going to be sick." He took an actual swig of the alcohol, then set the glass down and got up. "Can we bring the cavalry in now?"

"Soon," Moran said. "Money needs to change hands. Then we'll call it."

Dean growled softly.

"Smile," Max said. "You look like an ogre."

"Good. Give me a club, and I'll beat all these sickos." He huffed a sigh. "Sorry. I'm done now."

"Who's Simon talking to?" Sam asked her.

"I don't know. No one I recognize."

The meet and greet portion of the evening went on for another twenty minutes before Geoffrey got up in front of everyone with a microphone. Audra listened as he laid out the ground rules for the auction.

"Those of you who've been here before know the rules, but we have some new faces tonight, so I'll lay them out for you. There aren't many. My lovely ladies here are distributing numbered paddles. Raise it to bid. The women up for auction will appear on this screen." He pointed up, and a screen dropped down from the ceiling. "All transactions will be done immediately after the close of each round of bidding, and all sales are final. None of the women will be released until the auction is finished. At that point, you may collect your merchandise. We have several rooms beyond the lounge where you may have some time alone with them, or you're free to leave. The rooms are first come, first served."

Audra wrinkled her nose and glanced at Agent Dorset. "We need to get people in place now, so we can get in there before any of those girls are harmed."

Jessica nodded and reached for the phone.

Tuning her out as she circled the wagons and fed the entry team the warehouse layout, Audra paid attention to the auction, taking notes of names Geoffrey mentioned as the men bid and matching them to a paddle number. He was making their job too easy.

It took over an hour for him to go through all thirty-seven women. The moment the last buyer paid, Jessica gave the signal for the team to move in.

Audra pushed the button to communicate with all three men inside. "Get ready."

Muffled flash-bangs erupted, both outside the van and through Max, Dom, and Dean's microphones. A murmur went through the crowd.

Movement near the bar caught Audra's attention. Donny was heading for the rear exit. She hit her intercom button, connecting her to Dean. "Dean. Donny. Door behind the bar."

"I see him."

The camera image shook as Dean hurried after him. Sam's screen wobbled as well. Max was on his heels.

"I'll watch the Powells," Moran said. "Go." The brothers and Celine were heading for the curtained entrance.

Another bang sounded, this one inside the warehouse. Several of the women in the room screamed. A few of the men yelled that it was time to leave, even as the group scattered.

Dean and Max went through the door after Donny. The man glanced back, his eyes widening as he saw them.

"Callahan, stop!" Dean started after him.

Donny took off at a run.

Dean cursed. "I can't run in these damn shoes. Stop, you bastard!" Despite his words, he ran through the warehouse at a good clip.

Audra slammed her fist on the arm of her seat. "Dammit! I want to be in there. I should be." She kept her eyes on the screen. The picture bobbed wildly as Dean ran, growing darker as they went deeper into the warehouse.

"Where did he go?" Max asked.

"I'm not sure. You go left. And be careful."

"You too."

They split up.

"Do you see anything?" Audra asked Sam.

"No. Shelves. You?"

"The same. Bloody hell! He better not get away."

"I've got movement on the backside of the building." A new voice cut in over the radio that sat in front of Jessica. It was someone from the entry team. "Single male. Gray suit. Running northbound."

"That's Donny. He'll have to hop the fence to get out."

She hit the intercom that let her talk to all three men. "Guys, he's outside."

"Copy," Max said.

A unit replied that they were on their way over. Seconds later, a state patrol car raced past their van and around the corner.

Both Max and Dean's cameras lightened as they made it out of the building.

"Dean, do you see him?"

"No. Audra, does anyone have a visual on him?"

She relayed the message to the entry team.

"Negative," came the reply. "He ducked behind some ISO containers and I lost him."

Audra shoved her chair back. She reached for the box containing the comm units and grabbed an earpiece and button mic.

"Aud, what are you doing?" Sam frowned up at her from his seat.

"Going after him."

"Max and Dean will find him."

"No. This is my op. That bastard isn't getting away." She stuffed the earpiece into her ear and stuck the small mic on her collar.

"Aud—"

"You can't stop me, Sam. You're welcome to come along, but you can't stop me."

With a curse, he got up. "Give me the box."

She handed it to him, then headed for the door.

"Audra, would you wait?"

She hesitated a couple of seconds while he scrambled to take out a set of comms. Once he had both pieces, she stepped out of the van and took off to the north. A few moments later, she heard the thud of his shoes on the pavement, and he soon caught up to her.

"Babe, slow down. You need to keep your head about you." He grabbed her wrist, slowing her. "We can't go into this without a plan. It'll get us killed."

She sucked a breath in through her nose, his touch grounding her some. "You're right. We need to approach with caution." She shook her hand free. "When we get there." She took off running again. Her hip twinged, but she pushed through it. It was just pain. The joint was sound.

They rounded the corner and passed the end of the scrapyard's fence. It butted up to the taller chain link fencing surrounding the Powells' warehouse property.

Sam activated his mic. "Max, Dean, we're outside to the north. You see him?"

"No. It's a maze in here," Max said.

"Let's find an opening and get inside. We can help search." Audra began walking, pushing on the chain link at each pole they passed to see if it was loose.

At one of them, the fencing pushed inward. "Here." She hooked her fingers over the metal and shook it. "I think it's loose enough we can get under."

Sam bent down and grabbed near the bottom, pushing it up and in. "Go."

Audra slithered under the fence. On the other side, she grasped the metal and leaned back with all of her weight, pulling it back as far as she could so that Sam could get his larger frame under it.

His shirt caught, but he made it under and freed himself.

"You all right?" she asked.

He nodded. "Let's go."

They crept into the yard with cautious steps. Sirens blipped in the distance and angry male voices carried through the night air. The raid was in full swing. She hoped Moran was all right and had stopped Simon and Geoffrey from getting away.

"Jesus, Max was right. This place is insane." Sam glanced from side-to-side as they entered the sea of ISO containers.

"We need to split up."

"No way. I'm flypaper on your backside, sweetie."

She huffed a laugh. "Nice imagery. But seriously, we'll cover more ground separately. And I'm armed." She removed the gun from her waist holster and held it at her side. The FBI had allowed her to carry a weapon, but refused it for Sam and his team since they were civilians. She knew they didn't need them to capture someone or protect themselves. They were just as deadly barehanded.

"Doesn't matter, babe. I'm not letting you out of my sight."

She sighed. He wasn't giving in. Instead of wasting time arguing, she waded deeper into the containers. "I am a trained operative, you know," she whispered as they came to a junction.

"Yep."

"And I can take care of myself."

"I know. Which way are we going?"

Audra ground her molars together. Damn stubborn mule.

Scuffling to their left drew her attention. Sam shifted on his feet. He raised a finger to his lips and tipped his head toward the sound. She nodded. Raising her gun, she led the way.

A flash of gray appeared between two containers. They hurried forward, but were forced to take cover when a bullet pinged off the metal above Audra's head.

"Damn, that was close." Sam activated his mic. "Dean, Max, we've got him. Near the north fence."

"Coming," Dean said.

"Sam, you go around. I'll come up from this side. We'll box him in."

"No."

She groaned. "Will you stop with the macho thing? I have the gun. If anything, I should be asking you not to leave. But I know what you can do with those hands and feet. You don't need a gun. Donny's going to get away if we don't split up."

His jaw worked. "Fine. But Aud—" He stopped and shook his head. "I love you. Be careful."

She kissed him quick. "I will. I love you too. Now go." She nudged his shoulder.

With a long look, he disappeared around the other side of the ISO container.

Audra drew in a deep breath, steadying herself. She rolled her shoulders to loosen the tension and crept forward on the balls of her feet. Silence reined in front of her. Where had he gone?

She reached the end of the container and swung around it, gun raised.

Nothing.

Moving forward, she glimpsed Sam coming up from the other side. She shook her head, then continued forward clearing space after several more shipping containers. She strained to hear any sound over the police presence at the warehouse.

A muffled whisper reached her. She stilled, then glanced back, looking for Sam. He wasn't there. She knew she could reach him on the comms, but didn't dare try. If that was Donny whispering, he'd hear her.

Audra slunk forward. The whisper grew louder, but she couldn't pinpoint it. This deep into the containers, sounds echoed wildly.

"Get your ass here now!" came a fierce whisper.

Back against the end of a container, she listened, but didn't hear anymore. She thought it had come from her right, but couldn't be certain. Edging forward, she peeked around the side. The aisle was empty.

A click sounded behind her. She froze, recognizing the sound of a hammer being drawn back. Slowly, she turned.

Donny stood there, a revolver in his hand. His eyes widened slightly as he saw her face, then he grinned. "Hello, Alexandra." He moved closer. "Though I don't think that's your real name. Who are you, really?"

Muscles stiff, she faced him stoically.

"Don't want to talk? That's okay. You can come with me, and we can talk back at my place. I'm sure you'll be more willing to open that pretty mouth there. Drop the gun."

She held on to it.

He sighed. "Don't make me shoot you. It'd be a waste of a pretty face."

When she still just stood there, he raised his gun. "One."

Audra's jaw worked.

"Two."

She glanced to the side, hoping Sam would come around the corner.

Donny tsked. "Don't make me say three."

The words were light, but an edge of steel ran behind them. Audra dropped her gun.

"Good girl. Let's go." He motioned her forward.

She kept her feet planted.

Donny's face turned hard as stone. He stalked forward. "I'm not playing this game with you all night." He grabbed her arm and stuffed his pistol into her ribs. "Move." With a hard shove, he pushed her forward.

"You don't need to do this, Donny." She slipped into her American accent. From the question in his voice when he asked her name, she didn't think he knew she was an undercover operative. He didn't know who she was. There was still a chance she could sweet talk him into letting her go or simply making a mistake.

"Yes, I do. You know too much, and I have questions about—"

A quick burst of gunfire sounded from the warehouse, interrupting him. Her heart rate sped up. That wasn't good.

Donny pushed her forward again, moving more quickly now. "I'm not even sure how much you do know. Just that you know enough. Why are you here, anyway? Have you been following me since I offed your lover in the park? That's what he was to you, isn't it? Your lover? You know, that weasel blackmailed me for a lot of money? I stole it all from Liam, but still. The audacity. But I took care of him. I thought I'd taken care of you too. But then your picture showed up on the news the next morning."

They reached the edge of the field of ISO containers. Audra moved her eyes side-to-side, looking for anyone on her team. Where *were* they?

Donny pushed her into the open and toward the fence that was now only meters away. "Liam was very upset to learn you'd betrayed him. He put a price on your head, but you'd vanished like a vapor. Are you here to take revenge for your dead lover?"

"Audra! Where are you?" Sam's voice echoed through her head.

She wanted to call out to him, but didn't dare. Instead, she decided to play along with Donny. "How did you know he was my lover? We weren't near each other at the park that night."

"I saw him at your house. He liked to sit outside and watch you. Just like I did."

Her eyes widened. Was Donny the one who took all those pictures?

"Liam was such a pansy when it came to you. It was obvious to everyone with eyes that you didn't want to be with him. And you manipulated the hell out of him so you didn't have to let him take you to bed. The men started to look at him like the weak man he was. A man who lets a woman lead him around by his dick. I wouldn't have let you do that."

"Why did you trash his house? What purpose did that serve?" she asked.

"I needed the evidence he had. Wasn't much point in killing him if the cops found pictures of me with that underage girl he blackmailed me with."

They reached the fence, and he pushed her against it, leaning into her back. She felt the hard ridge behind his fly on her butt. She tamped down the urge to puke and clutched the chain link. If he gave her half a chance, she'd destroy his bollocks and stick his gun into his own ribs. Hers ached as he pushed the weapon deeper.

"I should take you right here, but the risk is too great."

"Max! Dean! Do you see her or Callahan?"

Both men answered in the negative.

A car with its headlights off rolled through the parking lot across the street. She looked left and right. Where were the police? A state patrol officer had come down here earlier. A federal agent was supposed to be parked behind the warehouse property, watching the rear. Had they gone to help their colleagues?

"There's our ride." He pulled her away from the fence.

A few yards down, he pulled a section aside and pushed her through. Audra glanced back. If she used her mic and called for help, what would Donny do?

Kill you, dummy! her subconscious mind yelled.

For the first time, an edge of fear skated down her spine. She was on her own.

Forty

Sam reached another junction and spun around, trying to figure out where he was. He'd gone up an aisle, expecting to come out one way, only for the containers to be angled. It was like someone had put them all in a big cup and tipped them out onto the ground like pickup sticks.

He reached the edge. The area beyond the containers was empty. He touched his mic and tried Audra again. "Aud? Can you hear me?"

Silence met his question.

"Sam, where are you?" Max said.

"Beyond the containers. Near the fence." He walked toward the chain link, head on a swivel.

"I see you," Dean said.

A moment later, Max spoke. "Me too."

Sam continued toward the fence.

"Man, that place was a maze." Max caught up to him.

"Are we going back in?" Dean joined them. "Audra's still inside, right? And Callahan?"

Sam stared at the empty lot beyond the compound. His gut told him something was very wrong.

"Sam?" Concern colored Dean's voice.

"I'm not sure." He turned to his right, walking down the fence line. Twenty yards down, he found a break in the fence. The chain link was cut and rested against the pole. He hooked his fingers through and tugged, rattling it against the hollow pipe. He glanced down. A tiny piece of dull metal caught his eye, and he crouched down.

"What did you find?" Max shifted closer.

Sam's blood ran cold as he picked up what he saw. He held it out as he stood up. "Audra's mic."

Dean muttered a curse.

Sam yanked on the fence, pulling it back. "Come on. We need to get back to the van."

The three of them slipped out and took off for the surveillance vehicle at a sprint. Jessica looked up with a soft squeak when Sam yanked the door open and hopped inside.

"Jesus, you scared me."

"Sorry. I need every camera feed you can get me on the north and east sides of the property. Where's Moran?"

She blinked.

"Now!" he barked.

She jumped.

Dean laid a hand on his shoulder. "Calm down. We'll find her."

Sam clenched his teeth, barely holding on to his temper. He didn't want to calm down. He wanted to find Callahan and put his fist through the scumbucket's face.

"Audra's missing, and Callahan got away. We think they're together." Dean tipped his chin toward the monitors. "Can you please find any footage from those sides of the compound? And what's the status of the raid?"

"Holy crap. Um, sure." She spun around and started typing. "I'll look to see if any of the businesses on that side have security cameras. There were supposed to be a couple units parked over there, but everyone was recalled to the warehouse for shots fired. Moran caught the Powells, but some of the other guests didn't want to go quietly. Apparently, the weapons search at the door isn't too thorough."

"The Powells are in custody?"

She nodded.

"Where?"

"Moran scuttled them away to interrogate them a few minutes ago. They're headed to FBI headquarters."

Sam spun around. "Max, where's the SUV?"

"Dude, they're not going to let us in. We're better off waking up the business owners on that side of the property and asking for their camera footage."

With a growl, Sam thrust his hands through his hair, then turned to Dorset. "Can you get Moran on the phone?"

"I can try." She reached for her cell and dialed his number.

Her eyes flicked toward him, the gray depths wary. He knew he should care that he'd scared her, but he didn't. All he wanted were answers so he could find Audra.

"Sir—" She stopped, nodding. "I'm aware—" She paused again and looked up at Sam with wide eyes.

He could tell Moran was giving her the brush off. Reaching out, he plucked the phone from her fingers. "Audra's gone."

There was a short pause. "Brackley?"

"I need you to ask the Powells where Callahan might go. We know about the house up here, but he shares it with his brother. He won't take her there. Is there anywhere else?"

"They're not going to give up anything."

"Put me on speaker."

"That's not wise."

"Are you alone with them?"

"Yes, but—"

"Then put me on fucking speaker!"

Rustling came over the line.

"There. You're on speaker."

"Listen to me, you sorry sacks of human waste. You will tell me what I want to know, or I swear on a stack of rifles I will hunt you down and make you bleed from a thousand tiny little cuts while you're strapped naked to a drum of ammonium nitrate. I might even dip you in some salt—make those cuts burn like the fires of hell you'll meet once I blast your asses there." He paused for a moment to let that sink in. "Now, where did Callahan go?"

Silence came over the line. Sam clenched a fist. His voice dropped an octave. "Where? I won't ask again."

"You should probably tell him," Moran said.

"He has a ranch," Geoffrey said. He paused to clear his throat. "Outside of the city to the west; off of State Route 160. He bought it under a shell corporation to hide it from the feds."

"What's the full address?"

Geoffrey gave it to him.

"Good choice, Geoff." Sam hung up.

Jessica took her phone back. "It's always the quiet ones who are the scariest."

"Don't threaten the people I love." Sam grabbed a pad of paper and a pen and wrote down the address before he forgot it. He ripped the page off, then wrote it again and handed it to her. "Here. Send help. Or not. I don't care. I'm not leaving that ranch without Audra either way." He looked at his friends. "Let's go."

Max spun on his heel and hopped out of the van, Dean right behind him. Sam jumped out and closed the doors.

"You didn't stutter on any of that." Dean patted him on the shoulder.

"Too much rage for the words to get stuck." Sam rolled his shoulders, trying to dump some of the anger that had fueled his tirade. "Max, do you think we can get your SUV out of the mess up there?"

"Doesn't hurt to try. And if not, maybe we can commandeer one of those fancy sports cars."

Sam cracked a smile. "One of those is going to end up back home, isn't it?"

"Maybe."

"Not very kid friendly." Dean looked at Max with a smirk.

"Would you guys stop with the kid stuff? Margot and I are just friends."

"For now. Give it time." Dean grinned as Max glowered.

They reached the main gate. Two state patrol officers stood guard. Max activated his mic. "Dorset, call the dogs off at the gate so I can get my car."

The officer's radio crackled to life.

"To the gate guards, please let the three men approaching you through. They're UCs with us." Her dry tone came through loud and clear. Sam was glad he hadn't scarred her for life.

Frowning, the two men glanced up.

"She's talking about us." Dean waved and smiled.

The closest officer turned sideways and extended an arm, motioning them through.

"Do you see the car?" Sam looked around the crowded lot. It wasn't just guest cars there now. Half a dozen state and federal cars were parked haphazardly on the asphalt lot.

"Yep." Max stood on his toes and pointed. "Over there."

"I'll get the keys." Dean jogged toward the valet station.

Sam and Max continued toward the SUV.

"You think you can maneuver us out of here?" Sam eyed the crush of vehicles.

Max crossed his arms and assessed the lot. "Yeah. I think so."

Dean jogged up with the keys in his hand. "Let's roll."

FORTY-ONE

Drip-drip.

Audra glared at the open bathroom door. The steady drip of water from the sink would drive her mad if she didn't do something about it soon. But with her hands cuffed behind her back around this damn chair, even just feet away, she could do little more than sit here and wish she could fiddle with the taps.

She tucked her thumb against her palm and tried to slide her hand through the bracelet again. The cuff bit into her wrist and wouldn't go any further. She'd thought about bashing the chair against the doorjamb, but that would make too much noise. The house Donny brought her to was large, but she wasn't sure where he'd gone after he left her alone here.

At least he'd actually left her alone. She'd been afraid he was going to tie her to the bed and rape her when he'd shoved her into this room. But he'd just forced her into the chair and cuffed her to it. Something else must have drawn his attention that he needed to take care of first. She couldn't imagine what. He'd been quite eager to violate her earlier.

Audra glanced around the room for the umpteenth time, hoping she missed something that would help her get out of the bloody cuffs. But the room was sparsely furnished. It had a queen-size bed with a rust-colored quilt, a nightstand with a small lamp, and a chest of drawers. And the southwest-inspired rug under her feet.

Drip-drip.

She poked her tongue into her cheek, a fierce frown on her face. That sound was one of the worst. At one of her particularly nastier foster homes, the hallway bath had a sink that leaked. She'd lain awake many nights, unable to sleep because of the *drip-drip* that echoed through the upstairs.

Muffled footfalls came down the corridor outside the room. She heard a scratch of metal on metal, then the door opened.

Audra glared at Donny as he walked in.

"Sorry to keep you waiting. I figured I should make sure the property was secure before I partook of any pleasure. You don't mind standing in for the girl I intended to bring home tonight, do you?"

Not saying a word, she continued to glare.

"Oh, we're back to the silent treatment." His mouth flattened, and he walked closer. Crossing his arms, he studied her for a moment, then leaned down, putting a hand on either arm of the chair. "This can be as unpleasant as you want to make it."

Audra whipped her head forward with force. She let out a yell of anger as her forehead connected with his nose.

He stumbled back and covered his face. Blood poured from between his fingers. "Oh!" Angry blue eyes glared at her above his hand. "Bitch! Unpleasant it is."

She raised an eyebrow. "Good luck screwing me before you bleed out." Her aim had been true, and she'd crunched the bones of his nose.

Giving a short growl, he turned for the door. "This isn't over."

Maybe not, but she'd bought herself some time.

The door slammed behind him. She listened for the lock, then grinned when she realized he'd forgotten. Audra pushed to her feet and walked over to the door, bent in half, and listened. His footsteps had faded.

Drip-drip.

She looked at the bathroom. The bright white trim around the door beckoned. Did she dare try to break the chair now?

Do you really have a choice?

Audra huffed. Her subconscious mind was right. When he came back, he'd have a weapon.

Waddling over, she gauged the best angle to come at the doorframe. She couldn't ram it backward; she'd break her arms. But if she swung at it from the side, it might not break the back. She needed to hit it right where the seat met the side rails to make it work.

This was going to suck.

No way around it, Aud.

Taking a deep breath, she lined up her shot and swung her hips with all her might.

"Ah!" The chair bounced off the doorframe, still intact, sending a wave of pain through her arms. She'd missed, hitting the side of the seat.

Wiggling her shoulders, she moved her feet a bit and tried again. This time, she hit where she wanted and the rail cracked. Buoyed by her success, she pushed the pain away and swung a third time.

The rail splintered and the bottom of the chair broke free, dangling by the other side. She turned around and swung again. The bottom dropped off, leaving the fractured back trapped between her arms.

It had shifted when it broke, and the split rail poked her in the arm. She walked over to the chest of drawers and maneuvered the back over one of the knobs, then bent her knees. The broken wood scraped her arm, and she hissed.

But it worked. The back slid free of her arms and hung on the knob for a moment before it clattered to the floor.

Audra dropped down to the floor and laid back. Her wrists protested being smashed between her back, the floor, and the cuffs. Wincing, she brought her knees up to her head, forming a ball, and shimmied her arms around her hips.

With her hands now in front of her, she got to her feet. Cautiously, she opened the door. A trail of blood on the tile floor led away from the bedroom. She stepped out, following it toward the living room. It continued past the bright white sofas to the other side of the house.

Audra made a beeline for the kitchen. She pulled a knife from the block, then headed for the garage and hopefully a car with the keys in it. Hand on the knob, her gaze stopped on the white rectangle near the top.

"Of course it has an alarm," she whispered. It would emit a loud chime when opened, just like the front door had when Donny's driver dropped them off.

She let go and backed away. Time to find a different way out. One of the windows, perhaps.

Retreating down the hall, she ducked into the first bedroom and checked the window. It, too, had an alarm.

"Bloody criminals and their bloody security." Huffing, she turned away. Okay. If she couldn't escape without him knowing, she'd have to make sure he couldn't come after her.

Audra returned to the kitchen, hoping he had a chef who used kitchen twine.

With one eye on the hallway beyond, she searched the drawers.

A flicker of light from the front entryway made her pause. She squinted. Those were headlights.

Her heart leapt, hoping it was Sam, but her rational side quickly reminded her he had no idea where Donny had taken her. Whoever was coming up the drive was here because Donny wanted them here.

She plucked another knife from the block and slid it through a belt loop. She'd find a place to hide for now and fight her way out when the time was right.

Forty-Two

"That's some house." Dean leaned forward, peering through the windshield at the sprawling Spanish-style ranch house they'd come up on.

Sam studied the building, cataloguing entry and exit points. There were a lot of them. Lights blazed in the middle of the house, softened by the sheer curtains covering the windows. Only the sidelights around the door were uncovered, but they were too small to see through at this distance.

"We need to get closer." He got out of the car.

"That's a lot of open ground to cover." Max came up next to him. He'd ditched the suit jacket and tie and rolled up his sleeves. So had Dean.

"We still have several hours of darkness left, though. And there's no moon. We don't have a choice." He eyed his friends. "I understand if you want to stay back. But I'm going in."

Dean scoffed. "Do you hear him, Max? Stay behind... What an asinine thing to say." He looked at Sam. "You can dress my blisters now for that. Also," he turned to Max, "I've half a mind to take all your fancy shoes and dump them in the ocean when we get home. My feet have never disliked me so much."

Max lifted a shoulder. "They don't bother me."

"It's because you wear them all the time," Sam said, staring out at the desert. "Just let it go, Dean. He'll never change." He tipped his head toward the house. "Come on. We're wasting time."

The three of them set off into the darkness, staying low to limit their silhouettes. Halfway there, the sound of an engine made them pause. Sam looked back toward the road. Headlights rounded the bend.

"Down!" Sam ordered.

They all dropped to the dirt. The car slowed and turned into Callahan's driveway.

"Who's that?" Dean asked.

"No clue. Let's go." Sam began to army crawl toward the house. "Watch out for snakes and scorpions."

"Ow!" Dean hissed. "And cacti. Dammit."

Sam ran into one of the prickly plants too. Wincing, he came up to a crouch. "Maybe a duck walk would be better." There was enough low vegetation to offer them some cover.

As fast as their crouch allowed, they moved toward the house. The car pulled to a stop out front, and several men got out. A floodlight came on as they approached the front door. Sam muttered a curse as he clocked the identity of one of the men. "That's Liam Brogan."

"Donny said he planned to take Brogan out." Dean shifted closer.

"I know."

"So, what's he doing here?"

"Good question. Let's go find out." Whatever the man's reason, Sam didn't think it was a good one.

Liam and his men knocked on the door. "Donny! Open up!" The man's voice carried through the still desert night.

Sam, Max, and Dean continued to creep closer.

Brogan knocked again. "Donny!"

When another thirty seconds passed and there was still no answer, Liam stepped back. Sam saw him gesture to one of his men, then the door. The man stepped forward and kicked the door in.

"I think Brogan knows about Donny's plan," Max said.

"Yeah." Sam moved toward the house, increasing his pace. Audra wasn't just Callahan's captive now. She was in the middle of a power struggle.

FORTY-THREE

Audra jumped at the heavy bang that echoed through the house following Liam's shout from outside. He didn't sound happy. She didn't blame him. She'd be miffed too if someone she trusted tried to take her job.

But his appearance made her situation much more complicated. If Liam knew she was here, he'd rip the place apart to find her. While her hiding spot tucked behind the dryer in the laundry room right off the kitchen was a good one, it would only be a matter of time before someone found her.

"Donny! Where are you, you fucking bastard?"

The house stayed quiet.

"Fan out," Liam said. "Find him. Start with the blood trail."

She closed her eyes. That would lead right to him. She was safe for the moment.

A minute passed, then she heard Donny shout from down the hall, his tone more angry than panicked.

"No! Let me go! I can walk on my own."

Several sets of scuffling footsteps grew louder as they neared the living room.

"Donny, what happened to you? Did you fall in your haste to run from the human trafficking auction you fled earlier?"

Oh, how she wished she could see Donny's face right now. Liam was a lot of things, but forgiving wasn't one of them. Donny had an uphill battle to regain Liam's trust. Not that he would. He was a lying, power-hungry jackass.

"What are you talking about? I've been here all night. I fell. Off a ladder, putting something away."

"Don't lie to me, Donovan. I know you were there. You forget, I own this city. A lizard doesn't scamper without me knowing about it."

"Really? You didn't know your fiancée was cheating on you. That she was scamming you."

The sound of flesh meeting flesh reached Audra.

"Remember your place, Donny. It *was* as my number two. But not anymore. Not after you went behind my back to bankroll your own little skin trade ring. And don't you worry about Alexandra. I'll take care of that bitch in time."

"You can do it now. I caught her."

"What?"

"She was at the auction. Slinking around outside. I caught her. She's in the back bedroom."

"You have Alexandra here?"

"Yep. And you can have her if you let me go."

"You're in no position to bargain." There was a short pause. "Hold him."

Well-made dress shoes moved over the tile, the sound fading as Liam walked down the hall. Audra took a chance and stood, letting the blood flow back into her legs. They couldn't see her from here, and she needed to not fall on her face when she made a dash for the door.

Angry footsteps returned from the hallway. "You're a fool, Donovan. She's gone."

"What? She was handcuffed to a chair. And the door..."

He trailed off and then groaned. "I didn't lock it when I left to tend to my nose."

"No, you didn't. And the chair is in pieces on the floor. I didn't see any cuffs, though."

"She couldn't have gone far. She's probably still in the house. I didn't hear the door or window alarms chime."

"Find her."

Bloody hell. Things were about to get hairy. She returned to her crouch, hoping none of Liam's men looked too hard.

A crash sounded in the kitchen. One of the men had opened the tall closet door and pulled out the broom and mop to look behind it. She kept tabs on their footsteps. They were getting steadily closer.

The light above her lit up. She kept her eyes glued to the top of the dryer, ready to pounce.

Marcus, one of Liam's bodyguards, came into view. His eyes widened, and he opened his mouth.

Audra sprang from her squat and plunged the kitchen knife into his throat. He gurgled and put a hand out as his legs gave way, crashing into the dryer with a bang. She backed away, pulling the second knife from her belt, and ran for the back door. It chimed as she opened it. As she stepped through, she heard shouts from inside. Her only chance now was to flee into the darkness and let the night give her cover.

Glancing back, she didn't see the man step out in front of her. She screamed and brought her blade up as his arms closed around her.

"Whoa! Aud, it's me!"

The voice registered. "Sam?" Her body sagged into his.

"Yeah. Come on. We need to get away from here."

"How did you find me?" she asked as they ran around the house.

"Geoffrey Powell. He gave up this location."

"What? How did that happen?"

"I used my powers of persuasion."

"Oh boy." She could imagine how that went. Not well for Geoffrey.

Sam paused at the corner of the house. He touched his collar. "I've got her. Get your asses out here."

She heard his voice in her ear and smacked him on the chest. "Why didn't you let me know you were here? I was hiding behind the dryer with a kitchen knife!"

"I didn't know if he'd found your earpiece. I didn't want to give away the element of surprise."

She tipped her nose up, unable to argue with his logic. "I guess that makes sense."

He gave a little snort and smiled. "Also, thank you for the breadcrumb. It's how I knew you were gone and not lost in the container maze."

"I knew it was a longshot, but I couldn't let him take me away from there without doing something."

"Well, it worked. It saved us a bunch of time." He peered around the corner again. "We need to make a run for the car. Someone's going to come around the building looking for you soon enough."

"Lead the way."

He clutched her bound hands and guided her around the front of the house. Two men ran out the front door. It took her only a moment to recognize Dean and Max. Together, the four of them dashed across the desert.

"We knocked out Callahan and tied up Brogan. His two goons ran out the back door after Audra," Dean said, coming up alongside them.

A shout from behind made her look over her shoulder. A flashlight bobbed near the side of the house from where she and Sam had run. Another appeared from the other side. Neither of the men had seen the group running away yet.

In the distance, she saw a line of headlights.

"Sam, you see that?" Max asked.

"Yeah. Here's hoping Dorset sent help, and it's not more of Brogan's men. We're not going to make it over the road before they get here."

They pulled up behind a clump of cacti. Audra's heart thundered in her ears.

"I see light bars." Dean shifted, rising slightly.

Max grinned. "It's the good guys."

The lead squad car braked hard and swung into the driveway. He hit his lights as the engine revved; the car roared toward the house. Four other vehicles followed.

Audra tipped her head into Sam's shoulder. "It's over. Oh, thank God."

Sam stood up, pulling her with him. A bright smile sat on his face. "Come on. Let's go get one of those guys to take these things off of you." He touched the metal cuffs circling her wrists.

"Yes, please."

Shouts filled the air as the state troopers and plain-clothes agents piled out of their vehicles, guns raised. Brogan's men stopped and raised their hands as the law enforcement officials swarmed them.

Audra and the others hung back until both men were cuffed. In the flashing light as they walked closer, she recognized both the man in cuffs and the one who now held his arms. "Hey, that's Moran."

Max and Dean shared a look. Dean looked at Sam with a chuckle. "You want to talk to your buddy Geoffrey again?"

"No. Too many witnesses. Besides, I got what I needed." He looked at Audra. "You're okay, right? I haven't asked."

"I'm fine. Sore, but fine."

He put a hand on her head and tipped it toward him, pressing a kiss to her hair. "Good."

Max waved a hand. "Moran!"

Several officers turned, guns drawn.

They froze.

Moran paused, then lifted a flashlight and flicked it their way. A wide smile spread over his face, his eyes on Audra. "Well, I'll be damned. You're like a cat, Ridley. Do you always land on your feet?"

She walked up to him, smiling. "Only when I have the right people at my back."

Sam, Max, and Dean came up behind her, forming a human shield. Moran looked at each of them, then nodded once. "With them on your side, I don't think you'll need to worry."

"Nope." She raised her hands. "Do you have a key?"

He chuckled. "Yeah. Let me stuff this one into a car." He gave his prisoner, Kieran, a small push, but the man didn't budge. Instead, he stared at her with wide eyes.

"You're British?" he finally said.

Audra grinned. "I'm a lot of things you didn't know I was."

Moran tugged on Kieran's arms. "Let's go." The two walked away.

Audra lowered her wrists and rolled her shoulders. She needed a hot bath and a massage. Her shoulders ached something terrible.

She glanced around while they waited on Dominick to return. Through the open doorway, she saw two state troopers with Liam. One held his cuffed arms while the other checked his pockets.

"Hey." She nudged Sam with her elbow, then tipped her chin toward the house.

He looked in the direction she indicated. "You want to go talk to him, don't you?"

"Uh-huh." She turned and smiled up at him. "You can stand behind me and glare."

"Can I punch him too?"

"You sure are aggressive tonight." Her smile turned naughty. "I kind of like it."

His lips twitched, ruining the fierce expression on his face. "I get a little mean when people I love are in danger."

"All right." Moran returned. "Let's get those things off of you." He reached for her hands, a silver handcuff key in his fingers.

The metal gave way and Audra shook her wrists out. They'd be sore for several days, and she'd have bruises. But she was alive and relatively unharmed. "Cheers."

Freed, she walked around him, Sam on her heels.

"Behave," Moran called after them.

Passing through the doorway, Liam stilled when he saw her. Then his eyebrows slammed into a vee and red dotted his cheeks. "Bitch!"

"Such language is rather uncouth, don't you think?"

His eyes widened at her accent. "Who the hell are you?"

"I'm the spy you willingly let into your organization, and the woman who's brought down your whole family."

The redness on Liam's face increased. "Donny was right. I should have forced you to submit to me. Taught you to be a proper lady."

Her smile disappeared, and she took a step closer. "You'd have lost something rather precious to you." Her gaze flicked to his crotch. "And learned that this *lady* runs the show. It will be a pleasure to watch you rot in jail, you son of a bitch."

From the floor by the sofa came a low laugh. Audra stepped back and looked past Liam and the cops to see Donny sitting on the floor, an officer holding a rag to his nose. In addition to the damage she'd inflicted, he now had a swollen left eye and cheek.

He looked past her at Liam with his good eye. "How does

it feel to be the bitch? Sucks, doesn't it?" Another crazed laugh followed.

Audra shook her head. She turned to Sam. "I'm done here."

He held out a hand to her, his gaze on Liam. "Have fun in prison."

Lacing their fingers together, Audra walked out without another glance.

FORTY-FOUR

F*ive weeks later...*

Audra rubbed her temples as she left the SIS building for the last time. That exit interview process had been grueling. But her case was out of her hands now. Dee had everything; the prosecutors did too. She just had to wait for the trial. But for now, her role as a spy was done.

"Hey, pretty lady. Can I buy you a drink?"

For a split second, the words "Get lost" were on the tip of her tongue before the voice registered.

A wide smile covered her face as she turned.

"Hi, Aud."

She let out a squeal and launched herself at him. "You're here!"

Sam caught her and wrapped her in his muscular arms. "Of course I am. You're officially retired. Which means you're all mine."

She leaned back in his embrace to frame his face in her

hands. "I am. And I'm so very excited. My bags are packed and waiting. All I have to do is run by my flat and grab them before heading to the airport."

A gleam entered his eyes. "About that…"

Audra tipped her head, trying to read his expression. "What?"

"I was wondering if you'd be open to a little detour before we catch our plane. And yes, I booked myself on your flight."

"I'm glad. What do you mean, though? What kind of detour?" She couldn't imagine what he meant. They didn't have a lot of time before their flight left. Only tonight. Her move to Costa Rica had been in the works for over a month. Ever since the day after they took down Brogan, Callahan, and the Powells. She'd decided she was done with spy work. Bright and early tomorrow morning, she was supposed to fly down to Costa Rica.

He dropped a quick, but heated kiss on her lips, then released her. "Come on."

"What? Sam, where are we going?"

"You'll see."

He led her to the tube station, where they boarded the train. After two line changes, they ended up at Southwark, where they got off. Audra still had no clue where they were going.

Outside the station, they crossed Blackfriars Road, then went up Union Street before turning right onto Great Suffolk Street. He stopped in front of a building with colorful windows.

She frowned and read the sign. It was for a theater. "Are we seeing a play?"

"No. I googled Spanish places in London. This came up. I'd take you to a restaurant, but that's too crowded and noisy."

"Okay?" She drew out the word, still confused about what was going on.

He reached into his back pocket. When he brought his hand around, he held a small burgundy booklet. Audra frowned as she realized it was a British passport. "Why do you have a British passport?"

"It's one of yours." He handed it to her.

She opened it. It was her Angela Brackley ID. "I'm so confused. Why are you giving me this? I can use my real one now."

"I know. I was wondering if you wanted to make that last name official, though?"

Audra's lips parted on a soft gasp.

He dropped to one knee, producing a small fabric pouch from another pocket. Opening it, he dumped a ring into his palm.

"Oh my goodness," she breathed, covering her mouth.

"Aud, you know I want you to be part of my life for the rest of my days. I've been thinking about this since the moment we met again. We're here"—he pointed at the theater—"because it's about as close as I could get us to Spain without leaving the city. I wanted the forever part of our lives to start in the place where our relationship began. I love you. Will you be my wife?"

A bright, happy smile started behind her hands, crinkling her eyes. She dropped her arms to her sides. "Yes!" She didn't even have to think about it. Secretly, she'd hoped he'd propose soon now that she was retiring. She wanted nothing more than to build her new life with him right by her side.

Standing, Sam took her hand and slid the square-cut diamond solitaire onto it. "No more fake names and false identities. From now on, you're just Audra Brackley."

Happiness propelled her into action, and she threw her arms around his neck. The noise of the busy London street faded away as she sealed her mouth to his. She liked the sound of that.

Epilogue

A small child's laughter, followed by a splash, put a broad smile on Audra's face. She turned her head against the spray of droplets Em's mini-cannonball threw into the air. Max lifted her from the water and tossed her up, catching her.

"'Gain!"

"Again?" He groaned. "Em, my arms are tired."

Audra chuckled, watching the pair. For nearly fifteen minutes, one of Margot's twin toddlers had been jumping into the pool at Max. He would pluck her out of the water and toss her high into the air, then set her on the pool deck, where she'd jump in all over again.

"Honey, let's give Max a break. How about you come over here and play with the fishies with your sister?" Margot sat in a wading pool with Em's twin sister, Lily. She waved a colorful plastic fish at her daughter.

"That sounds fun." Max tucked the girl to his chest and walked toward the steps. Em protested, but he kept going.

"She is a handful and a half." Sam sank into the chair next to Audra's and took her hand.

"That's for sure. He's really good with her, though. After seeing them together this week, I understand why you all say he's taken."

Sam grinned. "Yeah. It's only a matter of time, I think, before he realizes he's in love with Margot and asks her to marry him. He might be already and is just waiting for her to be ready. What she's been through—" He stopped and shook his head. "It hasn't been easy."

Audra didn't know much of the story, except that Margot's husband had left abruptly and they hadn't had any contact since.

"Edie, come on. You can't go to your wedding in flip-flops and shorts."

Audra turned to see Edie exit Max's house, her sister, Esther, on her heels.

"I'm already married, Essy. It doesn't matter."

"But this is for the wedding pictures."

"I have those."

"And they're crap! Mom and Dad want the perfect, glorious picture of you two to set on their mantle."

Sam chuckled as the sisters continued around to the other side of the pool, still bickering. "You sure you want to be here for Jordan and Edie's vow renewal? It's chaos around here."

She squeezed his hand. "I'm sure." Truthfully, she found the liveliness of Sam's Costa Rica family thrilling. She'd never had the big, happy family before. But in the month since she'd retired from the SIS, they'd embraced her fully. "I'm going to miss everyone when I go back to testify next month." The U.S. District Court that covered Nevada was finally ready to take Donny and Liam's cases to grand jury for their formal indictments. She'd been recalled to give a deposition for both cases. Sam wasn't going with her, so she hoped it went by quickly. His bar manager had threatened to quit if he left her again anytime soon. Max and Dean were going, though. They had to give testimony for the Powells' grand jury case.

"I hope that really only does last a couple of days. I want to go with you but—"

She laid a hand on his arm, cutting him off. "It's fine. Really. When I get back, I'll make it up to you." She sent him a hot look. After several days apart, she was sure their reunion would be explosive.

He leaned in, a hint of a smile on his full lips. "Yeah, you will."

Audra let out a girly giggle as his mouth brushed hers.

"Yuck. Cut it out." Asher nudged Sam's chair with his leg as he sank into the chaise next to them. "I can't go anywhere anymore without seeing someone smooching on someone else." He flipped his sunglasses down over his face and leaned back in his chair.

"You're just jealous," Sam said.

Asher scoffed. "No."

Audra grinned. She had a feeling Sam was right. Asher was the odd man out. While Max and Margot weren't officially together, they spent most of their time with each other. He needed someone.

"What are they arguing about now?" Asher nodded toward the redheaded sisters across the pool.

"Whether Edie should wear a wedding dress this weekend," Sam said.

A smirk lifted one side of Asher's mouth, baring his perfect teeth.

Audra still couldn't get over how movie-star handsome he was. If she wasn't head over heels in love with Sam, Asher would turn her head.

"Edie doesn't stand a chance. Esther knows which buttons to push to get her sister to do things. But Edie likes to push her buttons, too, I've noticed. She's probably already decided to wear whatever her sister wants and is just stringing her along now."

"You know Esther that well, huh?" Sam asked. "After three days?"

Asher lifted a shoulder. "I'm observant."

Audra covered a chuckle with a little cough. He was observant of Esther, she'd noticed.

"You all right?" Sam glanced at her.

Heat curled in her belly like it did every time he gave her that caring look. This man made her feel so cherished and loved. "I think I could use a drink." The direct look she gave him said she wanted far more than a drink. "You?"

He nodded once and sprang from his chair. "That sounds nice. I could use a drink." He took her hands and helped her up.

Asher snorted. "You're not fooling anyone." He waved a hand and wrinkled his nose. "But go. I'll stay here and monitor the kids." He gestured to Edie and Esther.

This time, Audra didn't bother to hide her laugh. She tugged on Sam's hand and led him away from the pool.

"So, I was thinking..." Sam said as they ducked into the house.

"About?"

He didn't answer right away. Instead, he pulled her through the living room and out the front door. When they reached his car, he pushed her against the door, trapping her against the vehicle.

Audra bit her lip as she lifted a leg, eager to ease the ache in her core.

He growled and leaned down to nip at her neck before he lifted his head to look her in the eye. "I was thinking we should get married when you get back."

Married? She froze and stared at him with wide eyes.

"I know we talked about having the big wedding with the flowers and the white dress—and I'm totally fine with it, if that's what you want. But I really just want to call you my wife. Maybe make a holy terror or two of our own in the not too distant future." He hooked a thumb toward the house and the twin toddlers they'd left behind.

A slow, happy smile spread over her face, stretching her cheeks so far they hurt. "I don't need a fancy dress. And any old flowers will do. How about we get started on the baby-making now, though?"

An answering smile crinkled the corners of his dark blue eyes. "Yeah?"

She nodded, framing his face in her hands. "Yeah."

Thank you for reading *Sam's Salvation!* I hope you loved it! Want to see Asher finally get his happily-ever-after? Check out *Asher's Assignment* on Amazon: *https://books2read.com/u/3y9g7J*

If you'd like to read more about Sam and Audra (and the other characters in this series), join my mailing list. Subscribers get a bonus chapter or scene after every book! You'll also get access to exclusive teasers, giveaways, and the occasional book recommendation, as well as sneak peeks into my world as I create my stories. Scan the QR code below to sign up and get your bonus scene!

Keep reading for a sneak peek at *Asher's Assignment*...

ASHER'S ASSIGNMENT

WAGNER BRIGADE
BOOK 5

ONE

Days like today were ones where Esther Campbell questioned her life choices. Rain pelted the window to her classroom, doing little to drown out the sounds of the twenty kindergartners busy at their desks. No one was screaming, so she took a moment to glare at the weather. She had to drive in that soon. And not to her house, which was only a few minutes away. No, she'd picked up a tutoring job and now she had to drive across the city in this weather.

At least it wasn't snowing. She very much disliked driving in the rain, but she disliked the snow more.

The shrill screech of one of her students turned her head. A moment later, Zoey stomped toward her. The girl held up two ends of a crayon, a fierce frown on her face. If kindergarteners could have a murder face, it would be the look on Zoey's.

"Evan broked my favorite blue crayon."

Esther glanced up, looking for the boy. He sat at his desk, tongue poked into the corner of his mouth while he concentrated on his work. He didn't look like he'd been causing trouble. But with a classroom full of five- and six-year-olds, she didn't always see everything.

"Let's go talk to him." She put two fingers on the girl's shoulder and turned her around.

The little girl marched over to Evan's desk. She slammed the two pieces of crayon onto the tan surface. "You're in trouble now!"

"Zoey." Esther waited for the girl to look at her. "Let's be calm and polite, okay?"

The frown on the little girl's face deepened. "He broked my favorite blue crayon," she said, like that explained it all.

"I didn't do it on purpose!" Evan yelled. "It fell!"

Esther patted the air. "We need to keep our voices on the indoor setting. No one needs to yell." She looked at Zoey. "Is that true? Did it fall off the table?"

She nodded. "It rolled off, then he stepped on it."

"Not on purpose!" Evan glared at her, then looked up at Esther. "Zoey's always tattling. I didn't do nothing."

Esther counted to ten. These two had been bickering all day.

"Zoey, I'm sure Evan is sorry he stepped on your crayon. Right, Evan?" She cast a quick look at the boy.

He nodded. "I didn't mean to break it, Zoey."

"See? Now, what do you need to say to Evan?"

The girl's bottom lip popped out. "Sorry," she grumbled. She held up the pieces of crayon. "What about this?" That bottom lip started to quiver. "I liked this one. It colored nice."

"Come here." She took Zoey's hand and led her over to the cabinet where she kept all the art supplies. Opening the door, she pulled out the bin that held all the blue crayons. "How about you pick a brand-new one?"

Zoey handed her the broken pieces of the one she held, drama forgotten, as her eyes widened at the sight of all the fresh crayons. She peered into the bin and picked one.

"You think that one will work?"

"Yep!" She scampered away. "Thanks, Miss Campbell!"

Esther sighed and put the bin back, shutting the cabinet door. Sometimes, all a girl needed was a sharp crayon.

The last thirty minutes of her day passed without incident. Once the kids were packed up, Esther led them down to the dismissal area, where they were split into car rider and bus rider groups. She was on car rider line duty today, so she stayed with those kids from her class.

"Yuck!"

Esther looked down at Zoey, who'd come up to her side. The girl stared out at the rain, her nose wrinkled.

"I agree, Zoey. I'm ready for some sunshine." They'd had several days of rain. Sometimes it was no more than a drizzle. Other times, it was a deluge. But it hadn't stopped since it started Monday morning. Right now, it was somewhere in between.

An image of a pristine beach, soft waves, and warm sunshine entered her mind. It was hard to believe two months ago, she'd been sipping cocktails on a beach in Costa Rica with her sister, Edie, for Edie's vow renewal. Her sister was living it up, surfing every day, and walking in the soft sand with her sexy husband. All while Esther was stuck here, mitigating arguments over broken crayons and contemplating how fast she could run to her car in her high-heeled boots.

The radio in Esther's hand crackled to life, pulling her from her daydream. The teacher outside, reading off the names on the placards in the parents' vehicles, called Zoey's name.

"Bye, Miss Campbell!" The girl ran out the door before Esther could even lift a hand in farewell.

Esther chuckled. She might not be on a beach with a drop-dead gorgeous man, but she liked her life. Kids were great.

Once the car riders were all on their way home, Esther

hurried back to her classroom. Her day wasn't done yet. She'd picked up a side job as a home teacher for some extra money. Tickets to Costa Rica weren't cheap, and she intended to visit Edie and Jordan as often as she could.

Hitting the lights, she looped her big purse over her shoulder and left the building. Water dripped down the sides of her face as she got into her little white compact SUV. Esther swiped at her face and started the car. Digging into her oversize purse, she unearthed her digital thermometer and took her temperature, checking to make sure she was safe to visit Leah. An illness could be deadly for the little girl.

The thermometer beeped and showed a temperature well within the normal range. Satisfied she was well, Esther stowed the thermometer, buckled her seatbelt, and put the car in gear. With her windshield wipers swishing away the rain, she rolled out of the parking lot.

The steady downpour gave way to a drizzle as she reached the other side of town. She was glad. This family was a little... judgmental, and she didn't want to walk into their house looking like a drowned rat. They already didn't like the fact that the state made them let a teacher come into their home every day. But their daughter couldn't come to school. She'd had a heart transplant several months prior and was still recuperating. Honestly, Esther didn't understand why her parents didn't submit the documentation to the district that would allow them to homeschool the girl. But until they did, she would continue to show up with a smile and help Leah stay caught up so that one day she could return to school.

After parking at the curb, Esther walked up the crumbling porch steps, then knocked on the door. She heard the family's chiweenie set off a howl inside and smiled. The parents might be rude, but the dog was sweet. So was the kid.

The inner door opened and Leah's father, Rob, frowned at her through the screen door.

"Good afternoon, Mr. Tyler." She pasted a bright smile on her face.

He grunted and pushed open the outer door. "Leah's in the kitchen."

Esther stepped inside and hurried past him. She felt his eyes on her as she walked through the living room to the small kitchen at the back of the house. He wasn't someone she'd want to be alone with. Everywhere she went, he watched. While she and Leah worked, he'd always sit in the living room. The moment she stepped out of the kitchen to leave, his gaze was on her, raking over her body and lingering on the places that made her the most uncomfortable. Today was no exception.

Buster, the family's dog, ran over and sniffed her feet as she walked. She smiled and greeted the dog, but didn't stop. Rob didn't like it when she lingered.

The flooring changed from faded carpet to faded linoleum as she entered the kitchen. "Hi, Leah." Esther's smile turned genuine as she spotted Leah sitting at the small table pushed up against the cream-colored wall. At nine, the girl was the size of a six-year-old thanks to her long battle with myocarditis. She was sharp, though.

"Hi, Miss Campbell." The girl's voice came out quiet—quieter than usual.

Esther frowned and lowered herself into the chair next to Leah. "Everything okay?"

Leah pursed her lips and shrugged.

"Are you feeling all right? Should I get your dad?" She glanced over her shoulder toward the living room.

"No. I'm okay. Mom's sick, so I'm not allowed to see her right now."

"Oh. I'm sorry, honey." Esther's curiosity piqued. She'd never met Mrs. Tyler. She'd always been at work when Esther arrived. Rob Tyler was Leah's caregiver. Leah said her mom's job paid better and had better insurance, so her dad had quit his to take care of her.

"I hate this. I'm ready to be normal, but I know I'll never be."

"Eventually, you'll get to a point where it won't be so dangerous for you to get sick." Esther hastily rethought her lesson plan for today. She'd brought some worksheets for them to go over for math, but she thought a game might be better. It might help lift Leah's spirits.

"I know, but I miss my mom. She seemed fine last night, but dad said she's running a fever. She hasn't come out of her room all day."

That didn't sound good. "Well, how about we play a math game, then I'll help you design a get-well card for her? Does that sound fun?"

Again, Leah shrugged. "I guess so."

"Okay. I need to run back out to my car for a minute to get supplies for all of that." She kept a supply tub in the cargo area of her vehicle with all the materials she thought she'd need for Leah's home visits. That kit included a bag of candy. The girl loved M&M's.

Esther pushed to her feet and retreated from the kitchen. Rob's gaze looked up from the motor sports magazine in his hands as she entered the living room.

"Where are you going?"

"I need something from my car. Leah's a little upset she can't see her mom right now, so I'm changing things up today."

"Don't baby the girl. She's fine."

Esther balled her fists but forced her voice to remain neutral. "It won't hurt for her to have some fun."

"You're not here for fun. You're here to teach her."

"I know. And I promise she'll learn from this."

The skeptical arch to his eyebrow told her he thought otherwise, but he didn't stop her as she left the house.

Outside, she opened her SUV's rear hatch and popped the lid of the clear plastic tote. The candy was on top. She grabbed the bag and a few art supplies, then closed the car. Arms loaded, she turned to head inside.

Movement at the side of the house caught her attention. She paused and squinted through the drizzle that was rapidly turning to fog. Someone was there.

Knowing she wasn't in the best neighborhood, she hurried up the walkway. Rob wouldn't help if someone tried to do something to her. She didn't want to be inside with him, but it was safer than out here. Heels clacking on the concrete, she squinted into the fog, trying to get a better look, just in case she needed to identify someone later. She caught a glimpse of long blonde hair and a feminine figure, but nothing else.

Esther frowned, pausing at the base of the steps. It had looked like a woman. Was that Mrs. Tyler? But if she was too sick to go to work or leave her bedroom, why was she outside? Who else could it be walking up their driveway?

Rob pushed the door open. "You coming?"

Her gaze swung to his. "Huh? Oh. Yes. Yes, I'm coming." She gave him a tight smile and stepped inside. "Thank you."

His dark eyes latched onto her as she walked past him. Esther kept her gaze forward and said nothing else. She crossed the kitchen threshold and pasted another smile on her face for Leah's benefit. "Okay, kiddo. Let's have some fun."

The next hour flew by while they played some fun multiplication games and made a pretty card for Leah's mom. When their time was up, Leah had a smile on her face.

Esther gathered up all her supplies and picked up her bag. "I'll see you tomorrow. I hope your mom feels better soon."

"Me too. Thanks, Miss Campbell." Some of the melancholy came back to Leah's face.

It was all Esther could do not to hug the girl. Rob would not like that, though. Instead, she laid a hand on Leah's shoulder for a moment. "You're welcome. Have a good evening." With a quick wave, she walked out of the kitchen.

Eyes followed her as she moved through the living room. "Have a good night, Mr. Tyler. I hope your wife feels better."

He grunted from his chair, not bothering to get up and see her out. Esther opened the door and immediately breathed a sigh of relief when it closed behind her. She picked her way down the brittle stairs and hurried to her car. It beeped as she unlocked it.

A hooded figure emerged from the fog across the road, highlighted by the streetlamp. It was a man, about six feet tall, and thin. His baggy gray sweatshirt and dark jeans hung on his frame. He paused in the glow and watched her. She couldn't see his face. Freaked out, Esther yanked on the passenger door handle and tossed the things in her arms onto the seat. She'd sort it and put it all away when she got home. Where she felt safe.

Rounding the hood and keeping one eye on the stranger, she got in and pushed the lock button as soon as the door shut. From the corner of her eye, she could see the man still standing there. For the first time, she questioned whether the extra money was worth it. This was a rough neighborhood. The nights were growing darker sooner. Before long, she'd be leaving the Tylers' home in total darkness.

But if she didn't tutor Leah, who would? The girl's education would lapse while the district tried to find someone to fill her place. Esther couldn't let that happen. Maybe she'd talk to Edie about the best kind of pepper spray to buy. Or a taser. Something to help her feel safer.

Two

Esther's stomach growled as she rinsed the rice for her dinner. She'd forgotten to cook it when she cooked the shrimp and vegetables, so now she was doubly hungry. After she ate, she was going to sink into a bath with some wine and hopefully relax. Her brain was so scattered.

The phone rang. She glanced over her shoulder, but couldn't see who was calling from where she stood. Esther picked up the saucepan and held the dripping strainer over it while she took a few steps back to look at the phone where it sat on the opposite counter in her tiny kitchen. Her sister's face lit up the screen. She set the strainer in the pot, then swiped the phone screen to answer and put her on speaker. "Hi, Edie. I'm cooking dinner."

"Oh, yum. What are you having?"

"Nothing special. Stir fry. What's up? It's not movie night."

"Can't a sister call to talk?"

"Sure. But you usually have a reason. Is everything okay?"

"It's fine."

Something in Edie's tone told her otherwise. She put the

rice pot down and waited, knowing her sister would tell her what was wrong when she was ready.

Edie groaned. "Technically, everything is fine. I'm just— I'm just not—" She stopped again and huffed. "I'm pregnant."

Esther sagged into the counter. "You're what?" she squeaked.

"Pregnant. And I'm not sure how I feel about it. I mean, I'm happy," she hastened to add, "but I'm—scared? Nervous. Nervous is a better word."

"Does Jordan know?"

"About the baby? Yes. He figured it out before I did. When we sparred the other morning, I just didn't have the same energy I usually do. Then we made breakfast afterward, and I told him the bacon smelled rancid. After we ate, he disappeared for a bit, claiming he had an errand to run." She snorted. "His errand was to the drugstore. He came back with a pregnancy test."

Esther laughed. That sounded like him. She also wasn't surprised that he'd picked up on the changes in her sister. He was a perceptive man, and he adored Edie. "So, does he know you're nervous?"

"Probably. I haven't said as much, but obviously, he can read me like a book, so..." Edie blew out a breath. "I just wanted to talk to someone without any stake in things, you know? You always give it to me straight. Help convince me everything will be okay, Essy. Because I don't know how to be a mom."

Esther pushed away from the counter and picked up her saucepot. "Sure you do. You had a great example. Mom's going to be thrilled, by the way. And you better tell her soon. If you keep this from her like you did your marriage, she's liable to fly down there and skin you." She dumped the water out, then tipped the rice from the strainer into the pot.

"Hey, I had a good reason for keeping Jordan a secret at the time. I came clean as soon as it was safe."

Esther turned on the water and added some to the rice. "Maybe so, but you know you could have told us before. We wouldn't have said anything to anyone." Esther and her parents had been a little hurt when Edie broke the news of her nuptials. Edie claimed it had been to keep them safe from the person terrorizing Jordan, but Esther had a feeling she'd also done it so she didn't have to deal with the emotions involved. Edie only had so much emotional bandwidth.

"Well, you know now. And yes, I promise I will tell Mom and Dad soon. I just need to get a handle on it myself. It's only been a couple of days."

"How far along are you?" Esther shut the water off and set the pot on the stove, turning on the burner.

"We figure about seven weeks. With all the chaos around here lately, I haven't paid that close attention to my cycle."

"Chaos?"

"Margot and the twins officially moved down. Her divorce finally went through. We've been busy getting them settled."

"Hey, that's great. Hopefully, she can move on now." Margot's story was a complicated one. Her husband left with no warning, leaving her to raise twin toddlers on her own. Thankfully, Edie's friends had stepped up to help her. She wasn't alone, and the girls would grow up with a great group of role models around them.

"Yeah. She already looks more relaxed. I've been watching Em and Lily a couple times a week so she and Annabeth can work on the clinic. Their goal is to open right after the new year. I know the people around here are ready for them to open. There just aren't enough doctors here, especially pediatricians."

"Well, that will be one less thing you'll have to worry

about when your baby comes. There will be two doctors close by."

"True." She groaned again. "This is nuts."

Esther laughed. "You'll be fine. You've done some wild and crazy things in your life, Edie. And you've overcome even more. A baby is nothing compared to that."

Edie scoffed. "Hardly. Because this isn't only about me. I just found out about this kid and I'm already worried about everything that could happen. Not just in the delivery, but as he or she gets older. Like, what if they're born with some sort of congenital disorder or they get really, really sick some time?"

Leah flashed through Esther's mind. That would be rough, definitely. But her sister was the strongest person she knew. "You'll be fine. And you're not alone. Jordan will be there through it all."

"I suppose that's true." She sighed. "I'm being a worry-wart. That's new too. I don't fret like this. I'm a mess."

"Welcome to pregnancy." Esther grinned. Her brother-in-law was going to have his hands full over the next few months.

Edie moaned. "Okay, let's talk about something else. How's your week going?"

"Fine." She glanced out the window. The rain had stopped, but it was foggy now. "Wet."

"It's the Pacific Northwest. That's a given."

"I know. I wish I was down there, though."

"Uh-oh. I know that tone. What happened?"

"Nothing." She leaned her palms on the counter and stared at the phone. "I'm just in a bit of a funk, I guess." Truthfully, she had been since Edie got married. It had high-lighted how far she was from having the family she craved. Hearing Edie's baby news wouldn't help. She was thrilled for her sister, but she was also a little jealous. Esther had always wanted to be a mom.

"It's too bad you don't have a break until Thanksgiving.

I'd tell you to come down here for a little getaway. I could use an in-person movie night."

"Me too."

The bubbling of the rice pot drew her attention. She turned the burner down and put a lid on the pan.

"You need to shake things up," Edie said.

"I don't have time to shake things up."

"I'm not talking anything crazy. Go on a date."

Esther snorted. "With whom?"

"I don't know. Aren't there any cute, single teachers at your school?"

"Single, yes. Cute—well, if you like baby men, sure." There was a second-grade teacher fresh out of college who was easy on the eyes. But she didn't want to date a guy so much younger. She was twenty-eight, but Mark was only twenty-three. The only other single male teachers at her school were forty-something divorced dads. That was too far in the other direction for her. And as much as she wanted to be a mom, it would take a special man for her to consider starting that part of her life with teenagers already in the mix. None of her colleagues fit that bill.

"It's too bad Jordan doesn't have a brother," Esther quipped. Jordan MacDowell was a catch. Handsome, successful, kind—he treated her sister like a queen.

"No, but I have some friends..."

Esther could hear the smile in Edie's voice.

"Asher's single. So is Max," Edie said.

"Max is not single. He and Margot just refuse to admit it."

Edie chuckled. "He's too old for you, anyway."

"Margot's only a couple of years older."

"Yeah, but that woman's got life experience coming out her ears. But you're in luck. Asher's still available."

Dark hair, laughing brown eyes, and a bright smile beneath a full beard flashed through Esther's mind. That man was sex on a stick. And he knew it. He was also so not her type. "Asher would drive me crazy inside of a week."

"Eh, maybe. He's not as nutty as he first seems."

Esther raised an eyebrow but said nothing. If that were true, she hadn't seen it on her trip down there.

"I think Asher uses his humor to protect his feelings. The man's a genius, and it's hard for him to connect with people sometimes."

"Well, in any case, it wouldn't work. He's there and I'm here."

"Love finds a way, dear sister. That's something I've learned in the last year. It doesn't matter who you are or where you live. Love finds a way."

"Well, I wish it would find its way here."

"Maybe I'll send him your way. He could use a vacation."

"Edith, don't you dare!"

Edie laughed.

"I'm serious. You won't have to worry about Mom skinning you. I'll do it for her."

Edie continued to laugh. "I'll hold off for now. Maybe I'll ask you again in a few months."

"The answer won't change."

"We'll see. So what's got you in a funk? Other than the weather."

She wasn't about to admit she was jealous of her sister's life. Edie didn't need that burden, because it wasn't her fault.

"I've been thinking about my job."

"Your job? You love your job. Don't you?"

"I do." And that was true. "I adore my students. Kindergarteners are the best. And it's not really school that's bothering me. It's the home tutor job I took on."

"It's not going well?"

"The kiddo is great. Leah's bright and funny. Eager to

learn. But her family—I've never met her mother. She's always at work. And her dad gives me the creeps."

"Has he tried something?" Edie's voice turned hard.

A small smile toyed with Esther's lips. Her big sister would be on the next plane, pregnancy or no pregnancy, ready to beat someone if Esther said yes. "No. He just stares at me and grunts when I ask him questions. They don't live in a great neighborhood, either. I was going to ask when we had movie night on Friday, what's a good kind of pepper spray or taser to carry?" It wasn't just Rob who creeped her out. So did hoodie man.

Silence came over the line. It lasted so long, Esther frowned and looked at the phone to make sure the call hadn't dropped. "Edie?"

"We'll come up with a different way to pay for your plane tickets down here. You're a decent artist. Maybe Brooke will—"

"No. We're not exploiting your friends. I'll be fine."

Edie huffed. "I won't have to ask. If Brooke gets wind about any of this, she'll be the first to offer her help. All I was going to suggest was for you to paint a few pictures of the area and see if she liked them enough to buy them for the resort."

Esther hummed. She might. She had enough photographs to get her started. And it would give her some new material to work with. Lately, she'd been struggling with her painting. Nothing sparked her desire to paint.

"In any case, I think you need to quit that second job. Let the district send in a man."

"We'll see. I might broach the subject of quitting the home tutor position with my principal. Tell her to start looking for a replacement. I can't leave Leah in the lurch, though. That girl's already been through a lot."

Edie went quiet again for a long moment. "Fine," she eventually growled. "But if you feel more unsafe—"

"Don't worry. I will quit if I feel truly threatened."

"I'm still going to worry about you."

"I know. That's what sisters do. I'm going to worry about you too. And pity Jordan." Esther chuckled. So did Edie.

"Yeah, he's in for it. I'm all over the place. All right. I guess that's all I can ask for without flying up there and becoming your shadow."

"No shadowing is necessary. Do you feel calmer now?"

"I'm certainly distracted."

"Well, at least my problems are good for something."

Edie chuckled again. "I guess so. Okay, well, are we still on for Friday night?"

"Wouldn't miss it."

"Great. I'll talk to you then. Love you, sis."

"Love you too. Bye."

"Bye."

Esther touched the end call button and pushed away from the counter. Well, damn. That was a twist she wasn't expecting.

A slow smile spread over her face. Excitement pushed out the melancholy. She was going to be an aunt.

Discover what happens and get your copy at
https://books2read.com/u/mK2qEv

About the Author

Ashley started writing in her teens and never stopped. Her first novel, Smoky Mountain Murder, came out in 2016, and she has since published two more series and has plans for more. When not writing, you can find her with her nose stuck in a book or watching some terrible disaster movie on SyFy. An avid baseball fan, she also enjoys crafting and cooking. She lives in Ohio with her husband, two kids, three cats, and one very wild shepherd mix.

Website: https://ashleyaquinn.com
Facebook Reader Group: facebook.com/groups/
349932159616427

goodreads.com/ashleyaquinn

amazon.com/Ashley-A-Quinn/e/B07HCT4QST

facebook.com/ashleyaquinn.writer

instagram.com/ashleyaquinn.writer

ALSO BY ASHLEY A QUINN

The Broken Bow

A Beautiful End

Wildfire

In Plain Sight

Close Quarters

Scorched

Light of Dawn

Pine Ridge

Sweetness

Loner

Shark

Katydid

Homespun

Foggy Mountain Intrigue

Smoky Mountain Murder

Smoky Mountain Baby

Smoky Mountain Stalker

Smoky Mountain Doctor

Smoky Mountain K-9

Smoky Mountain Judge

Prequel to Wagner Brigade

Stranded with Ezra

Wagner Brigade

Ford's Fight

Dean's Dilemma

Jordan's Journey

Sam's Salvation

Asher's Assignment